JUST A LITTLE MADNESS

MERRY FARMER

JUST A LITTLE MADNESS

Copyright ©2021 by Merry Farmer

This book is licensed for your personal enjoyment only. This book may not be re-sold or given away to other people. If you would like to share this book with another person, please purchase an additional copy for each recipient. If you're reading this book and did not purchase it, or it was not purchased for your use only, then please return to your digital retailer and purchase your own copy. Thank you for respecting the hard work of this author.

This book is a work of fiction. Names, characters, places, and incidents are products of the author's imagination or are used fictitiously. Any resemblance to actual events or locales or persons, living or dead, is entirely coincidental.

Cover design by Erin Dameron-Hill (the miracle-worker)

ASIN: B08P52VJ6M

Paperback ISBN: 9798586279682

Click here for a complete list of other works by Merry Farmer.

If you'd like to be the first to learn about when the next books in the series come out and more, please sign up for my newsletter here: http://eepurl.com/RQ-KX

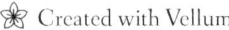 Created with Vellum

CHAPTER 1

LONDON – JANUARY, 1891

The theater was one of the only places in London where a man like Edward Archibald could truly hide. Of course, it was rather like hiding in plain sight, because everyone with even a shred of sense knew that the world of the theater was and always had been full of inverts, women of loose morals, and every other sort of unconventional personality to be found under the sun. Society was willing to overlook certain aspects of the character of theatrical types as long as they were entertaining and put on a good show, which playwright Niall Cristofori and star of the stage Everett Jewel always did. Almost no one batted an eyelash over the personal lives of those two men and their ilk, the lucky bastards. Members of Parliament weren't so lucky, as Edward most certainly knew.

Edward rose along with the rest of the audience to applaud the end of *Love's Last Lesson* from his seat near the back of a box in the second balcony. He'd seen the show six times since it opened in the fall and considered that night's performance one of the best. The rest of the crowd thought so as well, as attested by their enthusiastic applause. They clapped particularly loudly for up and coming comedic actor Martin Piper when Jewel shoved the man forward to take a second bow.

Edward tried his best to ignore the thrill in his chest and the way his breath caught in his throat at Martin Piper's affable, smiling face and strong, lean form. He absolutely refused to acknowledge the way his trousers suddenly didn't seem to fit properly as the man blew kisses to his adoring public, landing one relatively near him, before giving way so Jewel could take his bow. Jewel's prowess on the stage and magnetic appeal were a given, but Edward had been taken with Piper from the very first time he'd seen the play. His gaze stayed on the man once he resumed his place with the ensemble as Jewel preened and bowed. Piper made Edward laugh, and precious little made Edward laugh anymore.

Before the applause had fully died down, Edward scooted his way to the exit at the back of the box. He was not an actor. He was the very opposite of the theatrical luminaries who could get away with murder as long as they were charming and entertaining. He was a backbencher in the House of Commons. His job was to represent his constituency in York by staying as quiet as possible, never drawing untoward attention to himself, never, ever landing in the papers as part of a scandal, and shouting out "Aye" when his party told him to. Which was why he found sitting in the dark at the back of a crowded theater, not a soul in the world aware of his existence, merely looking on as other, better people than him shone like diamonds, to be the most enjoyable thing he could possibly imagine. And it didn't hurt that the male chorus for Cristofori's show was made up of some of the finest specimens of masculinity he'd ever—

"Archibald, is that you?"

A familiar voice startled Edward out of his indulgent thoughts, driving home the fact that his trousers still didn't fit right after an evening of feasting on the sight of Martin Piper and chorus boys.

"Lord Chesterfield." Edward jerked to a stop in the middle of his flight through the lobby and turned to his fellow parliamentarian with an uneasy smile. God, the man could probably see the state of his lower regions as if he were standing up like a sequoia. A man like Chesterfield would know exactly what he was thinking and exactly whom he was thinking it about. The whole world could see right through him, and he would be damned for it. He cleared his throat. "What a pleasant surprise."

"Likewise." Chesterfield approached him with a broad smile and extended a hand. He had to drop the arm of the attractive lady—who was years too young for him and who was most certainly not his daughter—to do so. "Smashing show, didn't you think?"

"Yes, it was rather droll," Edward replied with as bland a look as possible. He smiled and nodded to the woman with Chesterfield, debating whether he should appear to find her alluring so as to avert any suspicion his thoughts might cause.

"I never thought I'd see such a doggedly conservative man like you haunting a place like this," Chesterfield went on with a laugh. He turned to his companion and said, "Archibald never steps a foot out of line. He's the most boring and flaccid member Parliament has." He followed his comment with a raucous laugh.

Edward smiled warily at the comment. He heard that and much worse on a nearly daily basis, but it was better to be called boring than to be called out for the truth. "I was just on my way home," he said, swaying forward and trying to indicate to Chesterfield that he didn't want to chit-chat.

Chesterfield ignored his move, leaned forward, and lowered his voice. "Have you heard the latest about the raid in Marylebone? They broke up a very interesting party, you know." He leaned back and tapped a finger to his nose, then darted a sideways glance to his companion before touching his fingers to his lips in caution.

"Yes, I do believe I heard something about it in passing," Edward replied.

In fact, several prominent members of The Brotherhood—an underground organization of men who loved other men that Edward was a part of—had been arrested and were currently awaiting trial. It was all The Brotherhood had been able to talk about in the last few days. The party was of a sordid nature—the sort of thing Edward was both repulsed by and reluctantly fascinated with—and its organizer, Walter Borne, had accidentally invited a blackmailer. The blackmailer in question had spent months befriending the men in order to be invited to something like that, and he had jumped at the invite, bringing the police with him. The Brotherhood was livid, and David Wirth and Lionel Mercer were up to their eyeballs with work, pulling out every legal stop they could to exonerate the unfortunate bastards who had been caught up in the whole thing. The net result was that every invert in London was even more on his guard than usual. And that went double for Edward, who was *always* on his guard.

"That sort is a blight upon England," Chesterfield went on, puffing his chest up. "Their kind should be rounded up and thrown in the fire like the fags they are before they can corrupt the morals of the young. Why, my wife and her friends are intent on raising funds to do something about it. I believe they're meeting about it this evening, the blessed things." He turned to his companion—who was most certainly not his wife. The young lady giggled and cooed, hugging Chesterfield's arm and leaning into him in a way that exposed her ample bosom. "Come on, dearie," Chesterfield went on. "We'll be late to Monroe's soiree, and I hear he's had some of the good stuff imported from Burma." He laughed and kissed his companion's cheek before nodding to Edward and marching off.

Edward waited until Chesterfield had his back turned to scowl in frustration. A blight on England indeed. The hypocrisy of men like Chesterfield, with their mistresses, oriental narcotics, and who knew what other vices, insisting that men like Jewel—who just wanted to show off—or like Niall Cristofori and Blake Williamson—who only wanted to reunite Blake's family so that they could live in domestic peace for the rest of their days—was appalling.

The anger those thoughts brought with them burned in Edward's gut as he crossed the Concord Theater's lobby to retrieve his coat and hat from the booth near the front, then headed out into the frigid night. Maybe Walter had the right of things and he should make hay while the sun was shining, as the phrase went. Perhaps bending over backwards to avoid notice and deny the urges that were sometimes so demanding he couldn't sleep wasn't the way to go. He wasn't a total monk, after all. He should be bending over forwards with a strapping companion behind him. He'd been cruising in St. James's Park a time or two to find what he needed in the moment, which had never amounted to more than an impersonal hand, or even more rarely, a mouth, in the dark. Though he always felt miserable and dirty afterwards. But dammit, man was not meant to be made of stone, and he certainly wasn't.

His restless, winding thoughts took him around the side of the theater to the alley where the stage door stood. Already, a crowd of men and women huddled together in the cold and the dark, waiting, no doubt, for Everett Jewel to make his appearance. Edward grimaced at the pull he felt toward that crowd, walking forward to join them even as he warned himself he should go home and stay safe. The impish voice at the back of his head whispered that there might be a likely fellow loitering in the crowd who could do him a favor in a dark corner and end the relentless throbbing in his groin. When was the last time he'd had anyone, other than himself, do something about that merciless need? Months at the very least. One harmless little fumble wouldn't do him any harm. No one would have to know.

Edward glanced carefully at the men waiting for Jewel, keeping his eyes peeled for that particular look or a wink or any of the numerous signs their sort had to indicate they were game. He spotted a handsome young fellow with a wide mouth and teasing eyes leaning against the wall of the building beside the theater. The man's smile widened when Edward met his eyes. He touched the back of his hand as a signal. A rush of bittersweet excitement pulsed through Edward, and his cock stirred to life. With a mouth like that, he might get exactly what he needed from the man. He inched closer.

The stage door opened, and there was a roar of applause and adoration as Everett stepped out to greet his admirers. Edward noted the ever-present form of

Everett's lover, Patrick Wrexham, with a smirk. Anyone who thought they could get a piece of Everett for the evening would be sorely disappointed. Everett and Patrick were devoted to each other—a fact that had Edward's heart aching in his chest. What he wouldn't give for a man to adore and protect him the way Patrick and Everett looked out for and loved each other. When Patrick spotted him in the back of the crowd and nodded, Edward nodded back with a wistful grin. They knew each other from The Brotherhood, of course, and Edward had secretly envied Patrick and what he had for months.

That only increased his mad determination to get at least a modicum of pleasure that evening. And who knew? Perhaps a wicked assignation in the dark could lead to a lifetime of happiness. Men had met in stranger ways. He focused forward again, turning his hopeful grin to the young man leaning against the wall.

The young man's smile widened, and he stood straighter. He pushed away from the wall, walking with purpose toward the mouth of the ally and the street. Edward knew the signs well. The man probably had rooms nearby, or at least knew of a relatively private area, like a public toilet, where they could complete their transaction. Edward's heart thumped against his ribs in anticipation as he followed the man, taking care to keep behind him enough to deflect any suspicion, but close enough so that the man would know he was following.

They walked halfway across Covent Garden that way. The young man was definitely heading toward one of the public toilets. Edward was tense with expectation and arousal, though a large part of him felt tainted and gross already over what he was about to do. He told himself that he was only human, that he had every right to steal a moment of pleasure if he wanted to, and that both parties would be willing and eager. There was nothing wrong with what he wanted or what he was doing.

"Got a match?" the young man said, stopping near the entrance to the public toilet.

Edward reached into his pocket for the coins the man likely wanted to see before heading into the toilet.

"Charlie! Thank God. There you are."

Edward nearly jumped out of his skin at the shout from behind him. He whirled around, expecting to see someone who knew the young man. His heart dropped to his feet and his hands went numb at the sight of none other than Martin Piper striding toward him with a smile and something like determination in his eyes, as illuminated by the streetlights. For a fraction of a second, he was convinced Piper knew the young man, but a moment later, he realized Piper was marching straight toward him.

"You didn't have to come all this way to use the toilet you know, Charlie," Piper said, grabbing Edward's elbow and steering him away from the young man. He barely nodded to the fellow, then dragged Edward off toward the main street. "You could have used the one at the theater."

"Oh...I...sorry. Um, that is to say...." Edward stammered, no idea what was going on. He glanced over his shoulder at the young man, who had pulled up the collar of his coat and was rushing away. "Er, my name isn't Charlie," he finished.

"I know," Piper whispered, urging Edward to pick up his pace as well. He glanced around anxiously before letting go of Edward's arm and rubbing his mittened hands together. "You're Edward Archibald, MP. And that bloke was Jerry Rivers, one of the very worst blackmailers you'd ever want to come across."

Edward's nerves frazzled so quickly and so hard that he missed a step. "Good God," he hissed, pausing to lean against a lamppost for a moment so his legs didn't give out from under him entirely. "Thank you," he panted. "You're an uncommonly clever fellow." If he'd been caught cruising in Covent Garden...the scandal that would hit the papers by morning...his reputation, livelihood, and life ruined.... He didn't even want to think about it.

Piper seemed inordinately pleased with Edward's offhand compliment. "Of course, I know I'm clever. Few others tend to see it that way."

"Well, you are," Edward said. "I will forever be in your debt."

"It wasn't solely my doing. Patrick spotted you at the theater door, saw Rivers hook you, and sent me after you before you could do yourself a harm," Piper explained. When Edward dared to look the man in the eyes, Piper's face brightened into a charming smile, and he held out his hand. "Hello. Martin Piper."

The tightness in Edward's groin flared to life again at the kindness in Piper's eyes and the genuine happiness in his smile. He straightened and took the man's hand. "Edward Archibald," he returned the greeting.

"But I already knew that," Piper finished as though that was what he was about to say. "Come on. Let's get you home, safe and sound." He thumped Edward's shoulder once they were finished shaking hands and steered him toward the main road. "Where do you live?"

Edward blinked and shook his head slightly, unable to believe that *the* Martin Piper was walking him home after rescuing him from disaster. "Er, just on the other side of Birdcage Walk, off of St. James's Park."

"Ooh, fancy." Piper's eyes lit up even more. "Close to the halls of Westminster, I see."

"Yes, something like that." In fact, Edward had taken a small flat there in a fit of wickedness, as St. James's Park was one of the most fruitful and notorious cruising grounds for men like them. Whenever he couldn't stand denying his urges for a moment longer, there was always a likely fellow to be found in the park after dark.

That thought was as embarrassing as it was immoral, and heat flooded Edward's face and neck as they walked on.

"Did you enjoy the show tonight?" Piper asked as though they were strolling through Hyde Park in the middle of summer. "I assume you saw it, since you were at the stage door."

"I loved it. I've seen it six times now," Edward blurted before he thought better and stopped himself.

Piper's handsome face lit with delight. "You have? How lovely."

"I have always enjoyed the theater," Edward went on, feeling stilted and utterly incapable of the conversation he was supposed to have with a famous—or soon to be famous—actor.

"So have I," Piper said with a teasing wink. "That's why I made my home there. Though the roll in *Love's Last Lesson* is my first major part. Niall—that is, Niall Cristofori—is a personal friend of mine, and he took a chance on me. Up until now, I've mostly worked behind the scenes, stage managing, running props, working in the fly space. I've always wanted to be on stage, though. And I must confess, I love it. Especially this comedic part. And Everett is such an excellent foil to play off of. A man couldn't ask for a better introduction to the London stage. And I'm boring you by talking your ears off now, aren't I?"

"Oh, no, not at all," Edward insisted, his pulse racing, a strange, giddy feeling of joy filling him just by being near Piper. "I love hearing you talk. You're more of a draw than Jewel."

He snapped his mouth shut with a wince. Piper would probably think him the worst sort of boob for slavering all over him. But Piper was devilishly attractive, with soft brown hair and kind hazel eyes. He was an actor, after all, and actors had a certain reputation. Perhaps he would be game to come up to Edward's flat for a drink once they—

No, that was utter madness. He couldn't possibly proposition the man when they'd only just met, and under such embarrassing circumstances...could he?

"You were very good tonight," he spewed before he could humiliate himself further.

"Thank you." Piper beamed. "It's very kind of you to say so, especially since you've seen the show before. I was rather feeling my oats this evening, as the saying goes."

"More than other nights?" Edward blinked at him, wondering how the life and the mind of an actor worked.

"The audience was very responsive tonight," Piper said. "We were all on. And when everyone is having an on night, it lifts the entire production."

"Fascinating." Edward nodded. "Is it like that every night?"

"Heavens, no." Piper laughed. "We had a performance last week that was utterly wretched. I went up on half my lines, Dolores got the verses of her song switched around. Someone in the orchestra pit vomited in the middle of Everett's Act Two solo." He gave an exaggerated shudder, then laughed. Martin Piper had the most charming laugh Edward had ever known. "There's never a dull moment in theater, that's for certain." He paused, then said, "Here's Birdcage Walk. Which one is yours?"

Edward's mouth flopped open as he glanced around,

surprised he was nearly home. He'd been so wrapped up in Martin Piper that he hadn't noticed how far they'd come. "That's my building there." He pointed down the road.

"All right, then." Piper smiled, staying right where he was and seeming to study Edward for a moment.

The man was, simply put, beautiful. He didn't have Everett Jewel's flashiness or the bold masculinity of some of the members of The Brotherhood. He wasn't fey and delicate, like Lionel Mercer, either. His brown hair wasn't anything out of the ordinary, but his mien was filled with goodness and merriment. He was of the same height as Edward, which instantly filled him with the thought that their bodies would fit together perfectly.

He could ask. He could just ask Piper if he'd like to come up for a whiskey and a tickle. He might even want to kiss Piper and hold him and do more than the utilitarian acts that were necessary to get them both off. Things he'd never done before, never dared to do. He leaned closer.

A moment later, he shook himself and backed away. What the hell was he thinking? He was an MP and Piper was a nearly-famous actor. The press would go mad over the connection.

"Well, thanks again," he said, certain his face was pink, feeling like a coward.

"Any time at all," Piper said, his eyes still shining, even when Edward stepped away and walked toward his building. He glanced over his shoulder to find Piper continuing to watch him, as though waiting to make certain he made it home safely, and waved. "Good night. Sleep tight," he called.

"You too."

It was the maddest thing Edward could imagine. Piper was still watching over him when he opened the door to his building and stepped inside. He let out a breath and leaned against the door for a moment after closing it, letting out a heavy breath and indulging in a wide smile. His heart felt as though it were dancing around his chest.

But no, that was utter foolishness. He pushed away from the door and took the hall stairs two at a time until he reached his flat, then launched inside, slamming the door behind him. He tore off his coat and practically threw it and his hat onto the rack by the door. Piper was just being a good citizen and responsible member of The Brotherhood by seeing him home. The man's smiles couldn't possibly be anything more than kindness and the affectations of actors. Edward knew full well he wasn't lovable in any way at all. He'd had that much drilled into him since childhood. Piper was gorgeous and kind and had a voice that cheered him and a face that made him feel all was right with the world and a form that made him want to peel the man's shirt off....

Wicked though it made him, he had his trousers loosened and his hand on his cock within seconds. A deep groan of need escaped from him as he let his imagination run wild. Once again, he would spend the evening with nothing but his hand and his imagination. It got the job done, but he would have given anything for contact with another man, even if it was just—

He stopped abruptly when he noticed a small envelope on the floor, as though it had been shoved under his door. With a rush as though he'd discovered an intruder in his flat, he yanked his hand out of his trousers and bent to pick it up. After the near miss he'd had that evening and the things Chesterfield had talked about at the theater, an unexpected note could mean doom.

But when he tore it open as he walked deeper into his flat, he was relieved to find it was just a note from John Dandie, asking him to drop by his new offices at his earliest convenience the next day. Even so, the summons made Edward frown. No doubt, it was something having to do with his miscreant brother, Ian, who had run off with Lord Selby's wife, Lady Annamarie Selby, and still had his son, Alan. John had asked for his help before, but there must have been a new development in the case. At least the note hadn't been some sort of blackmail.

He tossed the letter aside, then continued undressing. And as soon as he cleaned up and got into bed, he'd continue abusing himself with a sigh. Without a doubt, his self-indulgent fantasies that night, and for many nights to come, would be about Martin Piper.

CHAPTER 2

*E*dward Archibald was positively lovely. Martin couldn't stop thinking about their walk the evening before as he went about his business at the theater. Edward had been so lost—but in a way that stirred Martin's blood—and so charming. He'd paid Martin the highest compliments anyone could, calling him clever and revealing that he'd seen *Love's Last Lesson* multiple times. Those two things alone were enough to leave a smile on Martin's face, a song in his heart, and veritable oak of an erection in his trousers. He laughed at himself for that last one and busied himself around the Concord Theater, repairing some of the props that were a little worse for wear after three months of performances, and helping the stage crew move bits of the scenery so they could make similar repairs.

"All right there, Lily?" he asked Lily Logan as she muscled one of the barrels that had been nicked a few too many times by Everett's prop sword backstage for a fresh coat of paint.

"Right as rain," Lily replied with a happy smile.

It was good to see the young woman so happy at the theater after the ordeal she'd gone through the year before. Once a kidnapping victim and forced prostitute, Lily was enjoying her life as a stagehand now, and enjoying wearing men's clothes as she went about her work.

Edward Archibald had lovely clothes, or so Martin assumed. His thoughts drifted back to the happy walk the two of them had had the night before as he worked at the table that had been set up backstage, pasting fake flowers onto parasols where they'd come off. At least, Edward's winter coat had been fine. He didn't know how much money MPs made or whether the things Archibald had on under his coat were of good quality, but he guessed as much. The man was quite prim and proper, or so he seemed on the surface, and young for an MP. Martin didn't think Edward could be much older than his early thirties, like him, even though he carried himself as a stodgy old man.

Underneath those fine clothes and stiff demeanor, something else must have been going on. The poor fool had been attempting an assignation, which meant he had needs that were far from prim and proper. Martin had a fair idea that the man had been seconds away from propositioning him as well. And why that made Martin smile wider and hum a bawdy tune to himself as he dabbed paste on flowers was anyone's guess.

No, it wasn't, he scolded himself. He found the naughty goings on of an otherwise stodgy politician fascinating because he'd fancied the man on sight. Or, if not on sight, from the moment he'd called Martin clever. After a lifetime spent being called a dunce because he was clumsy—something that had nothing to do with his intelligence—being praised was like catnip. He would have happily dropped to his knees, if Archibald had followed through and asked for his company. And who wouldn't? Archibald was quite good-looking, in an understated way. He needed to smile more, obviously, but one really couldn't blame him for being so withdrawn, considering the circumstances under which they'd met the night before. It would be delightful to spend a little time getting to know the MP under more relaxed circumstances.

He'd noticed Archibald in the various social rooms of The Chameleon Club, the central gathering spot for members of The Brotherhood, but even there, Archibald kept himself to himself. Perhaps he was simply shy. Drawing out shy men had always been something that gave Martin great joy, and not just for his own, lascivious purposes. That is, he enjoyed a good tumble as much as the next man and had few qualms about getting what he wanted when he needed it, but it was even more enjoyable to coax someone out of their shell and see the smile on their face when they realized the world was a beautiful place.

"You're away with the fairies again, aren't you, Martin?" Jacob Ruhl, one of the other up-and-coming actors attached to Niall's latest play asked him, shaking Martin out of his thoughts.

"I beg your pardon?" Martin asked with a smile, blinking. His thoughts had been rambling, that much was true. But rambling thoughts often brought back other thoughts worth thinking about, so he let his mind wander whenever it wanted to.

Jacob snorted and shook his head. "What are you doing repairing props, you fool? You're a star now, not a lowly stage hand. Only a blithering idiot like you would forget something like that."

The cozy joy that had buoyed Martin as he thought about Archibald flattened. "I haven't forgotten," he said in a brittle voice, narrowing his eyes slightly as he looked up at Jacob from his seat at the table. "And I'm no idiot."

Jacob crossed his arms, looking like every schoolmaster or theater owner that had ever sneered at him. Martin despised the sanctimonious look. Jacob seemed to enjoy the fact that, seated, Martin was at a lower level than him. Martin suspected Jacob had had his heart set on the part Niall awarded to him and was holding a grudge now. "Stars don't loiter around the theater during the day," he said, as though schooling a child who didn't know any better. "And they certainly don't lug scenery around. Leave that for the peons." He nodded over his shoulder at the hard-working crew.

Martin finished with the parasol he'd been repairing and set it aside. "I like helping out backstage. It brings me joy. I thought the entire point of life was to do things that bring us joy."

Again, Jacob snorted. "Which is why, if I was a rising star like you, I'd be living it up, eating good food, drinking good wine, and bedding good women. But I suppose you don't know anything about that either," Jacob sneered.

"I prefer bedding good men," Martin said without a shred of irony. He stood and gathered the parasols that had already dried, intent on taking them back to the dressing room where they were stored. He dropped one as he did, but simply reached to pick it up again without bothering to feel awkward about his clumsiness. Awkwardness and shame were wasted emotions, as far as he was concerned.

"All the more reason you're a fool." Jacob followed him across the backstage area. "I never did understand why your lot is willing to settle for what you already have instead of enjoying a fine pair of titties."

Martin rolled his eyes and huffed an impatient sigh, hoping Jacob would leave him alone. There was no point in explaining why he liked what he liked, whether it was his favorite food, his preference for the color green, or whom he liked to go to bed with. What he resented with every fiber of his body was the fact that Jacob—and plenty of others like him—believed him to be an idiot simply because he chose to be happy with what he had in life instead of miserable because of what he didn't have yet. The fight to prove himself was an exhausting one, and he was bloody well over it.

"Is there something I can actually do for you, Jacob?" he asked, ducking into the dressing room Everett Jewel used, to store the parasols on the shelf Everett wasn't using.

"No." Jacob shrugged. "I'm simply bored."

Martin arched one eyebrow at him as he crossed Jacob and headed back to his workspace. "Just bored, so you decided to follow me around, vexing me."

"More or less," Jacob said with a mean grin.

Martin paused halfway to the backstage area and turned to him with a wry grin. "Are you certain you don't like men? Because I can't think of any other reason you'd dog me like this."

A flush came to Jacob's startled face, and he dropped his arms as if offended. "Not if we were stranded alone together on a desert island."

Martin chuckled and marched on. Like so many other men Martin had known, Jacob would do better to dip his toe in the waters of what he was curious about to discover what his feelings on the matter actually were. He probably didn't fancy men, but why more men didn't at least try things out before making up their minds was a mystery to him. He'd dabbled in those experimental waters as a young man and found that he liked them quite a bit.

That thought had him wondering how Edward Archibald had first discovered he was what he was. Had it been a passing attraction to a schoolmate? Had he been cornered by an older man with nefarious intent, only to learn he rather liked that intent? Had he known his whole life, or had it hit him as an adult? The possibilities were endless. Perhaps it was because Martin was an actor and his entire profession was portraying other people, but he was fascinated with lives and thoughts and the things that had made people into who they were.

"Aren't you supposed to be at John Dandie's office?" Lily asked him as he made his way through the backstage work area to his table.

Once again, his thoughts had wandered, and he'd let them go. "Oh! I am," he said with a start, twisting this way and that, as though someone had a clock nearby that he could check. "The fairies I was away with aren't very good at keeping time."

Lily laughed, stepping over to his table and handing him his coat and hat. "You are a curious fellow, Mr. Piper."

"I wouldn't have it any other way." Martin smiled and let Lily help him into his coat, as though she were the gent and he were the lady. He didn't mind at all. There was nothing fixed in the world, let alone the roles either gender was meant to play, no matter what moralizing priests said.

He headed out of the theater, turning up his collar against the cold, wet wind that blew fog in from the river.

London in January was almost as bad as London in July, but it was his home, and he loved it. Where else could one observe all the varieties of human life while walking from Covent Garden to offices in The City?

He wondered if Edward Archibald ever had thoughts like that. Perhaps not. The man was probably too busy thinking about politics and ways he could make the lives of the people who voted for him better. Martin adored the idea of someone who was willing to devote his life to helping others. He never could have made a go of it in politics. He was too nice, for one. He wouldn't have lasted a second on the floor of the House of Commons, debating policy and arguing for sport. He would have worked too hard to see the other side's point of view, then offered to take them out to the nearest pub for a pint afterwards.

The thought had him laughing at himself as he walked, which drew the attention of a pair of street sweepers, who looked at him funny. He paid them no mind. What other people thought of him was their business. As long as he didn't do anything stupid, he had nothing to worry about. And if there was one thing Martin was certain of, it was that he was far and away more intelligent than anyone ever gave him credit for.

Except, perhaps, John Dandie, which was why John had called him to his office that morning, he was certain. John was still hard on the trail of Lord Selby's missing soon-to-be-ex-wife and son. Hand-in-hand with that problem was the search for a missing Egyptian medallion that Lady Selby's lover had demanded in exchange for Selby's son. As it turned out, Martin might very well have been the last person to have seen the medallion, since Selby had donated it to a theatrical troupe based out of Leeds that he'd once been a part of. John had questioned Martin about the medallion a month before, as had a detective, Arthur Gleason, who was also searching for it. John must have had a break in the case, a break Martin might be able to help with. Why else would he—

Martin's rambling thoughts and his footsteps stopped abruptly as soon as he stepped into John's office and came face to face with Edward Archibald. He held his breath, bursting into a smile, as his chest swelled with fondness. The man looked even more handsome in daylight than he had in the lamplight the night before. And his suit was fine indeed and fit his well-formed body perfectly. Archibald had broad shoulders and a narrow waist. He also had hands that were surprisingly graceful for a boring politician.

Martin shook his head to banish his wayward thoughts and stepped deeper into the office. "Mr. Archibald. We meet again." He extended his hand to shake the man's, getting a sensual thrill at the brush of their palms together.

"Mr. Piper." Archibald nodded.

"Do the two of you know each other?"

Martin had barely registered that John was standing right there, as if he and Archibald had been conversing before he entered the room. John's attractive, young clerk was in the room too, fiddling with papers behind the desk and looking as though he believed himself to be in over his head.

"We met last night," Archibald said in a voice that couldn't have sounded guiltier if he'd been standing in the witness box at a trial, about to be handed a death sentence.

Martin laughed, hoping to put the man at ease. "Mr. Archibald came close to getting himself into a spot of trouble. Patrick sent me after him to make sure he made it home safely."

John glanced between the two of them, his brow inching up. He studied them a bit longer than Martin would have expected, a hint of a grin forming on his lips. "I see. Thank you, Patrick."

"Quite," Martin agreed, smiling at Archibald.

Archibald blushed and focused on John instead of him. Good Lord, but the man was fetching in his shyness. He was downright adorable. What Martin wouldn't give to put a little snap in the man's step, in every way imaginable.

"I suppose you'd like to know why I asked you here today." John got down to business, but Martin couldn't tell who, precisely, he was talking to. Both of them, by the look of things. "As you know, I've been working tirelessly on behalf of Blake Williamson, Lord Selby, to locate his wife and son."

"Have you had any luck?" Martin asked, genuinely hurting on Selby's behalf.

"Not enough," John sighed, scrubbing a hand over his face. "We thought we had them pinned down right after Christmas, but the lead turned out to be a false one. That or they've moved from where we thought they were in Southampton."

"Are they still trying to take a ship to America?" Archibald asked.

"We believe so," John said hesitantly. "But it also appears as though Archibald has unfinished business in England that's keeping him here."

Martin blinked at the mention of his name, snapping out of the way he'd been staring and grinning at Archibald. For a moment, he stood there dumbly, confused. Then he sucked in a breath. "Oh, that's right. Lady Selby's lover is *Ian* Archibald, your brother."

"Yes," Archibald sighed, looking as though he regretted it.

"In that case, would you mind if I called you Edward? It would make things less confusing."

A charming, pink flush came to Edward's face. "Yes, that would be fine."

"And you can call me Martin. Or darling, I'm not picky." Martin winked at him.

Edward went scarlet. John made a sound that he tried to cover with a cough. Martin caught the tail end of a smile as John wiped it away, then went on. "Since our previous leads fell through—and I know this is a last resort—I was hoping you might be able to contact your brother for us," he told Edward.

Edward rubbed a hand awkwardly over his face. "My brother and I are not close," he said. "We never have been, but the last few years have been particularly strained. I haven't seen him more than a handful of times. I have barely spoken to my family at all since Lady Selby's disappearance."

Martin wasn't sure why, but his heart suddenly bled for Edward. He wasn't particularly close with his own family, small though it was. They hadn't approved of his theatrical ambitions or his choice of bedmates. But he and his sister still exchanged cards at Christmas.

"Would you be willing to attempt to contact him?" John asked.

Edward sighed and shrugged. "I'll do what I can. Perhaps my parents have more information."

"I believe they do," John said with renewed energy. "Blake and Niall spoke with them a couple of times when they were in Blackpool in the fall, before the girls were returned to them."

Martin nodded as more pieces fit together. Lady Selby had returned Selby's two daughters, Margaret and Jessica, to him in Blackpool in October, though she'd absconded with the son. The girls were supposed to be exchanged for the Egyptian medallion, but Selby had given Archibald a fake medallion instead. Both men had double-crossed each other.

"I can travel to Blackpool," Edward said, though he didn't sound happy about it. "There isn't anything truly pressing up for debate in Parliament at the moment, and even if there were, I doubt anyone would notice my absence for a few days."

"Good. Thanks." John turned to Martin. "Now, as for you—"

"Yes, I've been wondering what I have to do with this whole thing," Martin said with a smile.

John grinned for a moment before saying, "You worked with The Shakespearian Society of Yorkshire, the troupe Blake donated the medallion to, correct?"

"I did." Martin nodded. "And I remember the medallion. I was in charge of props for a production of *Anthony and Cleopatra*," he explained to Edward. John already knew the full story.

Edward looked mildly impressed, but John didn't give him time to comment. "I've done a little research and discovered that the props and costumes for the Society ended up being bought by a theater in Liverpool, The Crown Theater."

"Oh!" Martin's spirits soared. "I know the place. A friend of mine is manager there, George Wharton."

John looked as though Christmas had come early. "So you have contacts at the theater?" When Martin nodded, he said, "Excellent," as though they'd won a major battle. "That cuts out several steps in the process. I need you to go there immediately to fetch the medallion, if they still have it."

"Immediately?" Martin glanced from John to Edward.

"Yes." John paused. "I trust you have an understudy for the show?"

"I do, but I'm not sure Niall would—" He stopped when he realized the ridiculousness of what he'd been about to say. "No, of course Niall would be more than happy for me to miss a few shows if it means I'm fetching the medallion that can get his lover's son back," he said it out loud.

"Perfect." John moved to clap him on the shoulder. "And since Liverpool and Blackpool are neighbors, I want the two of you to travel together." He glanced between Martin and Edward. "Safety and expediency in numbers, and all."

Martin couldn't have been happier if angels had parted the heavens and showered moonbeams down on him. "Brilliant," he said, brimming with all the possibilities of things that could happen on a trip with Edward Archibald.

Edward didn't look as certain. "Two men traveling alone together?" he asked, more than a little reticence in his voice. "Won't that be...suspicious."

"What on earth is suspicious about that?" Martin laughed, trying not to sound unkind. He shrugged. "For all anyone knows, we could be schoolmates or business partners or complete strangers who just happen to take the same trains and cabs to get where we're going."

Edward still looked uncertain.

"He's right," John told him. "I know you worry, Edward, but there really isn't anything to worry about.

JUST A LITTLE MADNESS

This entire mission shouldn't take the two of you more than a handful of days. Visit your parents in Blackpool to see if they know how to contact your brother, then accompany Martin to the theater in Liverpool to search for the medallion. You'll be back before supper on Friday."

"I suppose," Edward said, rubbing his chin. He peeked sideways at Martin.

Martin did his best not to grin and wink back at that look. His instincts were sharp where people were concerned, and it was as plain as day Edward was worried something naughty might happen between the two of them if they were left alone for long. That either meant that Edward was secretly up for anything at any time, or that he hadn't had any for so long he'd be at risk of snogging a horse if it were pretty enough. Judging by the way he'd let Rivers lead him astray the night before, it was the latter, which would be an absolute smash to play with.

"I'm all for it," he said, smiling at John, then Edward. "I've always wanted to visit Blackpool for a holiday anyhow."

"It isn't much in the middle of January," Edward said, almost as though confessing *he* wasn't much. The stoop of the man's shoulders and the reticence in his eyes was as intriguing as if he'd boasted as boldly as Everett always did.

"I have just one caution for you," John went on in a more serious tone. "Beware of Gleason."

Martin's teasing mood evaporated. "Detective Gleason is still on the case too, then?" He turned to Edward. "The man is terrifying. He's a private detective who cornered me to ask about the medallion in the fall, when the case was new."

"And what did you tell him?" Edward asked.

"As little as possible," Martin replied. "Which was all I knew at the time. The man has an uncanny knack for looking small and unassuming. I didn't think much of him at first. But once he began to question me, I could see he's a force to be reckoned with."

"He is that," John said, frowning. There was a fascinating fire in his eyes, though. If Martin didn't know any better, he would have thought there was something between John and Det. Gleason. But that was none of his business. "Gleason is still searching for the medallion too," John went on. "I can only surmise that he doesn't know what we now know about the theater in Liverpool. He'll be one step behind you the whole way, I fear. That's why I'm sending you immediately. Today, if you can manage it."

"I only need to tell Niall what's going on," Martin said.

Edward shrugged. "I don't think it matters if I attend this session of parliament or not."

Martin's heart squeezed. He would certainly notice if Edward weren't where he should be when he should be.

"Good." John nodded. "It's settled then. The two of you will catch a train north this afternoon. With any luck, we'll be able to contact Archibald by the end of the week, and we'll have the medallion he wants to trade for Blake's son."

"And we'll be back in time for tea," Martin joked.

Edward's lips twitched into a half-smile, and he glanced sideways at Martin again. Martin's heart swelled in his chest, and a burst of lust filled him. Who knew what might happen on the sort of mission they were being sent on? Perhaps Edward was right to be worried about the two of them traveling alone after all.

CHAPTER 3

A thousand different kinds of trepidation filled Edward as he stood in the center of Euston Station, hat pulled lower than he needed it to be, hands in his pockets, glancing through the bustling crowd in search of Martin. He couldn't believe the man wanted to be on familiar enough terms with him to use Christian names, even though that was the tradition within The Brotherhood in order to emphasize the breaking of social boundaries in favor of a far stronger bond. Not that he, or Martin, were in a lofty enough social class to strictly observe the rules to begin with. His father was a mere baronet, after all, which made him—

He let out a breath and dropped his shoulders, shaking his head. If he couldn't even keep his thoughts from flying off in a dozen different directions before Martin arrived, how did he expect to maintain a cool and businesslike mien once he was face to face with the man?

Martin Piper was a celebrity, and he was...well, he was a Member of Parliament. But not the sort anyone would remember or recognize. The faces of several of his colleagues in the House of Commons graced the newspapers displayed in a rack only a few feet from him. Any Londoner would have known Gladstone or Parnell on sight. But as far as Edward knew, his picture had never appeared in print, and his name was buried at the bottom of the list of influential politicians.

But all that would change in a heartbeat if he set one foot out of line. If he so much as looked at a man wrong, he would be—

"Hello."

Martin's loud and cheerful greeting from behind him had Edward jumping out of his skin. He whipped around to face the handsome, smiling man, clutching a hand to his chest. "You startled me."

"Sorry. I have a tendency to do that." Martin's smile grew. He nodded past Edward to the rack of newspapers. "Were you thinking of buying a paper to read on the journey?"

Without waiting for Edward's answer, he stepped past him and reached for a copy of *The Times*. Or, at least, he was probably reaching for *The Times*. As he attempted to pull the paper from the rack, his cuff caught on its edge, and when he pulled the paper away, the entire rack tipped over, spilling newspapers everywhere.

"Sorry, sorry," Martin rushed to apologize, lunging this way and that as he gathered up spilled newspapers.

The angry barker, who had been busy selling a literary journal to a lady in traveling clothes on the other side of his stand, shouted wordlessly and leapt toward the mess Martin had made. "I'll get it. I can tidy up. Things like this happen to me all the time."

The last bit was addressed to Edward as Martin glanced up from his crouched position. His smile was magical, but as much as it brightened Edward from the inside out, it terrified him. Martin's efforts to pick up newspapers somehow spiraled out of control as loose sheets of newsprint spilled away from the carefully folded papers, scattering as if there were a strong wind in the hall.

"No, no, I can get it. Really," Martin told the barker as the man grabbed the papers Martin had already picked up from his arms.

"Get away, you daft fool!" the barker shouted at him.

"Well, if you insist." Martin straightened and stumbled to the side, knocking into a man in a bowler hat who was unlucky enough to be passing at that moment. "Sorry. Terribly sorry."

Somewhere in the middle of the explosive scene, Edward's jaw had dropped open. In spite of the burst of clumsiness, Martin moved with command and grace, like an actor on the stage. He brushed his sleeves as though they had dirt on them, then turned back to the newspaper barker with one last attempt to help the man. The barker swore at him, so Martin backed away, but his smile was as luminescent as ever, and he nodded and tipped his hat to a pair of passing ladies before finding his way back to Edward's side, drawing as much notice to himself as was humanly possible.

"So, perhaps no newspaper after all," he said with a cheeky wink.

"How in God's name...what could you...do you have any idea...." Edward couldn't find the right words to put to his thoughts. It baffled him how someone like Martin could blithely make a scene, without seeming to worry one bit over who might notice him, who might ask questions that would lead to disaster.

Then again, Edward was completely certain that Martin wasn't a thing like him.

"All right." Martin clapped his hands together. "How about purchasing train tickets for Blackpool?"

Edward's jaw flapped for a moment before he said, "I've already purchased them. I wanted to make certain we had a private, first-class compartment, so I went ahead and paid for yours."

"First-class, eh? And private?" Martin wiggled his eyebrows in a blatantly flirtatious way that had Edward's hands and feet going numb. He darted a look around to see if anyone had picked up on Martin's teasing look.

"Don't you have any baggage?" Edward asked, bending to pick up his own suitcase.

Martin laughed. "I have loads of baggage. But I only brought one suitcase. I left it with the porter over there." He gestured over his shoulder with his thumb to a bored-looking porter. The man seemed to be keeping watch over several people's bags.

"You simply left your suitcase in the care of a stranger?" Edward blinked at him. "What if someone had opened it? What if they found...." He darted another look around in case someone was listening to them.

Martin sent him a look that was equal parts amused and pitying. "If they open it, all they're going to find is an extra pair of trousers, a few shirts, and several pairs of drawers that I've probably kept longer than I should."

Edward nearly choked at Martin's mention of his drawers. It was all he could think about as Martin gestured for him to walk by his side to fetch his suitcase, and as they sought out the platform their train would be departing from. Once he started thinking about Martin's drawers, his thoughts continued on to what was contained in those drawers.

His thoughts had reached the pinnacle of ridiculousness as he considered length and girth when Martin asked, "Would you like one to suck on?"

"What?" Edward barked, then shrank at the volume of his own voice.

Martin was clearly trying not to laugh at him and failing. They were passing a stand selling sweets, and Martin had plucked a brightly-colored lolly from a display on the counter. "Would you like a lolly for the journey?"

"Oh. Er, no. No thank you," Edward mumbled, his face going hot. What the bloody hell was wrong with him? He needed to sober up and focus on the mission

John had sent them on. Ian. His thoughts should be about tracking down his brother and talking sense into the man, and nothing more.

"You're probably right," Martin said, putting the lolly back as they walked on. "I'm sure on a journey this long, they'll have a trolley come 'round with food at some point. I always did love buying things off a trolley on a train."

"I wouldn't know," Edward said as they joined the flow of foot traffic heading to the platforms. He did his best to make himself as small and unnoticeable as possible so as not to run into anyone or draw attention.

Martin, on the other hand, seemed to grow to three times his usual size and nearly bumped into everyone they came across. "You've never bought anything off of a food trolley?" he asked, grinning amiably at a woman with three children in tow and tipping his hat to them. The children giggled back.

"No," Edward answered, ducking his head slightly when a middle-aged man coming in the other direction looked at him a little too astutely.

"But you must travel back and forth between London and York all the time," Martin went on, pausing to glance up at a notice board.

"I do, but I never buy food." Buying food would mean talking to someone, which would mean drawing attention to himself. Like Martin was doing right then.

"Oy! Ain't you that bloke from that play?" a man who

had been hurrying by but stopped to look at the notice board said, gaping at Martin.

"If you mean Henry from *Love's Last Lesson*, yes, that's me." Martin beamed at the man.

"Right good show, that were," the man said, slapping Martin's shoulder. "Oy! You know who this is?" he called out to another passing traveler. "This 'ere is Martin Piper, the famous actor."

The traveler whom the man had accosted didn't seem to care at all, but a few others stopped what they were doing to gape and smile at Martin. That led to a terrifying moment when Martin was asked to sign a few autographs. Edward stepped as far back into the shadows of the notice board as he could, waiting until the strangers left Martin alone.

"Gosh, that's the first time I've had anyone ask for my autograph outside of the theater," Martin said with an unmanly squeal as they continued on. His face glowed pink with delight, and there was an extra spring in his step as they showed the porter at the platform their tickets, then continued on to their compartment. "I suppose I really could be as famous as Everett." The possibility seemed to be a complete surprise to him.

"How can you stand to be noticed like that?" Edward asked in a low hiss once they were safely sealed in their first-class compartment.

Martin blinked at him as if the question made no sense. "I'm an actor. I think the point is to be noticed."

"Yes, but...." Edward inched closer to him, looking

out the windows to see if anyone was peering in, waiting to nab them for a stray, guilty word. "Aren't you afraid people will notice what you are?"

Martin stared at him, his eyes widening for a moment. Then his expression settled into an almost sweet grin as the train jerked slowly into motion, beginning their journey. "Darling, there's no point at all in being ashamed of who you are. You can't change it any more than you can change the arrangement of the stars."

A shiver of something warm and dangerous shot through Edward. No one, not in his entire life, had called him "Darling". Not in his youth, not in the heat of so-called passion, and never on a train speeding away from London. He didn't know what to do with it. He didn't know what to do with the decidedly inconvenient way his blood pulsed through him, particularly his cock. And his heart.

"But if it's something that worries you," Martin went on, as though he hadn't changed Edward's entire world with a casual comment, "throughout this mission, if anyone asks, even your family, you can tell them I'm your secretary. MPs have secretaries, don't they?"

"Some of them," Edward said, sinking back into his seat, hardly believing the mad situation he'd gotten himself into.

"There you have it." Martin spread his hands as though the point were made. "I'm your secretary, and I'm accompanying you on parliamentary business. I think I would be rather good at playing the role of secretary."

"I daresay you will be," Edward mumbled. He wasn't going to be able to concentrate on a damn thing through the entire mission.

"Now," Martin went on, as though nothing about the situation was out of the ordinary. "Tell me a bit about your family. What am I going to encounter in Blackpool? And what about this miscreant brother of yours?"

Edward stared at him for a few seconds, particularly Martin's sparkling, hazel eyes. Then he shook himself, sat straighter, and said, "My father, Sir Richard Archibald, is a proud man. He's a baronet, but he deports himself like a duke. He is a stickler for rules and propriety. He has always demanded that his sons live up to their potential and make the family proud, both in terms of profession and deportment."

"The poor bloke must be bloody disappointed," Martin laughed.

Edward was stung by the comment and his face heated with shame.

Martin seemed to catch on. His eyes went wide. "I wasn't talking about you," he said, reaching toward Edward with genuine alarm. "I meant your brother. Your brother ran off with another man's wife, and a duchess at that."

Edward let out the breath he'd been holding. "Right. You're right." But he was absolutely certain that Ian's crimes wouldn't hold a candle to what his father would see as his own depravity. "Ian has always been a bit of a black sheep," he went on. "He is incredibly clever and has made a good name for himself as the manager of an investment firm. But he has a temper, and he doesn't take kindly to snubs of any sort."

"Which would explain his bad blood with Selby," Martin said, rubbing his chin. "He and Niall told me the whole story of their interactions at university."

Edward shifted uncomfortably. "Yes, I was on the periphery of that feud as it happened. Ian was exceedingly jealous of what he perceived as Selby getting all the things he thought he deserved."

"Did he?" Martin asked. "Deserve the things Selby got?"

"No, not one of them," Edward said, then paused, tilting his head to the side. "Perhaps Annamarie. I seem to recall that they were genuinely fond of each other before the then Lord Selby stepped in to offer Selby as a groom."

"Ah, love," Martin sighed. "It's the most powerful and the most destructive force on earth."

Edward was suddenly filled with the burning need to know whether Martin had been in love before. It made him green with envy to think the gorgeous, carefree man in front of him had loved anyone. "Yes, well, it's what we're up against, I fear," he said.

"And I do adore being up against love," Martin added with a wink.

A hot and cold flush shot through Edward. It was a pass. Martin Piper had made a blatant pass at him. He couldn't think, couldn't do anything but gape at the man.

Martin smiled and settled more comfortably into his seat. "Well, we've got a long way until we reach Blackpool, which gives us plenty of time to work out how we're going to contact your brother and convince him to do what's right. In the meantime...." He sat straighter, looking into the hallway that ran on the inside of the train past their compartment. "I wonder when the food trolley is coming around."

Edward smiled in spite of himself. Martin baffled him, titillated him, and made him smile, but at least their mission wouldn't be boring.

JOHN DANDIE WAS A BLOODY GENIUS. THE FARTHER their train sped from London and the more time Martin spent closed up in the first-class compartment with Edward, the more convinced of it he was. John must have known Edward needed someone to bring him out of his shell and that Martin would leap at just such a chance.

"So. Our plans to retrieve the medallion once we've finished with your family and located your brother," Martin said, purposefully waiting until Edward's attention had drifted and the adorable man was staring out the window at the darkening countryside, unsuspecting. "How do we get off?"

Edward sat suddenly straighter, glancing at Martin with wide eyes.

"I mean, how do we pull it off," Martin corrected his

deliberate mistake. Good Lord, but Edward was fun to tease.

"I would think that's up to you," Edward said, his voice hoarse. He shifted uneasily in his seat.

It took everything Martin had not to giggle like a schoolboy about to pull a prank. If it were up to him, he and Edward would draw all the shades of their train compartment and get up to all sorts of naughtiness as the train sped through the night. But he suspected that would be the emotional equivalent of losing control and coming thirty seconds after getting down to business.

He put on a serious look and tapped his chin. "I telegraphed my friend, George, the manager of The Crown Theater, to let him know we would be stopping by in a day or so to search through their props."

"Did you receive a reply?" Edward asked.

"Actually, much to my shock and surprise, I did. I thought there was no possible way George could reply before we left, but either the telegraph office is near the theater or the telegraph boys in Liverpool are highly efficient, because the reply reached me just as I was leaving for Euston."

He reached into the pocket of his winter coat—which he'd removed hours ago, when the journey started—and pulled out the last-minute telegram.

"Turns out George remembers the medallion in question." He scanned the telegram, but didn't bother reading it to Edward before stuffing it back in his pocket. "He thinks it must be there somewhere."

"Good." Edward looked genuinely pleased, though he was still anxious for some reason. "With any luck, we'll be able to accomplish our missions quickly and return to London as quickly as possible."

A grin spread across Martin's lips. "You're in a hurry to get away from me, aren't you?"

"What? No!" Edward insisted, blushing up a storm.

"I make you nervous."

"You do not." Edward squirmed.

"You think I'm nothing more than a randy idiot who walks around wearing a sandwich board inviting myself to be arrested for gross indecency." An unexpected twist of genuine hurt hit Martin as he spoke. Edward wouldn't be the first person to revile him for being who he was.

But Edward surprised him by saying, "Certainly not," with insistence. "You're…it's just that you…well, you're an actor," he said in the end, gesturing vaguely to Martin.

"I am." Martin nodded. "But I'm much more than that." The burst of seriousness didn't seem to be in a hurry to go away. "Do you know that I scored top marks in my primary school?"

"You did?" Edward's brow inched up.

Martin wasn't sure he liked the degree of surprise in the man's expression. He nodded. "I passed the entrance exam for Cambridge as well."

Now Edward gawked at him. "Why didn't you go?"

Martin let out a sigh. "I passed the entrance exam, but I didn't win the scholarship." He shrugged. "My father was a greengrocer. We didn't have that kind of money. And thus ended my academic ambitions."

"But you could have—" Edward stopped, blinking, then shut his mouth.

"I considered offering to do the head of the scholarship committee a particular sort of favor," Martin confessed, feeling far more awkward about it than he anticipated. "But I decided to take gainful employment at a theater in Leeds, working as a stagehand, instead."

"You would have...." Edward nodded awkwardly toward Martin's trousers.

"No. The point was, I would not have," Martin said, crossing his arms. God, he hadn't been so serious in years. He'd intended to have some of his joviality rub off on Edward, but here Edward's gravity was rubbing off on him. It wasn't the sort of rubbing off he'd hoped would happen between the two of them.

"As it turned out, I rather liked the theater," he went on, forcing himself to smile again. "It suits me. Everything is exaggerated and fun. And yes, actors have notoriously loose morals. Which more or less taught me that morals are a waste of time in the first place. Living life is the greatest way to please the Lord, not denying it."

"I hadn't thought of it that way," Edward said.

They'd reached a part of the countryside where the train darted through several tunnels of various lengths. Each time they shot through one, it cast shadows and darkness through the compartment, only to illuminate things again with evening light when they came out the other side.

"I'm perfectly happy with my life," Martin went on as they came through another tunnel. "Mostly because I choose to be. Perhaps I long to be given more credit for my accomplishments, but doesn't every man?" And if he were being honest with himself, he would like to be truly loved, not just as a comic amusement or a temporary bedmate. He wanted to be wanted, not just lusted after or laughed at. "I would have liked the life of a scholar," he went on, shaking out of his uncharacteristically angst-riddled thoughts, "which would inevitably have led to me teaching somewhere. But no, the theater is what makes me happy. It's what makes me feel free."

The train sped into another tunnel as Edward said, "At least you had a choice. It was only ever politics for me at my father's insistence. I was the son whose duty it was to restore the family's name."

"Restore?"

The train emerged from the tunnel, and out of the corner of his eye, Martin caught sight of a man passing through the hallway.

"Father lost most of his fortune speculating, which was Ian's doing," Edward went on. "Thus the house in Blackpool, instead of the ancient estate in Yorkshire where—"

Martin had stopped paying attention, which Edward noticed. He shot up from his seat, throwing open the door and dashing into the hall. The man he'd seen in passing was Gleason. He would have known the detective anywhere. Gleason was shorter than average with an angular face and blue eyes that saw into your soul. It had happened in the blink of an eye, but Martin was certain the detective had been looking into their compartment, possibly listening in, as they passed through the tunnel.

"Have we been discovered?" Edward asked in a worried hiss.

"Possibly, yes. Unless I'm imagining things." Martin pulled all of the blinds on that side of the compartment down, waving for Edward not to get up, which he was in the process of doing. He returned to his seat, staring at the lowered blinds.

"I knew it was a dangerous idea for the two of us to travel alone together," Edward said.

Martin blinked, momentarily confused. Then he realized Edward had never seen Gleason before and wouldn't have known who he was. He opened his mouth to reveal they were being followed by the man John had warned them about, then changed his mind and closed his mouth. There was no point in giving Edward something else to worry about. The man was already a champion worrier. Instead, he rolled his shoulders, keeping his uneasiness to himself. He still couldn't shake the uncomfortable way Gleason had made him feel when he'd interrogated him about the medallion months ago.

"I'm sorry," Martin went on after a second, shaking his head and focusing on Edward once more. "What were you saying? Your father lost his money and moved to Blackpool?"

"That's more or less the entire story," Edward said, eyeing the closed blinds as warily as Martin was. "Father and Mother are bitter about their lot in life, but they've tried to make the best of it. Their bitterness is one of the reasons I'm not sure they'll know where Ian is."

"It's worth asking, at least," Martin said, distracted.

He frowned, scratching the back of his head and trying to think of an alternative plan. If Gleason really had followed them north, their mission might just have become considerably more complicated.

CHAPTER 4

*E*dward felt as though he and Martin had been traveling forever by the time they reached Blackpool. They'd checked into separate rooms at a hotel in Liverpool overnight rather than waiting in the Liverpool train station for the last leg of their journey to begin. That meant they were able to sleep—in theory, though instead of sleeping, Edward spent most of his time tossing and turning and wondering if anyone had found it unusual that two men had checked into the same hotel at the same time and been given rooms on the same floor—then catch a slightly later train the next morning.

"Let me warn you, my father and mother are not warm people," Edward told Martin as they walked the last few streets in Blackpool to the house on Banks Street.

It was just past noon and a cold sun shone down on the frosty, January landscape. Even though his parents didn't live near the beach, the tang of salt was in the air and seabirds squawked and sailed overhead. The entire town had the feeling of the sea about it, but in the dead of winter, it was more forlorn and forsaken than festive and comforting, like it probably was when holidaymakers were there. Or perhaps the forlorn feeling was in Edward's heart at the prospect of facing his family.

"Not to worry," Martin said, clapping him on the shoulder with his usual, indelible cheer. "People tend to like me."

Edward slipped into a grin before he could stop himself. He had no doubt about that. Martin was thoroughly likeable in every way. But the day before, as they'd sped across England, he felt as though he'd caught a glimpse of a whole other side of Martin. One he hadn't anticipated. There was a great deal of substance underneath Martin's shine. Unfortunately for Edward, that just made his insides wobblier and his shoulder tingle where Martin had touched it.

"No sign of Gleason," Martin said in a low voice, glancing over his shoulder as Edward let them in through the garden gate surrounding his parents' house. "John seemed to think he'd follow us every step of the way."

"Perhaps that wasn't him you spotted on the train," Edward suggested.

"Maybe," Martin mumbled, still glancing around, looking a bit guilty. He adjusted his grip on his suitcase's handle. "Or maybe Gleason thought he'd get a jump on us by searching Liverpool for the medallion first."

Edward stopped at the base of the stairs leading up to

his parents' front door. "Should we turn around and go back to Liverpool to search there ourselves?"

An unexpected grin split Martin's face. "Oh, no. I'm not letting you back out of facing your family and figuring out where your wayward brother is. I've been looking forward to meeting your parents for almost as long as I've known you."

Edward frowned at the slippery shiver that shot down his spine. "You've only known me for a matter of days."

Martin pushed his shoulder to force him to face forward and head up the steps to the front door. "Yes, but it feels like a lifetime already, doesn't it?"

As clearly as Edward knew Martin was teasing him, he had to admit that it *did* feel as though they'd known each other more than just a few days. The amount of time they'd spent in each other's company since Martin rescued him two days ago, and the quality of that time made it feel like weeks at least. Not to mention how many times Edward had sat in a dark theater watching him.

He didn't have time to think about it. Martin darted ahead of him and knocked on the front door, then leapt back with an impish grin, leaving Edward to face his family, whether he was ready or not.

A maid in her twenties opened the door with a somber look. "Can I help you?" she asked.

Edward cleared his throat. "Are my parents in?"

The maid blinked at him. "I suppose that depends on who your parents are."

"Abigail, who is at the door?" Edward's father's voice sounded from somewhere in the house. The deep timbre of his voice shook Edward in ways he hadn't anticipated, making him feel all of ten years old again.

"It's me, Father," he called into the house.

"Edward?"

The maid leapt back with wide eyes, throwing the door open fully, as if she'd made a grave error. Edward tried to smile forgivingly at her, but his heart was too busy quivering in his boots for him to know how to soothe a startled maid.

"Don't worry," Martin whispered to the maid behind him as they both entered the house. "I'm forever stuffing things up myself."

Edward caught the man winking at the maid—actually winking—out of the corner of his eye as he moved deep into the foyer. The maid giggled.

That was all the time there was for that exchange, though. Edward's breath caught in his throat as movement from a side parlor caught his eye. He watched in awkward horror as his father muscled himself out of a chair near a fire in the front parlor with the use of a cane. It had been too long since the last time Edward had visited home, and he was shocked to see that his father's condition had deteriorated to the point where he needed a cane to get around.

"What are you doing here?" his father asked with a

frown. Rather than walking into the foyer to greet Edward, he gestured impatiently for Edward to meet him in the parlor.

Edward glanced furtively to Martin—who was still smiling as though he'd been invited to tea with the Prince of Wales—and started toward the parlor.

"Edward? Is that you?" His steps were halted as his mother came down the main staircase. Surprise lit her face, but not delight. She was dressed in a warm, woolen skirt and blouse that was a few years out of fashion and had a hand knit shawl wrapped around her shoulders. "Good heavens, that *is* you," she said, tilting her chin up when she reached the bottom of the stairs.

"Hello, Mother." Edward shifted his suitcase into his other hand before stepping over to kiss her cheek dutifully. His palms were sweaty, and he came close to fumbling the suitcase entirely. The only thing that prevented that was Martin quietly stepping forward to take the suitcase from him. It was a relief to be freed of that weight, but even better was the way their hands brushed for a moment, even if both of them were wearing gloves.

"Come in here and explain yourself," his father grumbled from the doorway to the parlor. It was as if he were intent to hold his ground and not budge an inch to accommodate Edward. Which was usual with him.

"You should have sent word you were coming," his mother said as they moved into the parlor.

Martin followed, setting the suitcases down in the

hall. The maid stared at the suitcases without making a move to do anything about them, then lingered in the doorway.

"It's all been very last minute," Edward attempted to explain himself and to figure out whether he was supposed to stand or sit in his parents' presence, and if he was meant to sit, where. "I did send a telegram, though."

"We did not receive it," his father said in a gruff voice, resuming his seat with a heavy grunt. "You should have waited for a reply before coming." His father planted his cane on the floor in front of him and rested his hands on it as though he were a king with a scepter.

"It would have been nice to know you were coming," his mother added in a disapproving voice.

"I tried to let you know," Edward mumbled. Arguing with his parents had always been pointless. They saw what they wanted to see and nothing else.

"And who is this?" His father frowned at Martin.

"Martin Piper," Martin introduced himself with a smile that was likely brighter than anything either of his parents had ever seen. He stepped forward, hand outstretched toward Edward's father. "I'm Mr. Archibald's secretary."

Edward's father merely stared at Martin's hand until Martin withdrew it clumsily. His mother tilted her chin up all over again and stared down her nose at Martin.

"I've come to see if either of you are in contact with Ian, and if so, might you know how I could reach out to him?" Edward got straight down to business.

It was as if he'd sucked all the air out of the room. His father tensed so much his face went red and his knuckles turned white on the head of his cane. Edward thought he could see a vein throbbing in the man's temple.

His mother was equally as infuriated by the question. "We do not, nor would we accept, any more contact with your brother," she said in a thin voice. "After the way he imposed on us in the fall, we have made it clear that he is not welcome here."

Edward tried not to let his disappointment show too blatantly. "He did not come home for Christmas?" It was a pointless question and one he already knew the answer to. Furthermore, since he hadn't come home for Christmas either, it was cheeky of him to ask.

"He did not," his father said. "No doubt he celebrated the birth of our Lord and Savior by carrying on with another man's wife." He practically growled the last few words.

"I agree that Ian's behavior in this matter has been egregious," Edward said, miraculously managing not to mumble or trip over the words as he spoke. "That is part of why we are searching for him—er, I am searching for him." He cursed himself for drawing attention to Martin. Dear God, if his parents suspected for even a moment what kind of man Martin was, what kind of men they both were, hellfire would probably rain down on them all.

Sure enough, his mother and father both glanced to Martin with narrowed eyes, as though they weren't pleased to be reminded he was there.

"As Mr. Archibald's secretary, I have been organizing his affairs," Martin said, covering perfectly. His acting skills were as sharp as his intellect. "I have a detailed account of the case and his research on the matter if you'd like to see it." He started toward the parlor door.

Edward fought not to cough or to let his eyes pop out of his head. They had no such thing. But Martin seemed to have guessed exactly how his parents would react.

"That won't be necessary," his father said, waving as if dismissing a lowly servant. He frowned at Edward, ignoring Martin entirely. "I suppose you'll be wanting to stay the night?"

It wasn't lost on Edward that his father had only mentioned one night, not several or a week, or offered what might be considered the family home indefinitely. "We—I could stay in a hotel, if you'd rather."

"And risk having the neighbors say we are inhospitable?" Edward's mother said, then clucked her tongue. "No, you will stay here. Abigail." She stepped back into the hall.

"Yes, my lady?" Abigail leapt over from where she was ostensibly dusting picture frames in the hallway and blinked innocently.

"Prepare a guestroom for my son and a room in the servant's quarters for his secretary," his mother said.

"Mr. Piper is not a servant," Edward insisted, shocked by the vehemence of his words.

His mother looked at him as though he'd grown

another head. "I beg your pardon?" She spared only a split-second, sideways glance for Martin.

"Mr. Piper is a guest, not a servant," Edward said. It was too late to back down, and surprisingly, he didn't want to. The very least he could do for the man who had quickly become the closest thing to a friend Edward had had in years was to secure him an actual guest room instead of what was likely to be a drafty attic room.

His mother sighed. "Very well, then. Prepare the brown room and the back bedroom for my son and his employee." She said the last word as if it were filthy. If he were honest with himself, Edward wouldn't have expected anything less.

"I suppose you want to be entertained as well," his father grumbled, though he didn't look at all inclined to get out of his chair.

"Not at all," Edward said with a respectful nod. "We —I simply came looking for Ian. I understand he spent time here in the fall with...with his companions. Did he leave any hints at all about where they were going?"

"I don't have time to deal with this now," his father huffed, settling back in his chair and reaching for the newspaper that was draped over the arm. "Essie, you deal with it."

Edward turned to his mother, his heart sinking.

His mother sighed. "I suppose we'll have to have a formal supper, though not tonight."

"Really, that isn't necessary," Edward insisted. "We'll just have a look around town, see if any of the tradesmen

Ian might have done business with have a forwarding address."

"And deny my friends the opportunity to sup with a Member of Parliament?" His mother looked mortally offended. "Certainly not. I shall make out the guest list and send around invitations immediately. Cook will have to scramble to be at her best by tomorrow night. Abigail will have her hands full preparing rooms for you and setting the dining room for supper. Of course, she'll have to wait until after we dine this evening."

His mother swept on, barely looking at Edward as she passed him.

"You really don't need to trouble yourself if you don't want to, Mother," Edward told her.

"But of course, I want to." Her tone said anything but.

"I suppose we'll just settle into our rooms, then," Edward sighed. "If Abigail would be so kind as to show us where they are."

"And then we could see about those tradesmen," Martin said, moving closer to Edward's side.

Edward's father dropped his newspaper to stare incredulously at Martin. His mother wore a matching look of shock that Martin would dare to speak in their presence.

"Good Lord," Martin murmured, more than a little humor in his voice, close enough so that only Edward would hear.

Edward peeked sideways at him, and when he saw

the mirth in Martin's eyes, he widened his own, warning Martin not to crack.

His mother let out a heavy breath and turned to Abigail, who had paused halfway up the stairs, as if she didn't want to miss the spectacle. "Show my son and his secretary to their rooms, Abigail. Once they've gone out to see to their business, you can change the sheets on the bed and make certain the rooms are adequately supplied."

Edward shuddered to think what "Adequately supplied" meant. Probably half a cake of soap and a pitcher of cold water for washing up, and maybe an extra blanket. Maybe.

"Yes, my lady." Abigail curtsied, then smiled at Martin as he bent to pick up the suitcases and follow her up the stairs.

"I suppose you'll want to view Shell Cottage as well," Edward's mother said as Edward started to follow Martin.

"Sorry, Shell Cottage?" he blinked at her.

His mother pressed her lips together for a moment, looking excessively put out. "Your brother and his... companions did not stay under this roof during their short period in Blackpool. They took up residence at Shell Cottage, on the beach."

Edward glanced to Martin, who had paused halfway up the stairs and now looked back, intrigued. "We should go there first," Martin said.

"I must search for the key before you do," Edward's

mother said. "And that will have to wait until after I have sent around invitations for tomorrow's supper."

"Shell Cottage can wait until tomorrow," Edward said, giving up without a fight and following Abigail and Martin upstairs. "We have plenty of places to search today," he told Martin once he was on the steps. As a final thought, he turned back to his mother. "Thank you for having us, Mother."

"Yes, yes," his mother said, annoyed, waving him away as she marched down the hall and out of their sight.

"They're lovely," Martin said, his voice dripping with sarcasm, once they reached the top of the stairs and turned a corner.

They started down a small side corridor. "Yes, quite," Edward grumbled. "Growing up under their care was such a delight."

The trouble was, that statement, intended to be flippant, ran far deeper into the wounded core of Edward's soul than he wanted it to. It might not have been the house he'd grown up in, but being under his parents' roof made him feel as lonely and looked down on as he had as a child.

"This is the brown room for you, sir." Abigail opened the door to a small but reasonably well-decorated guest room halfway down the hall. She continued on to a door at the very end of the hall. "And this is the back room." She opened the second door to a tiny room with almost no decoration and a single bed. A strong, icy draft blew out of the room, and Edward could see at a glance the room's single window had a cracked pane. "If you gents want to put your things inside, I'll make up the fires and bring blankets while you're out."

"Thanks ever so, love." Martin winked at her.

Abigail giggled and blushed, then rushed off down the hall. She glanced over her shoulder at Martin, wiggled her fingers at him, then disappeared around the corner.

"What in God's name are you doing?" Edward hissed, leaning toward Martin.

"Being friendly?" Martin shrugged.

"You're flirting with the maid." Edward lowered his voice even more.

Martin grinned from ear to ear. "Jealous?"

"I am not...how could you...in my parents' house...no!" He could feel the heat seeping up his neck and lighting his face.

Martin leaned closer to him. "You're rather fetching when you're green with envy."

"I am not—" Edward huffed loudly, shoving a hand through his hair.

Martin laughed as he pushed past him into the back bedroom, setting his suitcase on the bed.

"No." Edward marched into the room, taking his own suitcase out of Martin's hand and swapping it for Martin's. "I'll stay in this room. It's criminal for my mother to toss you in here or to suggest you should stay in a servant's room."

"I don't mind. Really. I've had far worse accommodations," Martin said.

"No, I insist." Edward sighed. He truly wasn't looking forward to staying in such a mean and meager room, but he was so angry over his parents' treatment of Martin—and of him—that he wouldn't have things any other way. "It'll just be for a few nights anyhow. It would only be one if I had my way, but my mother must have her supper party."

"I'm looking forward to it," Martin said with a wide grin. "It should be a treat."

"It'll be a miserable and painful affair," Edward groaned.

"Which is why it will be such a treat," Martin laughed. He shook his head. "Really, Edward. You need to learn to see the humor in even the most untenable situation. That's what life is all about."

He leaned close to Edward as he finished. So close that for a moment Edward thought Martin might kiss him. His heart leapt in anticipation, then thudded with disappointment when Martin pulled away. Martin's eyes continued to shine as though it were only a matter of time before he actually did kiss him, though.

"Right," Martin said decisively. "Let's put our things away and head out, like bloodhounds on your brother's trail. And if we're lucky, we'll have the added excitement of running into Det. Gleason while we're at it."

"God, I hope not," Edward groaned. At the rate things were going, they were on track to have far more of an adventure than he'd bargained for.

CHAPTER 5

There wasn't really a significant enough amount of time left that day to carry out any proper search for clues about Ian Archibald and Lady Selby's whereabouts, but Martin rather enjoyed the tour of Blackpool. Edward's parents had moved there long after Edward himself had left the bosom of his family years ago, so he and Martin discovered the place together. They returned home empty-handed after the search, then had to sit through one of the most stilted and joyless suppers Martin had ever endured in his life.

It wounded him to the core that Edward's parents were so indifferent to their own son. Beyond indifferent. It was as though they actively disliked him. But Martin couldn't figure out for the life of him why. He'd inferred from things Edward had told him that his parents didn't know his true nature, and Martin was convinced that was true as supper wore on. In Martin's experience, suspicious parents continually asked when their single sons would marry and sent pointed looks as they asked, but Edward's parents didn't bring the subject up once. They asked him about parliamentary business, the weather in London, and then proceeded to talk about their neighbors and the plans Lady Archibald had for her formal supper the next day. They didn't speak to Martin once, or so much as look at him.

"That was delightful," Martin joked to Edward when the two of them made their way upstairs at the end of the night.

Edward was clearly out of sorts and only *humphed* and shook his head. "We'd better get rest," he mumbled as they proceeded down the hall. "We've a big day of searching tomorrow."

"Are you sure you don't want to...." Martin deliberately left his sentence hanging, waiting with an expectant grin to see how Edward would assume he wanted to finish the sentence.

Edward stopped in the middle of the hall as though he'd run into something. He glanced furtively at Martin, then cleared his throat, blushing up a storm. The energy that radiated from him was palpable, reminding Martin of the way Edward had been the other night, when he'd rescued him from certain doom. The man was positively gagging for it.

Martin truly hoped he'd make an advance, but all Edward did was shy away and clear his throat again with a frown. "I'm too tired to talk tonight. We'll regroup in the morning and search Shell Cottage."

"All right, then." Martin grinned, pretending not to be acutely aware of the undercurrents between them. He nodded to Edward, then retreated into his guest room.

Much to his surprise, he slept well. The guest room was nice enough, and the bed was comfortable. He fell asleep thinking about Edward and his lamentable situation with his parents and woke the next morning, determined to see if there was anything he could do about it. As soon as he was washed and dressed, he headed downstairs in search of breakfast and parents, hoping for good results with both.

"Lady Archibald, good morning." He found Edward's mother seated at the foot of the table in the dining room, which had been transformed overnight from a formal and rather dark place to a light and airy one, thanks to the addition of a white tablecloth and several vases of flowers.

Lady Archibald did not match her surroundings. She had a heaviness about her that seemed to suck in every bit of light and warmth to kill it. She paused in the middle of buttering a scone and reading a journal of some sort that lay open on the table beside her place and glared at Martin. "I assumed you would take your morning tea in the servant's quarters," she said.

"And deny myself the honor of your esteemed company?" He smiled affably, taking what he hoped was the right place at the ridiculously long table. The maid,

Abigail, rushed forward to pour his tea with a cheeky grin.

Lady Archibald noticed and let out a disgusted sigh. "My son should know better than to introduce an employee to our house," she said, then resumed buttering her scone and reading her journal, as if Martin weren't there.

"Thanks, love," Martin whispered to the maid when she presented him with a plate so that he could pick a scone from the platter in the center of the table. She replied with a wink before stepping back. Martin considered that perhaps he shouldn't flirt quite so blatantly with the poor girl, but he had to win *someone* over, and Lady Archibald wasn't a likely candidate. "You have a beautiful house, my lady," he tried all the same.

Again, Lady Archibald glanced at him as though he'd insulted her. "It will do," she said in clipped syllables, then ignored him.

Martin widened his eyes at Abigail, who rolled her own, as though she were used to the behavior.

Several minutes later, Edward joined them, and Martin could tell at a glance that his friend hadn't slept well. There were dark circles under his eyes, and the same bristling tension that had gripped Edward the night before seemed to have doubled overnight.

"Good morning, Mother." Edward nodded to the woman—who didn't acknowledge him—then took a seat at the table across from Martin. Abigail rushed to serve him the way she had Martin. "Will Father be joining us?"

"Your father takes his breakfast in his room these days," Lady Archibald said without looking up from her journal.

Martin arched a wary eyebrow at Edward, his mouth twitching into a wry grin. He wasn't at all surprised that Sir Richard and Lady Archibald had separate bedrooms. He was certain nothing would surprise him about Edward's family. They were all as mad as march hares, from Ian running off with a married duchess and holding Selby's son hostage to Edward putting up with his mother's cold demeanor as they continued through a silent breakfast.

The silence was deafening, as far as Martin was concerned. To make matters worse, every time he glanced up at Edward and opened his mouth to start a conversation, Edward shook his head, jaw clenched, lips pressed tightly shut. Edward's reluctance to shatter the silence his mother had imposed was so amusing to Martin that he started winking and making faces at Edward across the table in an attempt to get him to crack. Abigail seemed to realize what he was doing and carefully hid her mouth with one hand to keep from bursting into laughter.

At last, Edward had had enough. "We're going to search Shell Cottage," he said, rising from the table and finishing the last of his tea in one gulp. Martin stood when he did, trying not to laugh at Edward's stiff discomfort.

"I've placed the key on the table in the foyer," Lady Archibald muttered, turning a page of her journal, her teacup poised in the air in one hand, as though she'd forgotten to sip it, just as she'd forgotten her son was there.

Edward hesitated for a moment, studying his mother with a look that made Martin's heart ache. When his mother failed to give any indication she knew he was standing there, Edward shook his hand and stepped away from the table.

Martin followed him into the foyer. "No wonder you're all so fit and slender," he murmured, standing close to Edward as they took their coats and hats from the stand near the door. When Edward frowned questioningly at him, he went on with, "Meals like that are terrible for the digestion. It's a wonder you've put on any weight at all. Though you do look lovely."

He added the last bit purely for fun, raking Edward's form with a heated glance. Edward was a fine specimen of masculinity, but it was the bright flush that painted his cheeks and the uneasy, stilted way he put his coat on and buttoned it tight that warmed Martin's heart.

"Where is this Shell Cottage place anyhow?" he asked once they'd left the house and made their way down to the main road that ran along the coast.

"Apparently, it's about a mile north and right on the beach," Edward said, hands thrust in his coat pockets, giving him the appearance that he was holding himself together with all his might. "Abigail gave me the address."

"She's a lovely lass," Martin said with a breezy laugh.

"I don't think she'll last long in your parents' employ, though. She has too much life in her."

Edward turned his head to stare at Martin with wide eyes. "You can't possibly be thinking—"

"No, of course not," Martin laughed. "But just because I'm never going to want to bed her doesn't mean I can't find her to be an amiable person."

Edward snapped his face forward and picked up his pace. Martin shook his head and caught up. Edward was dear and darling, but the man had strange ideas about how humankind related to one another. Then again, after what he now knew about Edward's family, it wasn't much of a surprise.

Shell Cottage lived up to its name in a spectacular way at first glance.

"I've never seen anything like it," Martin said as Edward opened the garden gate.

The house was small and cozy, and it was decorated entirely with shells. They had been set into the walls, likely when the house was built. It gave the whole thing an artless, ramshackle feel, which was entirely at odds with everything Martin had observed about Edward's family.

"How did your parents end up with this?" he asked as Edward unlocked the front door and let them in.

"It's an investment," Edward said, stepping into the front room and looking around. "Father purchased it to rent to holidaymakers in the summer. It's actually their primary source of income."

Martin hummed and glanced around. "I can see how it would fetch a pretty penny."

The cottage was actually lovely and comfortable, though chilly with the winter breeze blowing all around it. The furnishings weren't new, but they had been well taken care of. The kitchen off to one side had been updated to include a modern stove, though he didn't see anything that looked like modern plumbing to compliment it. Two doors off of the main room led to small bedrooms, both of which were made up, but with an appearance of disuse.

"Right." Martin clapped his hands together. "Do we begin by looking for clues or by putting one of those beds to good use?"

He intended the question to be a joke, but Edward snapped to face him, glaring. "Is that all you can think about? Sordid thoughts of—" He waved his hand at Martin, seeming to vibrate with tension as he did.

"Who says sex is necessarily sordid?" Martin asked in return, blinking in surprise at the vehemence of Edward's reaction. Though honestly, he shouldn't have been surprised. The man clearly had trouble with the subject.

Edward puffed out a breath and turned away, his tension doubled. "Never mind," he muttered before making a quick circuit around the main room. "We need to look for any clues Ian might have left behind that indicate where he and Lady Selby are and what they intend to do next."

Martin watched Edward pace, removing his coat and

hat and tossing them over the arm of the sofa that faced an unlit fireplace. Never mind indeed. Edward was going to burst several blood vessels if he didn't take a deep breath and let himself unravel once in a while.

"Are we certain the place hasn't been cleaned top to bottom since the fugitives were in residence?" he asked, following Edward to peer into the kitchen.

Edward only glanced into the kitchen, and when he turned around, he jumped at finding Martin right behind him. His already pink face flushed darker, and his eyes glittered with repressed longing.

"I'm certain it has been cleaned," he said in a hoarse voice. "But something might have been left behind."

He pushed away from Martin, stomping across the main room to the fireplace and checking the mantel for anything that might be a clue.

"Take off your coat and stay a while." Martin followed him, grinning. Bless him, but Edward was as nervous as a cat in a room full of rocking chairs now that they were alone.

"I don't think that's—" Edward stopped and huffed out a breath. "Fine." He unbuttoned his coat and shrugged out of it, tossing it and his hat and gloves onto the sofa beside Martin's. He stared at the collection of their winter things in close proximity, then shook his head and stomped to the farthest corner of the room to continue his search.

Martin chuckled and shook his head. "Good Lord,"

he murmured, walking to a small desk near the door and checking its drawers.

"What?" Edward clipped. "What was that for?"

"Nothing," Martin called over his shoulder. The desk drawers contained only blank stationary and a few pencils. "I was merely mocking your severe sexual repression."

"I beg your pardon?" The question came out strangled and wheezy.

Martin turned to Edward with a smirk. "Love, you're the most locked up, repressed, inhibited man I've ever known."

"That's not true." Edward balled his hands into fists at his sides.

Martin crossed his arms and stared flatly at him.

"Just because I don't conduct myself like a…a telegraph boy in heat doesn't mean I'm repressed," Edward argued, sputtering and tripping over his words.

Martin walked slowly closer to him, still staring, still not saying a thing.

"I'm not a tart. I don't take these things lightly," Edward continued to insist. "That doesn't make me a…a…." He gestured uselessly.

"I'm sorry, what were you doing in Covent Garden the other night?" Martin asked with a teasing twitch of his mouth.

Edward turned so red Martin thought he might transform into a tomato. "A man cannot expect to go through life like a monk," he stammered.

"Of course not." Martin reached the sofa and sat on one of the arms while Edward paced like a fiend back and forth in front of him. "So when was the last time you had a lover?"

"I couldn't possibly," he said in a rush. "Not with my position in Parliament, not with the scrutiny it brings with it."

"Yes, of course, because no Member of Parliament in the history of the realm has ever had a mistress or lover or bit on the side." Martin arched one eyebrow. Edward scowled, but didn't look at him. "University, then?"

Edward shook his head. "I lived in a public dormitory."

"And I suppose men never got up to anything in a public dormitory," Martin drawled. In fact, he had it on good authority that public dormitories were as good as brothels for a certain class of men, and even those who went on to marry and father a whole passel of children often had very special friends amongst their fellow students.

Edward's pacing grew more clipped, and he clenched his jaw so tight Martin worried his teeth might break.

"Before that, then," Martin went on. "Some likely lad from home who you used to diddle with in the hayloft, or whatever they had where you're from."

"We would have been caught," Edward grumbled.

Martin dropped his arms to his sides. "Are you telling me you've never had a lover? That you've only ever cruised the parks of London for a bit of satisfaction now and then?"

Edward answered with the guiltiest sideways look Martin had ever seen.

"No wonder you're such an uptight prick." Martin shook his head.

"I am not—" Edward started to shout, proving Martin's words true instead of countering them.

"All right." Martin stood and walked over to him. "If you're not about to crack under the strain of years'-worth of self-imposed sexual denial, then prove it."

"I'm not...how could...I won't...we're supposed to be here searching for clues about Ian's whereabouts," Edward hissed.

"He's not here." Martin stated the obvious with a teasing grin. "Now that that's settled, why don't you let me give you what you were looking for the other night?"

Edward's brow shot up so fast Martin thought his eyebrows might fly right off his face. "I couldn't...you can't...you're not a...."

"I'm quite good, you know." Try as he might, Martin couldn't keep his grin in check. Edward was the single most charming thing he'd ever seen, the way he was squirming and writhing, even as temptation lit his eyes. He stepped closer to Edward. "We're all alone in this lovely cottage by the sea. It's winter, so no one is walking past and no one will come knocking. You won't even have to undress. I'll just unfasten these trousers—" He reached for Edward.

"You can't." Edward pulled away so quickly he nearly lost his balance. "You can't do that."

"Yes, I can," Martin laughed. "I actually like it. Lots of people do. There's nothing quite so satisfying as a cock, big and thick, in your mouth when you know you're the one who got it that way."

Edward's mouth dropped open as he stared incredulously at Martin.

"Right, like that," Martin laughed, touching a finger to Edward's bottom lip. "You can suck me if you want to. I definitely wouldn't mind."

Edward snapped his mouth shut and jerked away, but not that far. The tension and need that radiated from him was so strong it was making Martin hard.

"Come on, love." Martin lowered his voice and closed the distance between them. "You want it. I know you do. You've wanted it since the moment we first met. I want it too and have for just as long. I know we could be magnificent together. And there's nothing wrong with it, I swear to God. Let me take care of you."

"But we're friends," Edward said, hoarse and weak.

"Precisely." Martin slipped an arm around Edward's waist, pulling him close until their bodies were flush against each other. They were both noticeably aroused, which made Martin unbelievably happy.

"We're *friends*," Edward repeated. "I can't do that with a *friend*."

"Who better to do it with?" Martin laughed softly, though his heart was breaking. He brushed a hand along the side of Edward's face, adoring the raging tide of emotions that flooded Edward's eyes. He would have given anything to take the fear and the anxiety out of those eyes and to replace it with joy and life.

The thought was overpowering, so he leaned into Edward, closing his mouth tenderly over Edward's. The kiss was beautiful. He adored kissing and had probably kissed more men than he should in his life, but there was something about kissing Edward that eclipsed everything else he'd ever done before, in spite of—or perhaps because of—the fact that Edward didn't have the first clue how to kiss properly. Martin's heart caught in his chest at the idea that Edward had never been kissed the right way, or perhaps even at all. He threw his whole heart into it, clasping the back of Edward's head and teasing Edward's lips with his own until Edward relaxed. He then nipped his bottom lip and brushed his tongue against Edward's. He grasped Edward's face with both his hands and explored him fully. Edward hardly moved, but that was a good sign, all things considered. He didn't move away, he just let Martin devour him.

When at last Martin inched back, muscling an almost frozen Edward toward the sofa, Edward let out a sound of protest.

"We're not stopping there," Martin said, his voice deep with passion.

He managed to maneuver Edward to the sofa and nudged him to sit. Once that was accomplished, he knelt on the floor in front of Edward and pushed his knees open. Instinct told him to be careful and go slow, so he leaned forward, capturing Edward's mouth again and kissing him lingeringly until the tension in his body shifted.

"There," he said in soothing tones, unbuttoning Edward's jacket and waistcoat and pushing them aside before sliding his hands down his shirt to the fastening of his trousers. "Isn't this so much nicer than a faceless fumble in the bushes at St. James's Park?"

"I can't even—"

"Ssh." Martin touched a finger to Edward's swollen lips to shut him up, then continued with the fastenings of his trousers.

He figured he would have to be quick and take Edward by surprise if he wanted to see the whole thing through to the end before Edward second-guessed everything and forced him to stop. As soon as he had Edward's trousers undone, he yanked them down over his hips. Edward's impressive erection sprang free, standing up at attention, already shining with pre-come, as if it knew exactly what it wanted, even if Edward's mind lagged behind.

"You're lovely," Martin said with genuine appreciation, taking Edward's prick in hand. He smiled up at Edward's wide, disbelieving eyes. "Truly, you are a thing of beauty. You shouldn't be ashamed of that or hide it."

He felt Edward's willingness waver, so before he could change his mind, Martin bore down on him, teasing and tasting his head first before drawing him deep into his mouth.

Edward let out a pleasured moan that Martin echoed. God, the man's taste was divine, and the way he filled his mouth had Martin throbbing. He should have thought to free his own erection before starting in on Edward's. Edward was all heat and heart and salty musk as Martin took him as deeply as he could, moving on him and using his tongue to give him everything. He vocalized his pleasure, feeling in his soul that it was important for Edward to know he was enjoying the act as much as Edward was. And, God, did he ever enjoy it.

As Martin expected, Edward barely lasted through a minute of sucking and teasing and swallowing. He came apart with a loud cry, spending himself in Martin's mouth as he gripped the sofa cushions with both hands. The moment of abandon was so potent that Martin almost came himself. He swallowed reflexively, then inched back to catch his breath as Edward went lip.

"That was lovely," he reassured Edward, grinning up at him and stroking his hands over Edward's sides and hips as if to soothe any lingering doubt. "I enjoyed it."

Too quickly, Edward's hazy, post-orgasmic calm tensed and evaporated. "I should...it isn't fair...you're not...."

Martin arched one eyebrow, grinning impishly. "What's that? Are you saying you want to return the favor?"

Edward pressed his lips tightly shut, but there was a new kind of heat and longing in his eyes. And an affirmation.

Again, knowing the window of opportunity before Edward had second thoughts was tiny, Martin straightened as tall as he could while still kneeling and tore through unfastening his trousers. He reached for Edward's hand and brought it to his cock. The feeling of Edward touching him was a thousand times better than he'd expected it to be. Like kissing, he'd fiddled around with other men, getting each other off, more times than he could count, but there was something worlds different about having Edward's hand stroking him—tentatively at first, and then with surprising purpose. Edward actually seemed to know what he was doing, which was wonderful.

"Yes, like that," he gasped, gripping Edward's thighs for support as his full focus narrowed in on the pleasure Edward was giving him, as rudimentary as it was. "That's good, love. That's so—oh!"

He came hard, spilling across Edward's hand with a groan. Edward gasped, then let out a shaky breath of surprise. The whole thing was so simple and intimate and basic, and yet, Martin couldn't think of a single experience that had been sweeter. He tipped forward, resting his head against Edward's chest for a moment, smiling at the connection they'd made and enjoying the afterglow for as long as he could.

"What do we do now?" Edward whispered at last.

Martin used all of his effort to pull back and smile. He clasped the sides of Edward's face and stole a kiss before clumsily standing. "Now we clean up a bit, then continue searching the house for clues."

"We...do?" The way Edward glanced up at him, clearly at a loss, holding his damp hand awkwardly in front of him, made Martin want to drop back to his knees and pledge to hold him close and take care of him for the rest of their lives.

"Unless you want to...." He nodded toward one of the bedrooms with a grin.

Edward shot to his feet so fast Martin stumbled back. "We should keep searching," he said, dashing past him toward the kitchen.

Martin laughed, his heart overflowing as he watched Edward retreat. He was never going to be able to let the man go now.

CHAPTER 6

The search of Shell Cottage turned up nothing of any interest in locating Ian, but it left Edward with a soul-deep sense that he'd fallen off a cliff and changed his life in ways he would never be able to recover from. He couldn't decide if he wanted Martin to pretended nothing happened between them or not. Martin didn't pretend at all, though. He grinned and stole mischievous glances as they searched for clues about Ian, his gorgeous face pink with pleasure, taking whatever opportunity he could to stand near to Edward or to brush his hand or touch his back, or to straight up steal a kiss just when Edward was certain the whole thing was forgotten.

Kissing Martin. It was almost as good as the mind-shattering pleasure of having the man swallow his cock. True to his word, Martin was very good indeed. He'd practically made Edward's soul leave his body at the intensity of the pleasure he gave. In the moment, it was simply the most magnificent experience Edward had ever had to come in Martin's mouth. Afterwards, and with increasing intensity as they finished their search, then headed off into Blackpool for a spot of lunch, as casual as you please, the knowledge and memory of what they'd done burned in Martin like a brand on his forehead for all the world to see.

"Cheer up," Martin whispered, standing far too close to him as the two of them walked down the stairs to join his mother's supper guests that evening. "Whatever has that screwed-up look of panic on your face, it might never happen."

Edward glanced to him with disbelieving eyes. He couldn't bring himself to tell the man it had already happened, or that he'd relived the moment a dozen times over in his mind already since that morning. How Martin could bounce down the stairs, as cheerful as a child on Christmas morning, looking as handsome as the devil in a suit his parents would probably scoff at, was a mystery to him.

But, God, he adored the man.

That stray thought hit him just as he stepped into the parlor, which was filled with stiff, well-dressed, middle-aged and older friends of his parents. Their conversations died off in an instant as they all turned to stare at him. One grey-haired woman in a high, lace collar even raised a pair of lorgnettes to her eyes to get a better look at him.

"My son, Edward Archibald, Member of Parliament

for York," Sir Richard informed the guests. To Edward's ears, it sounded as though he were telling them a plague victim had arrived, so they'd better stand back. He said nothing at all to introduce Martin.

"How do you do?" Edward bowed, facing the nearly bald gentleman he supposed was the most important of the guests, judging by how his parents stood on either side of the man.

He was certain, beyond a shadow of a doubt, that he had the word "invert" emblazoned across his forehead in letters of fire. Every single one of his parents' guests could probably see right into his soul, could read his mind and view his memory of Martin fellating him that morning and him groaning in ecstasy as he did.

"Mr. Archibald." The balding gentleman extended a hand with a brittle smile. "It is a pleasure to meet you."

Hearing the word "pleasure" did nothing for Edward's composure. He shook the man's hand, then proceeded to have his mother drag him around the room, introducing him to her guests with a touch of distaste in her voice. What surprised Edward the most was that there wasn't a title among any of them, but they all behaved as though they were dukes and duchesses.

"Our cook has prepared her finest for us this evening," his mother said at last, looping back toward the parlor doorway as if leading her guests in a parade to the dining room. "I'm certain you will be impressed."

In spite of there being no peers or persons of note among them, the guests shuffled into lines in order of what they probably considered precedent. His father and mother took the front of the line, of course, but when one of the richly-dressed widows attempted to take Edward's arm and step in place right behind them, Edward's father turned and glared at him.

"Mr. Wright takes the place behind me," he growled, narrowing his eyes as though it were Edward's fault that protocol had been breached.

"Yes, of course," Edward mumbled, stepping back.

He caught Martin's eye as he waited for the widow to choose a better placement for them. Martin was smiling away at his companion, of course, though she looked to be about as old and dry as a tin of biscuits found in the back of a pantry. There was a spark in his eyes when they met Edward's that had Edward blushing and aching like a fiend. He forced himself to look away. Everyone would know what had happened between him and Martin if he so much as breathed the same air as the man.

When order of precedence was finally decided and the company made their way into the dining room, Edward was slightly relieved to find himself seated at the opposite end of the table from Martin. He still had a full view of Martin's irresistible, grinning face as he entertained his supper partner, but in all likelihood, Edward's full attention would be at his father's end of the table, where he sat.

"Don't embarrass me this evening," his father growled to him, leaning across the corner of the table.

"Of course not, Father," Edward whispered in return.

He couldn't imagine how his father thought he could be an embarrassment. Although he could think of a hundred ways that he might embarrass himself, from staring down the table like a lovesick fool at Martin all evening to blurting out that Martin had swallowed him that morning, to having an erection at the table, which—oh, God—he was well on his way to getting at just the thought of Martin.

He squirmed uneasily. His father sighed and rolled his eyes. Martin glanced in his direction, a brief cloud passing over his otherwise jovial face.

"I don't believe we were introduced to your friend," Mr. Wright said to Edward from his seat across the table.

"Mr. Piper is my secretary," Edward said, certain everyone knew he was lying and that Martin was his lover. But was he? His lover? After one incident that lasted less than five minutes.

Oh, God, he'd lasted less than five minutes. Less than one. How long would he last next time? Would there be a next time? Did he want a next time?

Yes, God help him, he did. Did that mean he wanted Martin to be his lover? Like Niall Cristofori was Blake Williamson's lover?

He reached for his wine as soon as the young man hired to play footman for the evening poured it and sloshed some of the red liquid onto the pristine tablecloth as he did.

His father hissed in disgust. "Your manners are as gauche as ever, I see."

"Sorry, Father," he said, hoarse, gulping his wine.

"Imbecile."

The insult was fired off loud enough for everyone at that end of the table to hear it. Judging by the way Martin glanced away from his conversation with a middle-aged man across the table, he'd heard it as well.

A quick hush fell over the company before conversations resumed.

"How goes parliamentary business these days?" Mr. Wright asked, a little too loud, as though he was purposely attempting to rectify the embarrassing situation. He only made Edward want to sink into the floor more, though.

"It's fine," Edward said. "The Irish Question is still on everyone's mind, but problems of basic growth and development, subsidizing housing and sanitation costs, for example, have taken up most of the session this time so far."

"Oh." Mr. Wright's shoulders dropped in disappointment.

"As you can see," Edward's father said with a sneer, "having an MP as a son isn't as scintillating as we were promised it would be. Edward is a dedicated backbencher."

His father and Mr. Wright chuckled together, leaving Edward feeling like a ten-year-old who had disappointed his parents' expectations.

"You must have quite a fascinating social life in London," the woman to his left, Mrs. Thompson, asked with a hopeful glimmer in her eyes. "I'm certain members of parliament never lack for invitations."

"My work keeps me too occupied for much of a social life," Edward told her, face blazing with heat. There was no way he could divulge that he spent most of his free time either lurking in the back of theaters or tucked away in a corner of The Chameleon Club, reading from their extensive library of books that had been banned in England.

"Not even balls in Westminster?" Mrs. Thompson asked.

"I'm afraid not," Edward said with what he hoped was a conciliatory smile. He couldn't imagine what she even meant by balls in Westminster. "I do visit the British Museum on a fairly regular basis." Although he would be damned if he'd tell her the museum was a known cruising ground for homosexuals. Not that that was why he visited. Most of the time.

He glanced down the table to Martin again, squirming in his chair and unable to find a comfortable way to sit. How lovely would it be not to ever have to worry about slinking through the shadows of public places just to satisfy an itch that would drive him mad otherwise.

"As I said." His father's voice pulled his attention back to his end of the table just as Martin glanced his way. "Dull, unoriginal, and disappointing in every way."

Edward hoped his father was talking about the food that the hired footman was quickly serving, but he knew better. He didn't even need to see the sneer his father gave him to know the truth of things. Dull, unoriginal, and disappointing were among the nicer things his father had called him.

Martin's laughter at the other end of the table left him with a bittersweet feeling of longing in his gut as he focused his full attention on eating without tasting and drawing as little attention to himself as possible. Martin was lively, fascinating, and colorful. What had happened between them that morning had to have been a fluke. Or something Martin did casually without it meaning anything. Edward was a fool if he thought it could be anything else. His father sneered at him and ignored him in favor of talking to Mr. Wright. Mr. Wright didn't give him a second glance as he launched into a political conversation with his father—as if Edward were the dustman and not an MP. Mrs. Thompson turned to talk to the gentleman seated on her other side. None of them wanted anything to do with Edward, and he wasn't surprised. It stood to reason that it was only a matter of time before Martin wouldn't want anything to do with him either.

MARTIN WAS ABOUT READY TO MURDER SOMEONE. He laughed and smiled and carried on a lively conversation with the people seated around him—much to Lady Archibald's disgust—but inside he seethed. Whatever had happened to make Edward shrink into himself, whatever his father or the people seated near him had said to put that hang-dog look on Edward's face, he wanted to stand up and flip the table over in anger. How dare those stodgy old nobodies kick a man when he was already down. And after the way things had unfolded between him and Edward that morning and afternoon, Martin was convinced that Edward was very much down. A man who felt good about himself wouldn't engage in a sexual act with a willing partner, then slink around as though he expected to be told off for the rest of the day.

"And how do you find Blackpool, Mr. Piper?" Mrs. Frost, the elderly lady sitting on Martin's right asked. He'd just finished telling the people around him about the way he'd had to haggle for a fish pie for lunch, making them laugh in the process. Of course, he'd left out the bit about eating the pie with a ridiculous degree of sensuality as Edward watched him, or the string of double entendres he'd teased Edward with, or the way he'd deliberately dripped the pie's creamy sauce onto his fingers so that he could remind Edward of their earlier activity and watch him squirm with arousal as he licked it off.

"I think it's splendid," he said, grinning back at all of the guests who were smiling at him. He knew full well that he had a captive audience in his hands, and he intended to give them their money's worth. "I would love to return in the summer for a little sea bathing. I hear it's all the rage up north."

"I dare say it's all the rage wherever one finds a beach and a sea," Mr. Jeffers, the middle-aged man seated across from him, said with a wink. "Why, when I was in Egypt as a young man, we used to see all sorts bathing and sunning themselves, both in the sea and the Nile. And some of the ladies were quite a sight to behold, I can tell you." He winked at Mrs. Frost.

Mrs. Frost laughed so loud she drew a scowl from Lady Archibald. "This is hardly an appropriate topic for supper conversation," Lady Archibald said, narrowing her eyes at Martin, as though it were his fault.

"I've never been to Egypt," Martin promptly steered the conversation in another direction, though he would never acknowledge to Lady Archibald that he was doing it for her sake. "I've never had a chance to go on holiday outside of England at all." He checked down the table, fuming all over again to find Edward staring at his food and being ignored by the others. Poor Edward wasn't even eating his food, just staring at it and looking as though the weight of the world were on his shoulders.

"I wasn't in Egypt on holiday," Mr. Jeffers said. Martin wasn't fully paying attention until he added, "I was there as part of an excavation in the city of Thebes."

In an instant, the man had Martin's full attention. "Thebes? Are you an Egyptologist then?"

"I am," Mr. Jeffers admitted, sending a teasing wink to Mrs. Frost. "I've uncovered tombs and worked with some of England's most prominent archeologists to bring the past back to life."

Excitement pulsed through Martin. "Did you ever work with a Professor Carroll?"

Mr. Jeffers looked surprised. "In fact, I did. Jolly old fellow, Carroll. I was sad to hear of his passing a few years ago. He was a good man, if somewhat absentminded."

Martin wanted to jump out of his seat and shout in victory, but he kept his face placid and asked, "Really? How so?"

"He was forever forgetting lectures he was supposed to give and mixing up artifacts from his digs."

"You know, I've heard something like that." It took every bit of Martin's acting skills to appear only casually interested when, in fact, he was reasonably certain he'd just stumbled across a major piece of information that was vital to the mission he and Edward were on. "I once heard that he gave away a priceless artifact as a prize for an exam," he said, glancing down the table to Edward, as if he could will the man to pay attention to what was about to be said.

"He did," Mr. Jeffers laughed. He paused, tilted his head to the side, then went on with, "Well, he did in a manner of speaking. I know the medallion you're talking about. Or at least I've heard the rumors. It was made out of an onyx and gold scarab beetle."

"Is it valuable?" Martin asked, his breath catching in his lungs. "That is to say, could the medallion be sold for a fortune?"

Mr. Jeffers winced. "I highly doubt it. On its own, it's just a pretty piece of jewelry."

"Oh." Martin deflated a bit. At least, until he noticed

Edward had caught on that something important was being said and had glanced his way.

"What gives that scarab value is that it was part of a set," Mr. Jeffers went on.

"A set?" Martin's heart sped up again.

"Yes. Several items were uncovered in a box in one of the tombs we excavated. The thought at the time was that it was the tomb of one of the pharaoh's queens. The set was a jewelry box, or perhaps a cosmetics box. Whatever it was, the set was rare in that it was completely and carefully kept together. At least, until Carroll gave that scarab away."

"Where is the rest of the set now?" Martin asked.

Mr. Jeffers shrugged. "I believe it was purchased by a private collector."

"Do you think they would pay a pretty penny to have the scarab reunited with the rest of it, to have a complete set again?"

"Possibly," Mr. Jeffers said. "But as I understand it, the scarab has been utterly lost, so there doesn't seem to be any hope of that."

"I suppose not," Martin said, pretending to be disappointed.

In fact, his hands were numb with excitement and his thoughts bounded in a hundred different directions as Mrs. Frost asked Mr. Jeffers more questions about Egypt. Ian wanted the medallion back. So much so that he had listed it in his demands to Selby. The medallion wasn't worth much on its own, but if Ian had the rest of the set—

or if he knew who owned the rest of the set—he could sell the whole thing for a fortune. Or, if someone else was looking for the scarab, Ian might have some connection to them. Either way, it seemed as though they'd discovered the motive behind why Ian wanted the medallion so badly.

The rest of supper couldn't pass quickly enough. The dull conversations that Martin usually found a way to be amused with, if only for their ridiculousness, only seemed dull to him. Edward became more and more withdrawn as they ground their way through to pudding, and then when the supper finally broke up. It was a reason for celebration that so many of the guests deemed themselves too old to stay around for cigars and brandy or tea and chitchat. Even though the meal itself had gone on for ages, the guests were quick to depart afterwards.

All the same, when Martin tried to catch Edward before his father drew him into the parlor for some sort of discussion, he failed. He lingered in the downstairs hallway as the guests slowly departed, saying goodbye to Mr. Jeffers and Mrs. Frost, but what he really wanted was to drag Edward aside and get him alone. For more reasons than just carnal ones, for a change.

"Why are you lurking in the hallway?" Lady Archibald snapped at him after the last of her guests departed. She narrowed her eyes suspiciously at him. "Are you thinking of stealing the silverware while it's all out on the table? Because I will have you arrested immediately, whether you are my son's secretary or not."

"Not at all, Lady Archibald." Martin smiled and made a show of deference to the woman. He would have found a way to tease her and attempt to get her to laugh in spite of her dislike, but the information he now had was too pressing to play games. He had to talk to Edward.

Unfortunately, Lady Archibald stared at him and stared at him until he was forced to retreat up the stairs, as if going to bed. Perhaps that was better after all, though. If he made like he was retiring for the evening then waited for Edward to come up to his room, they could have the conversation they needed to have with complete privacy.

He spotted Abigail in the upstairs hallway in the middle of his retreat and changed course to have a word with her.

"Psst, Abigail." He waved her over to the corridor where his and Edward's rooms were located.

Abigail's eyes went wide and her cheeks pink. She glanced around, then darted to join Martin in the secluded hallway. "Yes, Mr. Piper?" she asked with a spark of impishness in her eyes.

"What time do you think the master and mistress of the house will go to bed tonight?" he asked.

Abigail's eyes shone brighter. "I'd wager they'll be in bed and fast asleep in an hour or so. They don't last long after dark these days, especially when they've had company."

"So they sleep soundly, then?" A wealth of ideas for

things he and Edward could do after they'd talked about the medallion came to him.

"They do," Abigail said. "I'll even bring her ladyship some warm milk before bed. That'll do the trick."

"You're a peach, love," he told her with a wink.

"I think you'll find I'm much more than that," Abigail said in a coquettish voice. She stepped away, wiggling her fingers over her shoulder at him as she ducked back into the upstairs hall.

Martin continued on to his room. They might not have found Ian or any further information about him, but they'd made tremendous progress in their trip to Blackpool. Now that they knew why Ian wanted the medallion, once they retrieved it from Liverpool, they would have the bargaining chip Selby needed to get his son back.

CHAPTER 7

"And another thing," Edward's father droned on from his throne-like chair in the parlor, scowling at Edward as he did. "It's bad enough that you would sit sullenly at my supper table and refuse to engage in conversation with my friends—"

"I found their conversation to be cruel and designed to denigrate me," Edward muttered, wishing he had the backbone to meet his father's eyes when he said it.

His father's eyes widened. "The topics of conversation at my supper table are none of your concern. It is your duty to entertain my guests and to bring praise to me and your mother. You are a reflection of us, and—"

"And I suppose Ian is as well?" Edward interrupted again with slightly more vigor.

His father clenched his jaw, his face flushing. "Leave your brother out of this. It is you whom we are discussing now."

"Your parliamentarian son who has never set a foot out of line, never brought dishonor to the family, and is respected in both York and London, and who still somehow manages not to be good enough for you." Edward shocked himself with his statement.

"You are a sniveling coward," his father spit back at him. "At least your brother went after what he wanted and stood up for himself when confronted. You are nothing more than an elaborate doormat."

Edward flinched as his growing confidence withered. His father was right. His accomplishments were all undermined by the simple fact that they weren't what he wanted. He'd fallen into politics in a bid to please parents who he had known in his heart all along would never be pleased. He skulked around London, afraid of his own shadow. Worst of all, he knew he would continue to be afraid, continue to keep his head down and his collar turned up against life, because he couldn't bear to face the utter rejection of being himself.

"And as for that silly idiot you have forced me and your mother to entertain," his father went on. Edward snapped straighter as a wave of indignation on Martin's behalf washed through him. "If you ever bring such a frivolous jackanapes to my house again—"

"Martin Piper is the very best of men," Edward defended his—dammit, now was not the time for his mind to catch on whether to call Martin his friend or his lover. Especially since the thought of it all heated his face and made him unable to stand still or look his father in the eyes.

His father snorted. "The man is a buffoon with no decorum whatsoever."

"Mrs. Frost and the rest of your precious friends didn't think so." Edward took a half step toward his father. "They were clearly delighted with Martin's conversation."

A moment too late, he realized calling Martin by his Christian name could raise more questions than he was ready to answer.

His father didn't seem to pick up on what Edward believed was a major slip on his part. "Weak-minded fools, all of them," he said.

"Or perhaps you are jealous that someone else upstaged you during your precious supper?"

Edward's father glared at him as though he were a dog that had vomited on his shoes. "The matter is closed," he growled. "You are a woeful disappointment to me and your mother. You always were and you always will be. I want you gone from this house tomorrow morning. And don't bother to come back."

"As you wish, Father." Edward bowed stiffly and turned to march out of the room.

His insides were a Gordian knot of emotion as he mounted the stairs two at a time and stormed down to the drafty and miserable back bedroom. He wanted to feel free. He wanted his father's curt dismissal to make him feel as though he were a bird let out of a cage. That was how Martin would feel if their positions were reversed. Then again, if Martin were his father's son, he would probably find a way to make the bastard love him. Everyone loved Martin, but no one loved him.

Edward cursed himself for the maudlin thought as he marched into his room and shut the door behind him. It was absolutely true that no one loved him, not a soul on the earth, now or at any point in his life. But growing morose over it, like an adolescent girl, wasn't going to solve any of his problems. He tore at the buttons of his jacket and waistcoat, undressing for bed as quickly as he could. All he wanted was to go to sleep, put everything behind him, return to London, and forget the disappointments of his life. He wanted to finish his service as an MP, then leave politics altogether. Perhaps the British Museum was hiring docents or the Concord Theater needed an usher. He just wanted to forget himself and his boring, frustrating path through life.

The back bedroom was frigid, so he leapt into bed as soon as he was in his pajamas. The fire had gone out hours ago, by the feel of things, probably because Abigail was too busy preparing for the cursed supper party to keep it lit. His mother had kept the poor maid too busy to notice much of anything. Even with an extra blanket, Edward shivered as he hugged himself in bed. He'd forgotten to blow out the lantern before crawling under the sheets, and the prospect of getting out of bed to take care of that wasn't appealing. It all seemed fitting, though. He would just lie there in bed, cold, diminished, abandoned, miserable—

The door handle turned in the middle of his litany of complaints, and without so much as a knock, Martin let himself into the room.

"Oh, good, you're still up," Martin whispered as he shut the door behind him.

Edward's heart slammed into his throat, and his whole body heated in an instant. "What are you doing here?" he hissed, propping himself on one arm under the thin blankets.

"You will never guess what I discovered at supper," Martin took a few steps forward, his face lit with joy and excitement in stark contrast to the way Edward felt. "I was seated across from a Mr. Jeffers who is a—good God, it's as cold as monkeys' balls in here." He hugged himself suddenly, rubbing his arms. "Was it like this last night? No wonder you didn't sleep. This is intolerable. It's simply—" He lunged forward, reaching for the bedcovers. "Shove over. I'm not going to stand around freezing my willy off while I tell you what I've discovered."

Edward was utterly gob smacked by the flurry of words—not to mention the thought of Martin's willy—as Martin leapt into bed with him. The bed was relatively narrow, so there was no place for Edward to go to escape being fully caught up in what amounted to an embrace. Martin made no attempt to keep distance between them. On the contrary, he snuggled against Edward, humming happily as he nestled their bodies together, legs intertwined, touching in every possible way. The extreme intimacy was so sudden that Edward couldn't do a thing about it until it was too late.

"Mr. Jeffers is an Egyptologist," Martin said, eyes bright with excitement, his hand resting on Edward's side.

"A-all right," Edward stammered.

"He worked on an excavation in Thebes." Martin's eyes glowed even brighter, as though Thebes were somehow significant.

What was significant was the way Edward was swiftly getting hard with Martin's thigh lodged firmly between his legs.

"Is Thebes important?" Edward somehow managed to ask.

"Yes, of course." Martin burst into a giddy smile. When Edward just stared at him, captivated by the way the man smelled like the freshness of summer in spite of it being the dead of January, Martin went on. "The medallion. It was part of that excavation at Thebes. Jeffers knew all about it, knew that Carroll gave it up as the prize that Selby won without realizing what it was."

Edward blinked at the information, shocked that anything could startle him out of the acute awareness of Martin's body that had overtaken him. "Is it valuable, then?" he asked.

"Jeffers doesn't think it's particularly valuable on its

own," Martin reported as though they were sharing tea in a café in public. "But apparently it's part of a set."

"A set?"

"Yes." Martin nodded, shifting subtly. That simple action pressed their bodies together even more intimately, sending Edward's blood rushing to his groin. "And it stands to reason that whoever now owns the rest of the set—Jeffers said it's in private hands now—wants the medallion to complete things."

"Which could explain why Ian is so determined to get his hands on the thing," Edward thought aloud. His voice wasn't nearly as calm as it should be, which wasn't surprising, considering he couldn't catch his breath.

"Precisely," Martin said. "So it would stand to reason that if we can find the medallion in Liverpool, and if we make it known that we have it, we might be able to figure out who actually wants it, besides your brother. And if that person comes forward, they might know where Ian and Lady Selby and Lord Stanley are. They might even be willing to help us get little Lord Stanley back, which would eliminate Lady Selby's reasons for keeping away from Selby, which would mean Selby could divorce her and she would be free to marry your brother and *voila*! Everything will be solved."

Edward gaped, not just because of the leaps of logic Martin had made, but because of his optimism that everything could be resolved like the plot of a play in the second act. "You're forgetting that my brother holds a grudge against Selby," he said. "Spite could complicate things."

"Who cares about spite?" Martin shrugged. The movement rubbed their bodies together in ways that made it hard for Edward not to gasp at the contact. "Mark my words. As soon as we find that medallion in Liverpool, we'll be home free."

Home free. The two words echoed everything Edward had been thinking earlier, but with the most positive interpretation possible. That positivity was all Martin's, and yet, it was somehow contagious. He could feel lightness and joy radiating from the man as though he were the sun. Or perhaps that was just the heat of their entwined bodies and—dear God, Martin was as hard as he was. He'd been so focused on his own arousal and so distracted by Martin's flood of optimistic planning that he hadn't realized the thing pressing against his hip was Martin's erection.

His realization must have been painted all over his face. Martin's smile heated, going from excitement over their mission to something carnal and seductive. "I was wondering how long it would take you to realize the predicament you're in," he said. "And what a predicament it is." His voice was a delicious purr as he nudged Edward to his back and settled over top of him, parting his thighs so that he could nestle between them with the most intimate contact possible. "It would be a shame to waste all this delicious heat, don't you think?" He flickered one eyebrow as he gazed down at Edward.

A hundred different kinds of panic coursed through Edward all at once. Martin felt so good that none of them could fully take hold, though. They just buzzed around him like bees, menacing but distant. Exchanging a few coins for relief in the dark of a public park in London was one thing. Even letting Martin sink to his knees to swallow him came with a certain degree of distance. This was something else entirely. It was everything Edward wanted, but it terrified him to the point of immobility.

Martin must have sensed what he was feeling. His smile turned gentle, and he stroked the side of Edward's face tenderly. "You've never done this before, have you?" he asked with supreme kindness in his voice and eyes.

Edward shook his head tightly.

"Do you want me to go?"

The question was somehow heartbreaking. He absolutely did not want Martin to leave him, now or ever. It shook him down to his soul, but he knew beyond a shadow of a doubt that he needed Martin and everything he represented. He'd needed it for his whole life, but in a twisted echo of his father's accusations against him, he'd never been brave enough to ask.

He shook his head again, staring up into Martin's beautiful, hazel eyes, at an utter loss to know what to do.

Martin's smile warmed back to its previous, seductive level. "This is going to be a delight," he said, dipping down to kiss Edward's lips briefly before shifting to nuzzle his neck and suck on his earlobe. Edward gasped at the new sensations. "This is going to be simply amazing," Martin went on, his voice dropping to a deep, carnal register that had Edward shivering inside and out. "Let's start by doing away with these pesky pajamas."

He couldn't breathe. As much as he wanted to, Edward couldn't draw in anything more than shallow breaths as Martin wriggled out of his pajamas without breaking the cocoon of warmth under the blankets. Edward tried to move, tried to remove his own pajamas, but his hands felt like blocks of lead. He'd never been completely naked with another man before. He'd never felt another man's body fully entwined with his own, skin against skin, touching everywhere. With his usual, prescient magic, Martin seemed to know that instinctively and made the most of it, peeling off Edward's pajamas slowly and brushing his hands and mouth across his shoulders and chest and sides as they were exposed. His touch had Edward dangerously close to the edge in seconds.

"I'm going to come," he gasped, feeling the tell-tale signs building in his groin.

Martin immediately stopped, holding himself carefully above him. "We wouldn't want that, now," he said with a teasing grin. "Not for at least another three minutes."

The pinch of indignation that followed Martin's teasing cooled Edward's ardor just enough. "Are you mocking me?" he asked, hoping to use the emotion to last longer.

"Yes, darling, I am," Martin laughed. He relaxed

enough to press his body over Edward's so that the contact was pleasing without pushing him too far.

"I've never been with anyone like this," Edward confessed, staring up at Martin with wide eyes.

"I guessed as much," Martin replied in a wry voice.

"No, I mean, I've never—" Edward swallowed, feeling like an idiot. "I've never been naked and touching with anyone before."

"Which explains so much," Martin said without a lick of judgement in his voice. He stole another kiss that went from sweet and simple to deep and passionate in a matter of seconds. It was so good that Edward groaned. That, unfortunately, made Martin stop and pull up. "Too much?" he asked. "I want you to enjoy this to the fullest, and while reaching orgasm is wonderful, it's everything before that that makes the whole thing amazing."

Edward blinked as something in his heart coiled tight, then burst loose. He'd only ever pursued orgasms with forgettable men in the past. And yes, his body throbbed with the need for that kind of release. But an even bigger part of him loved what they were doing right then and there—touching, gazing into each other's eyes, feeling each other's heartbeats, loving each other. The power of it took his breath away.

"I just want to be with you," he whispered, not daring to speak the precious thought louder.

The heat in Martin's eyes shifted again. The man had so many emotions within him that Edward could barely keep up. The tension in Martin's body changed subtly as well. He kissed Edward slowly and lingeringly, earning another heartfelt sigh from Edward. Martin's hands stroked his sides, and the touch was magnificent. So much so that Edward barely felt embarrassment at all as Martin sought out his hands and placed them deliberately on his sides, as if reminding him he could play a part in lovemaking too instead of just lying there.

It was a whole different kind of revelation. Edward spread his hands across Martin's back, testing how it felt to press his fingertips into his lover's flesh. The firmness of Martin's muscles under his skin had Edward's heart beating faster. He reached lower with one hand, daring himself to stroke Martin's hip and cup his perfect, firm backside.

"Now I'm the one who's not going to last if you keep that up," Martin gasped, moving into Edward's touch.

"Oh. Sorry." Edward started to move his hand.

"No, no, no, no, no," Martin growled. "Keep doing that. I love it. I want you to touch me everywhere."

Edward could hardly believe it. He put his hand back where it had been and gripped Martin's backside tighter for good measure. Martin let out a sound of pleasure that sent shivers through Edward and began to move with purpose against him. Edward's eyes went wide and his breath caught in his throat at the pleasure those desperate thrusts gave him. It was rudimentary at best, but Martin moved on him at exactly the right angle to rub their pricks together. The friction of their bodies pressed so close added to the sensation. Edward was already excited beyond anything he'd felt before, and part of him wondered if something so simple would do the trick any other day, but even those thoughts were blasted away as his body tensed and soared toward orgasm as Martin moved faster.

He came with a gasp and a groan, spreading sticky heat between their bodies.

"Yes, love," Martin hummed against his neck, breathing heavily and jerking faster. "I'm right behind you. I'm—" He let out a long, heady cry as more, wet warmth spilled between them.

Contentment and pride like nothing Edward had ever known raced through him. Martin sagged on him, the energy completely gone from his body. Edward felt as though he were floating in a river of contentment, so much so that it drowned all of his inhibitions. He embraced Martin with his arms and legs, brushing his hands up Martin's body to thread his fingers through his hair. Martin responded by muscling himself up to grin down at Edward, which made Edward's heart feel like it was going to explode.

He arched up, kissing Martin and moaning in victory when Martin kissed him back. He wasn't sure if it was normal or even right that all he wanted to do now, as he basked in post-orgasmic bliss, was to kiss Martin. It just felt right for their mouths to mate the way their bodies had. He could have spent the rest of his life kissing Martin and been perfectly happy.

"Darling," Martin whispered between kisses, letting

his body press heavily over Edward's. "You are so lovely. So—"

With no warning whatsoever, the bedroom door flew open.

"Psst. Mr. Piper," Abigail whispered, eyes alight with mischief, a smile on her face. She wore nothing but a thin robe, which was evident from the way her nipples pressed against the fabric. "Mr. P—oh, my God!"

Abigail wasn't the only one who cursed loudly at the discovery. The layers of blankets covering Edward and Martin had slipped down more than enough to give away that they were naked, and with Martin on top, Edward's arms around him, and the fact that their mouths had been firmly fused together when Abigail burst in the room, there was absolutely no hiding what was going on in any possible way.

Of course, Martin only made it more obvious when he lifted himself enough to send the blankets dropping down to the level of his and Edward's waists, which exposed the sticky dampness on both of their abdomens.

"Abigail," Martin laughed nervously. It was the first time Edward had ever seen Martin nervous. "Fancy seeing you here. Didn't you know Edward and I switched rooms?"

"I'm sorry, I'm so sorry," Abigail gasped, eyes wide, lifting her hands to her mouth. "I didn't—I never would have—with Mr. Archibald?" Her last, stuttering question came with a fair share of indignation.

"Perhaps it would be best if you pretended you never

saw this," Martin said, shifting so that he could slide out of the bed, taking one of the blankets from the top to wrap around himself.

Judging by the way Abigail's eyes bulged and her face went even redder as she clapped her hand to her mouth, she saw everything there was to see and then some where both Martin and Edward were concerned. "Oh! Oh!" She backed toward the doorway.

"Abigail, you cannot say anything to my parents." Edward scrambled out of bed himself, clutching a blanket to himself and shivering violently with both the cold of the room and horror at the situation.

Abigail merely squeaked and fled the room.

Martin turned to Edward, eyes wide with shock and —damn him—humor as he clutched the blanket to his chest. "Do you know," he said in an almost conversational tone, "I think it would be a good idea if we packed our things and ran for it."

Edward agreed with a grim nod, dropping the blanket and dashing for the washbasin. "If we're lucky, it's not too late to catch a train out of Blackpool." He splashed water from the pitcher into the basin, practically throwing a wet rag over his torso to clean away the evidence of everything he and Martin had done before dressing.

Edward expected Martin to rush out of the room to clean himself up and pack for a whirlwind flight, but instead, he leapt toward Edward, dropping his blanket and throwing his arms around Edward in a mad embrace.

He kissed Edward fast and said, "This might very well be the best night of my life."

With an unbelievably giddy giggle, he kissed Edward one more time, then dashed out of the room, leaving Edward to wonder what in the hell had happened to his timid and structured life.

CHAPTER 8

It was the single most thrilling night of Martin's life—and that included his first performance in *Love's Last Lesson*, the night his primary school's football team won the county championships, and the night Billy Haverbrook proved to him that, yes, he definitely fancied men. Not only had Martin had the honor of playing Billy's role in helping Edward discover that same truth, in the course of everything he and Edward had done in bed and out of it—making a mad dash across Blackpool and barely catching the last train out of town—Martin had discovered fully and magnificently that he was in love.

He was head over heels, passionately, irreversibly, madly, deliciously in love. Edward was absolutely perfect in his imperfections. He was brave in the middle of his timidity, as evidenced by the way he took to lovemaking like a natural, once they'd gotten started. Edward had taken charge and gotten them out of Blackpool once they reached the train station, even though the last departing train was headed toward Edinburgh and not Liverpool. They'd gotten off at the next major station and waited for a train heading back to Liverpool, all thanks to Edward's quick thinking.

Once they reached Liverpool, after the sun came up, Edward's confidence flagged once more. But Martin even found that utterly charming and endearing.

"What if Abigail tells my parents what she saw?" he fretted as they walked through the chilly station, suitcases in hand, as soon as their train arrived. "What if she tells the local authorities? What if news reaches London or my constituents in York?"

"And what if Zeus strikes her down with a lightning bolt?" Martin asked, tucking his free hand into his pocket after turning up the collar of his coat. "Or, more likely, him being Zeus and all, he seduces Abigail and impregnates her with some sort of demonic demigod. I wouldn't put it past the cheeky little chit to go in for that sort of thing. I'm half surprised she didn't ask to join us last night."

"Ssh!" Edward hissed at him, hitting Martin's arm. Martin grinned back at him as if Edward had leaned over and kissed him unexpectedly. That only made Edward scowl deeper, which made Martin laugh contentedly to himself. "The train station is crowded," Edward whispered on. "Anyone might overhear us."

"So what if they do?" Martin shrugged. "Does

anyone truly listen to anyone else's conversations in public places?"

"Whether they do or not, if Abigail talks to my parents, I'm deathly afraid they'll listen to her," Edward grumbled.

Martin stopped and faced him. "And why should you worry about what your parents think? Are you twelve?"

"They are my parents," Edward said, emphasizing each word, seemingly at the end of his patience.

"Edward, darling, forgive me for saying it, but your parents are shits." Martin fixed him with a flat stare.

Edward's eyes popped, and he darted a look around as though they were on stage. "You cannot say that," he growled.

"What, that your parents are shits? Because they are. They treated you abominably, and I suspect they always have," Martin said.

"No," Edward hissed. "You cannot call me...." He paused, hunching in on himself and looking as suspicious as the Artful Dodger on his rounds through East London. "*Darling*," he finished in a whisper so low Martin almost didn't hear him.

Martin beamed, his heart full to bursting. "What would you prefer? Sweetheart? Lovie? *Mon petite chou*?"

"Stop it," Edward hissed.

"Maybe I should just call you 'Shoe'. No one would have the first clue what that means but you and I."

"You cannot call me anything like that." Edward

darted another suspicious look around, shrinking in on himself.

"Why not, Shoe?" Martin teased him.

"Because people will know." Edward lowered his voice to a seething whisper.

God, but he was precious. Martin wanted to wrap him up in cotton wool, then unwrap him and do naughty things to him until he had Edward screaming his name for joy. He leaned closer to Edward. "What will people know, Shoe?"

"That we—" Edward started, then stopped as a passing traveler knocked into him, causing him to drop his suitcase, as a particularly large group of people disembarking from the nearest platform walked past.

"Sorry, sorry," the gent said, gripping Edward's arm for a moment to steady himself. He picked up Edward's suitcase and handed it back to him, brushed off Edward's coat, then adjusted his own hat, which was pulled low over his face, before walking on.

"You see?" Edward grabbed Martin's arm and goose-stepped him away from the flow of the crowd and into a quieter corner. "Anyone could be close enough to hear anything we say."

"What, like the fact that you sighed like a virgin on her wedding night when I made you come last night?" Martin teased him, barely able to contain his grin.

"SSH!" Edward clapped a hand over Martin's mouth, then pulled away as though he'd touched a hot stove. He bristled with frantic energy as he glanced around to see if they were being watched.

"Nobody cares, Shoe," Martin laughed, slapping Edward's arm in an admittedly blokey manner. "Nobody is listening, nobody is watching, and nobody gives a damn what the two of us do when we're behind closed doors."

"They would care if they knew who we are," Edward argued.

Martin tilted his head to one side. "All right, I'll give you that. An MP and a rising star of the London stage would draw notice for committing the very grossest and indecentest of gross indecencies." He still couldn't stop himself from grinning at Edward's discomfiture.

Edward pressed his free hand to his temple, as if he had a headache, and let out an impatient sigh. "Is it always going to be like this with you?" he asked, opening his eyes slowly and meeting Martin's grin.

"Yes," Martin said with a nod.

"You're going to vex me and drive me mad at every turn, aren't you?" Edward narrowed his eyes.

"Absolutely." He leaned closer. "And then I'm going to make up for it by transporting you with pleasure and showering you with the sort of affection you've never known to the point where you will be on your knees begging me for another go."

Edward's face turned beet red, but his eyes shone with temptation. Oh, yes, the man wanted it, all right. No, he *needed* it. He needed it like he needed air and water. Particularly since Martin was now certain he'd never had anything close to what he needed in terms of basic love before. It shifted Martin's thinking from silliness and the need to play with the man to an uncomfortable twist of frustration and a desire to give a few people a piece of his mind, starting with Edward for letting himself be treated so poorly.

"Come on, Shoe." He looped his arm through Edward's and pulled him back into the flow of foot traffic through the station. "Let's go find something to eat. I'm starving after all the activity overnight, and I need to build up my strength if I'm going to have it in me to make you scream later."

"For God's sake," Edward snapped, yanking his arm away from Martin's and looking as though he might hit Martin with his suitcase. "You have no shame."

"No, none at all." Martin walked on, smiling and certain he was having the best day of his life. And so he was. Edward was perfect. He was exactly what Martin had always wanted—a man who needed him deeply, not just for a spot of fun. He could imagine all his dreams fulfilled when he thought of Edward.

Edward caught up to him. "Everyone who looks at us can see what we did," he grumbled.

"No, they can't," Martin laughed. "And even if they could, I'd wager that half the people around us were in a similar state of carnal enjoyment themselves within the last twelve hours. That bloke over there definitely was." He nodded to a middle-aged, balding man with a paunch who hurried against the flow of traffic toward the platforms. "Yes, he definitely wet his willy last night."

"Will you stop?" Edward sighed and shook his head.

"And her." Martin nodded to a young woman with a high, buttoned collar who held the hands of two children while she waited off to the side for something. "She definitely screamed someone's name last night."

"Martin," Edward warned him.

"And him over there." He gestured subtly to a young man who was selling newspapers and smiling broadly at every woman who passed him. "I bet he had it twice last night, and with two different women at that."

"You are impossible," Edward growled.

"And that's why you love me," Martin told him with a wink.

Edward flushed, his eyes going wide. Martin's own heart lurched in his chest at the understanding that passed between them. At least, he thought it was an understanding. And yes, he loved Edward ridiculously. But he wasn't entirely certain he was ready for any declarations yet.

He cleared his throat and nodded toward a cart where a man was selling meat pies. "I believe I see our breakfast."

He marched toward the cart, trusting that Edward would follow. Fortunately, he did. By the time they reached the pie seller, the frisson of the moment had dissipated and they were back to business.

"Two pies," Edward mumbled, beating Martin to the purchase.

"That'll be four bits," the pie seller said.

Edward reached into his coat pocket, but instead of pulling out his wallet, his eyes went round. He reached farther into his pocket, then checked the other pocket, then put his suitcase down and began frantically slapping his coat all over.

"What's wrong?" Martin was immediately serious.

"My wallet. It's gone."

"Are you certain?" Deep concern flooded Martin. He put his suitcase down and helped Edward search his pockets.

"It must have been that man," Edward said with a grimace. "The one who bumped into me."

In an instant, Martin knew he was right. Edward had had his pocket picked. He stood taller, searching around the station for any sign of the man, fighting to recall what he could about the short, nondescript man who had—

An uncomfortable suspicion hit Martin in the gut. The man who had likely picked Edward's pocket had been short. He also hadn't shown his face. And while any one of dozens of criminals could be short, Martin had the creeping suspicion that the devil wasn't a criminal at all, but rather someone with a vested interest in slowing them down.

"We should leave," he said with more seriousness than he'd projected in years.

"What? Leave?" Edward glanced around, as if trying to see what Martin had seen.

Martin drew in an uneasy breath. Just like when he'd spotted who he thought was Gleason on the train, he was not sure he wanted to alarm Edward with his suspicions. Edward was on edge enough already. He didn't need to add the fear that Gleason had caught up with them to his list of worries.

"I need a nap," he said, reaching into his own pocket for the money to purchase the pies. "It's been a long night."

"It has," Edward agreed, still looking around nervously.

Martin traded the money for the pies, nodding to the pie seller—who looked as though he couldn't have cared less about whatever was going on with Martin and Edward—and handed one to Edward. From there, he picked up his suitcase and munched on the pie, trying to appear casual, in case Gleason was still there and had his eye on them. There was no point in letting on to Gleason that he'd been discovered—if the man who had picked Edward's pocket was truly Gleason at all.

"What are we going to do without money?" Edward asked once they were on the street, heading away from the train station.

"Who says we don't have any money?" Martin spotted any number of hotels nearby and nodded to one that looked inexpensive but still reputable.

"My wallet was stolen," Edward reminded him.

Martin slowed his steps until Edward was walking by his side. "Am I a pauper, then?" he asked, nodding to Edward's half-eaten pie.

Edward blushed and stammered, "I didn't want to assume. I don't know how much actors make."

"I make enough to take care of you for at least one night, Shoe," Martin said with a wink, pausing at the street corner to wait for the traffic to pass.

"I didn't want to assume," Edward said again, frowning as they continued on. "And you aren't going to give up the shoe business, are you."

"Now why would I want to do a thing like that?" Martin grinned. He might not have felt fully safe again, not with the possibility that Gleason was on their tail, but teasing Edward settled something in his soul.

They finished their pies and stepped into the lobby of the hotel Martin picked out, heading to the counter.

"A room for the night, if you please," he told the man behind the desk.

"Two rooms, you mean," Edward muttered, looking anxious.

"I'm not made of money, Shoe." When the man behind the desk looked confused, Martin told him, "Just one room." And because Edward looked as though he were about to expire with anxiety, he added, "My erstwhile friend here just had his pocket picked at the train station and is skint at the moment. Which means we'll have to share."

The man behind the desk nodded in understanding.

"Tough luck, mate. You try going to the police yet? Not that there's likely anything they can do about it. We've a real problem with pickpockets and cutpurses at the station."

"We'll check with the police as soon as we get things settled," Martin said, taking out his wallet.

Minutes later, he had a room key, and he and Edward headed upstairs.

"See, Shoe?" he said with a wink. "Nobody cares. Nobody notices. All it takes is one clever excuse, and we don't have to worry about a thing."

"Until we do," Edward said as they headed down the hall to the room they'd been given.

As soon as they were inside with their suitcases thrown onto the room's two beds with the door shut and locked, Martin rounded on Edward, taking his face in his hands and kissing him soundly.

"What are you doing?" Edward protested through the kiss, though Martin could feel his resistance evaporating quickly.

"Kissing you," Martin said between more kisses. He lowered his hands to work open the buttons of Edward's coat, then his jacket and waistcoat under that so he could warm his hands against the heat of Edward's sides.

Edward broke away from his kiss. "It's not even noon, and your hands are freezing."

"I love your ability to tell time," Martin growled, slanting his mouth over Edward's to shut him up. He tugged Edward's shirt from his trousers and caressed his bare sides. "And I can't think of a better way to warm my hands."

"We have a medallion to find," Edward hissed.

Martin lowered one hand to the bulge in Edward's trousers. "Found it." He worked his hand over Edward until Edward was hot and hard and panting desperately.

"Is that all you can think about?" Edward asked, though it came out sounding more like a whimper as he reflexively arched into Martin's hand.

"Yes," Martin said, then moved to kissing Edward's neck when Edward tilted his head back to roll his eyes at the ceiling.

"You make me insane, you know." At last, Edward gave up with a sigh, throwing his arms over Martin's shoulders.

"I know." Martin smiled as Edward kissed him.

It was pure bliss. Few things had ever made Martin happier than pushing Edward to that point where his reticence and repression broke and he let himself go. They both relaxed as Edward concentrated on kissing him. Bless him, the man barely knew what he was doing, but Martin hardly cared. Teaching Edward everything he needed to know to be an amazing lover would be the most fun he'd ever had.

He slid his arms around Edward's waist, handing over the reins to him and playing the passive partner as Edward explored his mouth. It was like he'd died and gone to heaven, and there was Edward, an angel waiting to receive him.

At least, until Edward paused, seeming to sense that things had changed between them.

Edward leaned back, frowning slightly, his mouth looking sinfully delicious with his lips pink and swollen the way they were. "Aren't you going to continue groping me and vexing me until I come undone?"

Martin grinned so hard he thought his heart might leap straight out of his chest. "Only if you want me to." He paused, arched one eyebrow mischievously, and asked, "Do you want me to?"

Edward's hold on him loosened. He inched back a bit more, his gaze dropping to Martin's mouth. Martin could only imagine what kind of wicked thoughts were flying through Edward's fractured mind. He was ready to drop to his knees and suck Edward off like he'd never been sucked before the second the man gave him the word.

Instead, he ended up cursing himself for not jumping to it when he had the chance as his chest tightened in frustration. Edward pulled away entirely, clearing his throat and rolling his shoulders. He turned away before racing to do up all of his buttons with shaking hands. "We should really go to the police to see if there's a chance of retrieving my wallet."

Martin let out a breath of comedic disappointment. "And we were so close," he murmured, then ran a hand through his hair, attempting to steady himself.

Edward pivoted back to him with a look that was half guilt and half regret. "It's not that I don't want to," he said, not quite able to meet Martin's eyes.

"You're just not used to casually falling into bed in the middle of the day," Martin finished for him. "I know." He rolled his shoulders in an attempt to banish any lingering lust—which he would never truly be able to banish—and stepped closer to Edward, bussing his cheek. "Let's go find the police and ask them about pickpockets and wallets, then," he said with a cheery smile.

Deep down, though, a new twist of impatience formed in Martin's gut. Edward's bashfulness was adorable, but dammit, it wasn't what Martin hoped for. His own urge to be loved was as great as Edward's need to hide from the world. Waiting for intimacy was going to get old unless Edward let go of his inhibitions and accepted who he was and what he wanted.

CHAPTER 9

The rest of the day was accompanied by increasing annoyance. Martin didn't really expect anything more, but the police were woefully unhelpful where tracking down Edward's wallet was concerned.

"Your wallet is long gone, sir," the third officer they'd demanded to speak to said, arms crossed over his bulging stomach, glancing between Edward and Martin as if they were both simpletons. "Once a pickpocket gets ahold of something like that, you're never going to see it again."

"But surely there's a way to search," Martin said, forgoing all of his usual cheer when dealing with strangers. Perhaps it was the lack of sleep, but he felt anything but jolly in Liverpool. "Pickpockets tend to return to the scene of the crime to strike again, particularly when that scene is a bustling train station. You must have a list of known suspects. They generally don't hold onto their loot for very long. You must know of pawn shops or men who deal in stolen goods who you could question." He still thought there was more than a good chance Gleason had picked Edward's pocket, but he could have been mistaken.

The only bright spot in the whole fiasco was that Edward looked impressed by Martin's line of logic. Though that could also have been a sign that he hadn't thought Martin was capable of that sort of intelligence in the first place, just like everyone else in his life had assumed affability equaled imbecility. And that thought was likely due to his impatience with Edward's sexual insecurities. It was all one messy, circular muddle.

"I can't help you." The officer shut them down, turning away. Before he left entirely, he said over his shoulder, "If I were you, if it's money you need, I'd wire your bank and ask them to send you some."

The advice was so unhelpful that Martin threw up his hands and huffed. "I am swiftly coming to the conclusion that I don't like Liverpool," he said as Edward nudged him to walk out of the police station.

"I've been to better places myself," Edward grumbled.

They had even worse luck at The Crown Theater.

"I sent a telegram to George Wharton to let him know we'd be here to search through some old props," Martin told the stage manager at the theater's back door. "He's expecting us."

"George ain't here today," the man said, crossing his

arms and blocking the doorway, as if Martin and Edward might attempt to storm and rob the place.

"Could we speak to the assistant manager, then?" Edward asked in a far more diplomatic voice than Martin was inclined to use.

"You're lookin' at him," the manager said with a scowl. "And you're not gettin' in. Not unless George himself meets you here and vouches for you."

"We've come all the way from London," Edward argued.

"And you can go all the way back to London, for all I care," the manager sniffed.

In the end, they were forced to walk away empty-handed.

"You did send a telegram to your friend, didn't you?" Edward asked warily as they headed down the street toward their hotel.

"Yes," Martin sighed, rubbing a hand over his face in irritation. "We're technically a day early from when I told him we'd be here."

"Then I suppose we can only come back tomorrow."

Edward was right, and there was nothing Martin could do about it. He attempted to be sunny as they walked Liverpool's cold streets, venturing down to the docks to take a look at the massive, trans-Atlantic ships, then looking for a likely pub for supper. Martin was well aware that his usual good spirits were gone, but rather than talk to fill the space Martin left blank, Edward remained silent as well. He watched Martin constantly, frowning slightly as he did, as though trying to make sense of the new side of himself that Martin was showing him. The trouble was, Martin wasn't certain Edward was reaching positive conclusions about him.

After their long, exhausting, and disappointing day, there was nothing to do but return to the hotel.

"If it's all the same to you, I just want to crawl into bed, pull the covers over my head, and sleep until next Thursday," Martin said as they crossed through the lobby.

His glance was drawn to a short man in a bowler hat sitting in the corner of the lobby, reading a newspaper. The paper was held up so that it hid his face. Martin sucked in a breath, narrowing his eyes to study the man and determine whether it was Gleason.

"What, you mean you don't want to find new and unique ways to drive me mad?" Edward asked with just a hint of humor in his voice.

Martin's questions about the man in the bowler hat blew straight out of his mind, and he turned to Edward with wide eyes as they started up the stairs. "Did you just make an off-color joke?"

"I'm not very good at it." Edward shrugged.

The smile that Martin had been missing all afternoon returned. "It's only a matter of time, Shoe," he said with a wink.

By the time they reached their room, Martin's frustration returned in full force. The hope he had that Edward would follow up his quip with action evaporated when he turned away from Martin as soon as the door was shut instead of advancing on him. Martin waited where he was, watching as Edward took his pajamas from his suitcase, then stepped behind the screen in the corner of the room where the chamber pot stood. Nothing happened, no suggestive looks, no teasing comments, no goodnight kiss.

That was the end of that. The most Martin could hope for was that George Wharton welcomed them into the theater the next morning and they were able to find the medallion and head back to London quickly. He changed into his pajamas as quickly as he could, since the room was nearly as cold as the back bedroom at Edward's parents' house, and dove between the sheets of the lumpy hotel bed.

He was asleep long before he figured he would be, but he didn't sleep particularly peacefully. All through the night, he dreamed that he was searching for the medallion in a room piled floor to ceiling with old chests packed with thousands of nonsense items. Every time he thought he was close to finding what he needed, catching a glint of the medallion underneath other rubbish, he pushed that rubbish aside to find nothing there. Over and over, all through the night, until sorting through trunks of props turned into looking for Edward in the cluttered, disorganized theater. Every time he caught a glimpse of Edward's face or the flicker of his hand at the other end of the room and chased after him, he disappeared even farther into the mess.

Which was why he flinched in surprise when he awoke with the first, hazy light of dawn to feel Edward's warm, solid body spooning him from behind. Edward had one arm thrown over Martin's side, and his breath was soft and steady against the back of his neck. At least, until Martin's knee-jerk reaction startled Edward awake as well.

"You're in bed with me," Martin slurred, sleep leaving him quickly.

"I was cold," Edward mumbled in return, snuggling closer to him. Close enough that Martin felt the spear of Edward's morning erection against his backside. Edward must have felt the intimate contact as well, but he didn't pull away.

"Now who's the one driving the other mad?" Martin sighed, twisting so that they lay face to face in each other's arms.

Martin studied Edward's sleepy face in the dim, morning light. Edward wasn't fully awake, but he couldn't resist sliding his arm over the man's side and pulling him closer. He surged into him, slanting his mouth gently over Edward's and kissing him with a lazy passion. When Edward sucked in a breath of surprise, Martin pressed his fingertips into his back and kissed him harder, and Edward gave in with a sigh.

It was as if the coil of tension that had been pulling tighter and tighter in Martin's gut suddenly loosened. Edward was there with him, in his arms, giving in to what they both knew was growing between them. He didn't pull away or seize up when Martin reached between them to tug the drawstring of Edward's pajama bottoms, then his own, then fumbled to push them down to their thighs so that their erections could be free. He caressed Edward's backside, teasing his hole, and wondering when they would have the chance to take things to the most intimate extremes.

Edward made a sound of pleasure and spread his hand across Martin's sides underneath his pajama top. The contact was as intimate as possible with the two of them still mostly dressed, and the way Edward moved against him was a clear indicator that he was ready for release already. All Martin wanted to do was give it to him, and to himself. He kicked off his pajama bottoms so that he could throw one leg over Edward's hip, bringing them closer together in all the places that mattered. Even that wasn't enough, so he rolled Edward to his back, straddled him, and thrust franticly against him.

The friction of that contact was so perfect that he let out a deep sign and moved from kissing Edward's mouth to gently biting his neck as the tension grew in his groin. There was so much more they could be doing, far better ways they could pleasure each other, but like a green boy, Martin didn't need any of that. He was going to come in spectacular fashion, and soon, he could already feel it, but he wanted Edward to enjoy the moment fully too. He seemed to be doing exactly that, if his increasingly desperate pants and the way he gripped Martin's backside and met his thrusts with jerking movements of his own was any indication.

Visions of fucking Edward properly, Edward's legs spread wide and his hips tilted up to allow Martin deep inside of him filled Martin's head as he passed the point of no return. He spilled himself across Edward's belly with a deep cry of release, then reached between them to fist Edward's cock. He sighed in victory as Edward came with a gasp that resolved into a long, "Oh!"

But just as Martin was determined to float on the high of orgasm and to wrap Edward in his embrace, hopefully snuggling them both into sleep again for another hour or so, Edward's body went tight with tension.

"Oh," he repeated, but with an entirely different emotion.

Edward wriggled restlessly under Martin, trying to get away. At first, Martin was too spent to realize what was happening, but with a painful lurch in his heart, he tipped to the side, letting Edward go.

"What were we thinking?" Edward hissed, tugging up his pajama bottoms and diving across the space between the two beds, hiding himself under the covers of his own bed. "My God, what if someone discovered us again?"

The bliss that Martin had felt moments before slammed back into the frustration and disappointment of the previous day. "Who is going to discover us, Shoe?" he sighed, sagging onto his side and hugging himself to combat the sudden coldness that reached deep inside of him. This was not how he'd envisioned morning sex with Edward ending.

"The hotel staff, another guest, a maid," Edward rattled off a quick list. "The police."

Martin rolled to his back, rubbing his eyes, disturbed by how close he was to crying. He was a fool to let his emotions run away with him. Edward had legitimate concerns. He had almost no experience with a lover. They were in a strange city, far from home, and he'd been robbed the day before. After being rejected by his parents and having the maid walk in on them. A hundred excuses for Edward's behavior flashed through Martin's brain, but none of them eased the sting in his heart. What he'd thought would be a delicious game of seduction that would end in a clear victory was turning out to be a war of attrition that he wasn't certain he was up for.

"No one cares, Shoe," he said with an even deeper sigh. "No one cares except you. You're the only one who's shocked by your behavior and the only one who is going to condemn you for it."

"I'm not—"

Martin rolled to his side, facing away from Edward before he could rattle off whatever excuse he'd come up with now. Sex was supposed to bring two people closer together, not drive them further apart. Edward wasn't the only one who felt vulnerable because of the things they'd done. And while Martin understood the situation fully in his head, his heart was furious. Once again, the love he craved was woefully out of reach.

He forced himself to take a few deep breaths to calm down. They had a mission ahead of them that day, and it wasn't resolving two lifetimes of vastly different experiences and emotions. Though if they didn't work things out soon, Martin wasn't sure he'd be able to remain sane.

It came as a shock to Edward to realize there were worse things than being discovered and branded an abomination. Worse things like the sound of Martin's wounded sigh and the way he turned his back on him. Like the awkward silence that stretched between them as they washed and dressed and made their way to a café across from the hotel for breakfast. Like the sight of Martin's eyes without their usual mischievous sparkle and his mouth without its smile as they sipped tea without speaking. Like the deep and certain knowledge that he was a disappointment—not to his parents, who expected duty and honor, but to his lover, who had needed comfort and been given coldness instead.

He'd climbed into bed with Martin in the middle of the night because Martin had been muttering and thrashing in his sleep. For the space of a few hours, Edward had felt as though he were useful, as though he could do some good for Martin on an intimate level, when Martin's restlessness stopped and he fell into a deeper sleep while Edward held him. He was in no way Martin's equal, but for a moment, he'd tried. He'd tried and failed when old habits got the better of him.

Now, as he sat across the café table from Martin, watching Martin stare out the window with pursed lips and a frown, Edward wondered if he was capable of changing. He knew he was unlovable—his parents had drilled that lesson into him ages ago—but the horrifying thought gripped him that he was also incapable of loving someone else. At least, of loving Martin the way he deserved to be loved. He should have stayed in Martin's bed, even though it terrified him. He should have taken a more active role in their lovemaking, even though he didn't know what he was doing. He should have apologized the moment he realized he'd hurt Martin, when he turned away, instead of worrying he'd say the wrong thing and make it worse.

He was an utter disaster, and the worst of it was that the only person he could imagine cleaning him up and turning him into something other than a disaster was Martin, the man he'd just offended into silence. And Martin was not the silent type.

"I can pay you back for all the expenses we accrue on this trip," he said as they walked swiftly through the freezing drizzle blowing off the sea on their way to the theater after breakfast. He didn't want Martin to think that he was a financial drain as well as an emotional one.

"It's fine, Shoe," Martin told him with a short, sideways smile that didn't quite reach his eyes, hinting that Edward had offended him even more. "I've got more money than you might expect."

"I just don't want you to think—" He gave up with a

sigh when it was clear nothing he could say was going to put the smile back on Martin's face.

He would have given anything to go back to the day before, to the way Martin had kissed him as soon as they'd reached their hotel room. He never should have pulled away. He should have let Martin have his wicked way with him right then and there, even though the risk would have been astronomical.

But would it, really? No one had been listening in on them or peering through the window. No one would have known if they'd been quiet. No one would have walked in on them that morning if he'd just stayed tucked in bed with Martin either.

Edward sighed heavily as they turned onto the street where The Crown Theater stood. "I'm sorry," he mumbled, feeling sick in his soul.

"I know you are, darling." Martin veered closer to him, bumping Edward's arm with his elbow. It probably looked like a casual mistake to any passersby.

The show of understanding made Edward feel worse. He was out of his depth in every way with no idea how to claw his way back to where he'd been the day before.

They reached the theater, and Edward hung back as Martin inquired after George Wharton. Fortunately, Wharton was at the theater, and he was expecting them.

"Martin. How magnificent to see you again," Wharton greeted him with outstretched arms that turned into a hearty embrace.

Edward's heart sank to his feet. George Wharton was

devilishly handsome, with blond hair, startling, green eyes, and a build that made even Edward's depressed spirits stand up and take notice. Worse still, the way he looked at Martin and didn't seem to want to fully let go of him once they'd embraced made it clear as day to Edward that the two had been lovers at some point.

"This is my friend, Edward Archibald," Martin introduced him once they were inside the theater's grand lobby. Friend. Martin introduced him to the god of a man that must have once known him intimately as his *friend*.

"Pleased to meet you." Edward offered his hand, and Wharton shook it with a smile.

"Any friend of Martin's is a friend of mine," Wharton said, though his smile was less exuberant than it'd been for Martin. Wharton barely gave Edward a glance before turning back to Martin. "So you're looking for that funny Egyptian medallion we used during *Anthony and Cleopatra* all those years ago?"

"That's the one," Martin said, his usual joviality back in place and his smile as bright as ever as Wharton gestured for them to continue across the lobby to a door leading backstage. It killed Edward that someone else had been the one to bring the light back to Martin, even if that light didn't reach his eyes. "You remember the piece?"

"How could I forget it?" Wharton laughed. "It was so heavy that it swung around and hit Lettice in the face more times than I can count."

Martin laughed out loud. "I'd forgotten about that. She was furious with you."

"Not as angry as she was when you filled her glass with real wine during that Ibsen play in Nottingham."

Martin laughed out loud, gripping Wharton's shoulder as they passed through the backstage door. "I'd forgotten about that. Poor dear was so inebriated by the end of the performance she kept going up on her lines."

"She would have murdered you if she'd been able to stand up after the curtain call," Wharton laughed.

Edward pressed a hand to his roiling stomach. Jealousy did not sit well after a full breakfast. Nor did the reminder that Martin had an entire life that had nothing at all to do with him. He was nothing more than an albatross around Martin's neck.

Martin and Wharton continued to laugh and relive old memories as they climbed a narrow flight of stairs to a room on the first floor. A musty, antique smell wafted from the crowded room once the door was opened.

"I really need to clean the place out," Wharton said. "Or have some of the stage hands sort through the rubbish to see what's worth saving."

Martin made a mock scolding sound as they all stepped into the room. He took off his coat and tossed it onto a rack that was probably meant to be a prop. "When I was property master, I kept everything in order. You should see the storage rooms at The Concord Theater in London."

"Good job of that, by the way." Wharton clapped Martin's shoulder again. A wave of bitterness and possession hit Edward. He wanted to growl that that was his shoulder to touch, not Wharton's, but he knew that was a pitiful lie. "I've heard you're making quite a splash in Cristofori's new play."

"I do my best." Martin smiled modestly, then turned to Edward. "You should ask Edward here. He's seen the show half a dozen times at least."

"Is that so?" Wharton turned to Edward with a new sort of assessing look. "And what do you think of our Martin?" he asked. The question was clearly not about Martin's acting prowess.

In an instant, Edward's hands went numb. He detested being put on the spot, but there was nothing he could do about it. "Martin is perfectly lovely," he said, ashamed of how stilted his words sounded. He cleared his throat and went on. "He's going to be one of the brightest stars of the London stage before long."

"As I always knew he could be," Wharton said, winking at Martin.

That wink decided things. Edward was going to die. He'd been a fool to think that Martin would want him for more than a handful of satisfying dalliances. Martin could have any man he wanted, so why would he want a repressed, cowardly, unlovable buffoon like him? His own parents didn't even care for him.

A cloud passed over Martin's amiable expression as he glanced in Edward's direction. "Everything all right, Shoe?" he asked.

"Shoe?" Wharton asked with a chuckle.

Edward held his breath. The silly nickname

suddenly felt a thousand times more important than the risk of being walked in on while in bed, and he didn't want another living soul to know the story behind it. It was his, his and Martin's, theirs alone.

"It's a long story," Martin laughed in return. A split-second of fondness filled his hazel eyes before he turned back to Wharton, clapping his hands together. "Right. Let's find this medallion."

"It could be anywhere," Wharton said, leading Martin toward a row of shelves that were packed full of crates that were practically bursting at the seams.

"I need to go to the bank," Edward blurted, feeling as though he were frozen to his spot.

Both Martin and Wharton turned to stare at him questioningly.

"My wallet was stolen yesterday," he explained to Wharton. "It had all of my money for this journey. I need to go to a bank and have them contact my bank in London to wire more funds." He felt like the worst sort of fool for coming up with the excuse to flee, but he didn't think he'd be able to stand a morning of watching Martin and his former lover catch up on old times and good days, not after the way he'd hurt Martin that morning.

"If that's what you need to do, Shoe," Martin said in a gentle voice, meeting and holding Edward's gaze for a moment.

It made things so much worse that Martin was trying to be understanding and compassionate, particularly since he saw a thread of anger behind those softer emotions. If Edward were smart, he'd leave the theater, return to the hotel to pack his things, and catch the next train back to London, alone. He knew how to navigate "alone". It was his life. He was out of his depth with Martin.

"There's a bank on the corner," Wharton said, glancing uneasily between Martin and Edward. "I don't know if it's the one you need, but it's there."

"Thank you." Edward nodded to him. "I'll investigate it right away."

He met Martin's eyes for a painful moment, then turned to flee the room, the theater, and the turmoil of emotions that he had no idea what to do with.

CHAPTER 10

The second Edward left the room, Martin exhaled as though he'd been underwater and come up for air. He pivoted and leaned heavily against the shelves he and George had started to remove crates from, rubbing his hands over his face.

"Would you care to explain what the hell that was all about?" George asked with a knowing grin.

Martin laughed ironically and shook his head. "I wouldn't know where to begin."

George shrugged, taking another crate from the shelves and stacking it on top of the first one. "I take it he's your lover."

Martin stared at the empty doorway and chewed his lip. It wasn't that he was afraid to talk about such things openly. They were in a theater, for Christ's sake. If there was such a thing as an ironclad safe place to discuss homosexual love affairs openly, it was in a theater. What held him back wasn't the fear of discovery, but utter confusion over what had already been discovered.

He settled on saying, "I love him." As soon as the words were out, a wave of powerful emotion flooded him, making his knees weak and his throat close up. "God. I love him." He buried his face in his hands, gob-smacked and wrung out with the truth.

George pulled one more crate from the shelves and stacked it on top of the others, making the stack tall enough to sort through without the need to bend over. "Does he feel the same way?"

Martin rubbed his eyes, then moved his hands away from his face, shaking them and sucking in a deep breath. He blew it out deliberately and rolled his shoulders to clear what was becoming a dam of emotions holding him back from dealing with everything that needed his immediate attention.

"I believe he does," he told George with a glancing look before facing the crates on the shelf behind him. With the others cleared away, there was enough room to empty each crate of its contents for sorting. "But there are extenuating circumstances."

"There are always extenuating circumstances," George laughed compassionately. "I take it he's uncomfortable with himself?"

It was Martin's turn to laugh, though there was little humor in the sound. George always had been perceptive of people. It was what made him such a brilliant actor. "I've never met a man more uncomfortable with himself.

And I mean that on nearly every level you could imagine."

George hummed and nodded. "Leave it to you to give your heart away to that sort."

Martin paused in the middle of removing a sack of what felt like wooden disks—which were probably painted to look like coins, if he had to guess—to stare at George. "What is that supposed to mean?"

"You're a butterfly, Martin," George said with a shrug. "You always have been. You flit about without a care in the world, sipping from whatever flower catches your fancy."

Martin raised one eyebrow. "I'm not certain if that's a compliment or not."

"It's a compliment if you choose for it to be," George said. He pulled a carton of mismatched scarves from the crate he was sorting through, made a face at the remaining contents of the crate, then put the scarves back and shifted the entire crate to the side. "You enjoy people," George went on. "You *enjoy* them as well," he added with a particular look. "You're not an idiot, mind you."

"I most certainly am not," Martin muttered, bristling over old wounds and people who assumed he was a dolt because he smiled.

"So it stands to reason that a man who can barely look at his own reflection would be drawn to you," George continued, pausing before diving into another crate. "I'm assuming your Mr. Archibald is afraid of his own reflection."

"Oh, it terrifies him," Martin said, sending George a wary look before pushing his first crate aside and reaching for the one tucked in the back corner to search next. It was easier to explain things to George when he wasn't looking directly at the man, so he continued. "Edward isn't just afraid of his reflection, he's afraid of what everyone around him might think of him. He's an MP, you know."

"You don't say." George glanced up from his search with an amused grin. "Well, no wonder he's such a stick-in-the-mud."

"He's really not," Martin defended him. "He might have given that impression just now, but it's because of the awkward morning we just had."

"Awkward how?" George asked.

Martin let out a breath, his shoulders sagging. "I suppose there's no use in hiding anything from you, seeing as you used to be one of my closest friends."

"*Used* to be?" George put on a mock offended look and pressed a hand to his chest. "I'm wounded, Martin, *wounded*."

Martin sent him a sarcastic look, then returned to his search and his story. "I am reasonably certain that, up until very, very recently, Edward was a virgin."

"I take it you did the honors." Martin's back was turned to George, but he could hear the grin in George's voice.

"I did, more or less," Martin said, feeling even more protective and possessive of Edward. "I have every reason to believe his fears kept him that way until I came along. But it's those same fears that appear to be driving a wedge between us every time I so much as touch him now."

"So it's sexual frustration, then?" Again, Martin could hear the teasing in George's voice, even though they had their backs to each other as they worked.

"Yes and no," he went on in a softer voice. "You've known me long enough to know I'm not the type to deny myself."

"No," George said pointedly, making Martin's face flush hot. They'd taken care of each other that way years ago while traveling with the troupe, but Martin wouldn't classify it as a love affair of any sort.

Which brought him right up against the problem. "I love Edward, truly, I do. Even though our acquaintance is new. It's like I've been waiting for him my whole life. I've never felt this way about anyone, and I don't want to waste a single second. His problems with sex don't just frustrate me because I end up unsatisfied, they frustrate me because I can't bear to see him suffering."

"Ah," George said, as if he understood. "It's emotional dissatisfaction, not physical."

"Yes, it is," Martin said with a surprising burst of relief. Perhaps George did understand, and if he understood, he might be able to—

A flash of black and gold in the bottom of the crate he

was sorting through caught his eye. He pushed aside a bunch of crushed fans and handkerchiefs soiled with fake blood to uncover it fully. His heart leapt into his throat as he reached into the cart and pulled the medallion out. *The* medallion. He knew in an instant, beyond any shadow of a doubt, that it was exactly the medallion they were looking for.

"I take it you would like this relationship with Mr. Archibald to be more than just a dalliance?" George asked. It sounded like his back was still to Martin.

Acting on instinct alone, Martin quickly tucked the medallion into his jacket pocket, then pretended to continue to search the crate. He scrambled to remember the question George had just asked.

"I would," he admitted, once his brain had caught up. His heart beat fast, both over the fact that the medallion they'd all been searching for was safely in his pocket and for the way that victory sent renewed determination through him where Edward was concerned. "I adore the man," he said. "If I had my way, we would spend every spare moment together. I'd take him out to all the pubs and theaters, I'd travel the continent with him and giggle over everything from French brothels to Italian seaside resorts with him."

"You always were a giggler," George laughed, giving no indication at all that he'd seen Martin pocket the medallion.

"I'd take him to bed and keep him there for as long as it took to fuck the fear right out of him," Martin went on.

"That's an interesting metaphor," George laughed, turning to face Martin. "It's not in any of these," he said, hefting one crate back toward the shelves.

"Nor in these." It wasn't technically a lie. The medallion wasn't in any of the crates. Not anymore. Martin didn't know why he wasn't telling George, but his instinct screamed at him not to. "The thing is, I think Edward is gagging for it," he went on. Talking about sex and relationship troubles was the very best way he could think of to both distract George and possibly find a solution to those problems. "He holds back and holds back and holds back, then races forward like there's no tomorrow."

"That sounds exciting." George smiled impishly.

Martin made a wry face. "And then he pulls away again, like he believes he's committed a cardinal sin, the second we've finished."

At least, he had that morning. He didn't know how Edward would have reacted in Blackpool if Abigail hadn't walked in on them. Things had turned rather cozy before the maid showed up. And in Edward's defense, even though he'd only engaged in real, horizontal intimacy that resulted in orgasm one time in his life before that morning, that meant a hundred percent of his experiences of making love had ended in disaster. All those other times cruising in London parks must have been fraught with the fear of being caught as well.

"It sounds to me like what the man needs is more experience," George grinned, then shrugged. "I'd be willing to step in and show him a thing or two, if you'd like."

"Over my dead body," Martin growled. He knew George was joking, but his reaction was anything but a joke. Edward was his, and anyone who thought otherwise would have to battle him to the death.

George laughed, holding up his hands. "All right, young man. You've proven to me that you're besotted with your MP. Therefore, I stand by my previous statement and yours. I think you really do need to fuck the fear out of him."

The prospect didn't sound half bad to Martin. He just knew that getting them to that point would be a Herculean feat.

"The medallion has to be here somewhere," he muttered, using the continued search as an excuse to disappear into his darker thoughts. He shifted a few crates on the shelf and pulled a few down to search. As he did, he subtly patted his jacket pocket. They had the medallion. Half of their troubles were solved. But the medallion had turned out to be the easy part. Love was proving to be much more complicated.

Edward turned up his collar against the freezing drizzle as he walked to the end of the street where the bank Wharton had mentioned was located, hating Liverpool more with every step. He hated the cold and the damp, hated the dreariness of the buildings around him and the grey sky, and he especially hated the handsome, smirking face of the man who was probably ten times the lover that he would ever be for Martin. The sound of Martin and Wharton laughing together haunted every one of Edward's steps. The friendship between the two men was undeniable.

"Don't be a fool, Shoe," Edward whispered to himself. His heart squeezed as he called himself by Martin's silly nickname for him. He was a damned Member of Parliament, for God's sake. He was a respectable subject of the crown, a grown man, and a responsible person. He had enough money to live comfortably, food in his pantry, clothes, shelter, far more than too many other men could say. He had no right to go skulking around feeling sorry for himself because the man he loved was probably locked in a passionate embrace with an ex-lover who could make Greek statues jealous, or on his knees with Wharton's cock down his throat, making those same lovely sounds he had when the two of them were—

"For God's sake, stop," he hissed at himself, reaching an intersection and pausing for traffic before crossing.

Martin would not fall instantly into a sexual encounter with Wharton just because the man was there. And even if he did, it was Edward's own fault for rejecting him that morning. What madness had possibly made him shrink away from Martin at a moment when they should have cozied up together to enjoy what they'd just done?

He was broken. That was all there was to it. He was a pitiful, broken man who wouldn't have known love if it had—

"Don't say a word."

Edward nearly jumped out of his skin at the hissed command, and at the way the strange man had come up behind him, grabbed his arm, and was now dragging him into the alley beside two buildings. His heart instantly hammered in his throat. He was about to be robbed, and it wasn't going to be as quick and impersonal as it had been at the train station. He could be murdered.

"I don't have any money," he said, praying he didn't sound like a cowering fool. "I was robbed yesterday."

"I know." The stranger jerked him into a shallow alcove within the alley, then stepped in front of him, blocking his way out. "You were a pitiful target too. I thought John Dandie warned you about me."

Edward gasped. "Gleason?"

He knew the detective only vaguely from The Brotherhood, but up close, he was unmistakable. Gleason was shorter than average, but his presence more than made up for his lack of height. His blue eyes were as sharp as daggers, and his angular face lit up with triumph as Edward recognized him.

"Looking for this?" Gleason reached into his pocket and held up Edward's wallet.

"As a matter of fact—" Edward made a grab for his wallet, but Gleason pulled it out of his reach, tucking it back into his coat.

"I want the medallion," he said, simple and to the point.

Edward gaped for a moment, shaking his head and shrugging. "I don't have it."

"You've just come from The Crown Theater," Gleason told him. "You and Piper were only there for a matter of minutes, which means George Wharton must have handed it to you."

"No, he didn't," Edward said truthfully.

"You're taking it back to the hotel while Piper catches up with an old friend." Before Edward could deny it, Gleason narrowed his eyes with a sympathetic look. "Sorry about that. It must sting. Especially after the way the two of you have been carrying on this trip. But Martin always was a bit of a tease."

"Take that back," Edward said with sudden ferocity, leaning into Gleason and grabbing the front of his coat.

Gleason stumbled backwards, eyes going wide. "Maybe I have the situation wrong."

"You most certainly do," Edward spat. "Martin is a good man with a heart of gold. He makes friends wherever he goes. That doesn't mean he's—"

Gleason didn't let him finish his sentence. He grabbed Edward's arm and twisted it in such a way that, before Edward knew which way was up, Gleason had his arm wedged behind him and his face pressed up against the brick wall of the alcove. A split second later, Gleason kicked Edward's feet apart and proceeded to pat down his coat, thrusting his hands into the pockets as if searching for the medallion. For such a small man, Gleason had surprising strength.

Only when he'd searched every inch of Edward's coat did Gleason let him go.

"Where is it?" Gleason demanded, looking extraordinarily put out at coming up empty-handed.

"I told you, I don't have the medallion. It wasn't at the theater." The second bit was a lie, or at least it might be, but Edward prayed it was a convincing lie. He summoned up all the courage he had and rounded on Gleason. "Where is my brother?" he demanded.

"I don't know." It was Gleason's turn to lie.

"I know you're working for him," Edward insisted. "Tell me where he is."

Gleason remained silent, his eyes narrowed.

"All right, then send him a message from me," Edward went on. "Tell him that he's the worst sort of reprobate for running off with another man's wife and holding his child hostage. And for what? A silly piece of jewelry? Money? Tell him he's abominable and that we're on his tail. Tell him that if he doesn't return Lord Stanley to his father immediately and come forward with Lady Selby so that Selby can divorce her, he'll be arrested for kidnapping and extortion, and neither I nor our parents will raise a finger to defend him. You tell him that."

Edward was surprised by his vehemence, and more than a little delighted that he'd been so bold. If he could hold his own against a man like Gleason, there was no telling what he could do.

JUST A LITTLE MADNESS

But Gleason didn't answer him. The man didn't so much as blink. It took the wind right out of Edward's sails. Before Edward could launch into another speech, Gleason turned and dashed out of the alley.

"Bloody hell," Edward grumbled, leaping after him. He couldn't let Gleason slip away without giving him so much as a hint of where Ian was.

He made it as far as the street, but as soon as the brighter light of the main thoroughfare hit him, when he glanced up and down to see which way Gleason had run off to, Gleason was gone.

Edward let out a heavy breath, raising a hand to his forehead as he searched up and down the street. The man had vanished entirely, and Edward hadn't learned a bloody thing about his brother's whereabouts. He swore under his breath, then traced his steps back to the theater.

The only bit of luck he had was that the doorman who had let them in to meet Wharton earlier recognized him and let him in again. He had to find his own way back to the prop storage room on the first floor, though. By the time he found it, he was out of breath and his nerves were frazzled. At least when he burst back into the room, he didn't find Martin and Wharton snogging, or worse. In fact, they were searching through crates at opposite ends of the room, though Edward could tell he'd walked into the middle of a cheerful conversation.

Martin noticed him immediately, and his friendly smile dropped to a look of deep concern. "What is it, Shoe?"

"It's Gleason," Edward said, gulping for breath. "He accosted me in an alley just now, before I got to the bank. He was the one who stole my wallet at the station."

"I knew it," Martin growled.

"Did you get it back?" Wharton asked.

Edward almost didn't hear the question. "You knew Gleason stole my wallet?" he demanded of Martin. "How?"

"I thought I saw him at the station," Martin said, abandoning the crate he was searching through and marching over to where he'd left his winter coat by the door. "What did he want?"

"You saw Gleason and you didn't think to tell me?" Deep inside, Edward knew now was not the time to be hurt by something like that, but it stuck in his throat like a burr. Martin really didn't think much of him.

"I'm sorry. We were distracted. What did Gleason want?" Martin snapped.

Edward gaped at him, then shook his head. "He wanted me to give him the medallion. I said I didn't have it. He didn't believe me at first, so he manhandled me and searched me."

"He what?" The indignation in Martin's eyes and voice would have been endearing if Edward's nerves weren't already frazzled.

"I told him to send Ian a message, telling him to give Lord Stanley back to Selby, but he ran off," Edward went on.

Martin's eyes went wider. "He ran off?"

"Yes."

"Just like that?"

"I could hardly have stopped him," Edward argued.

Martin made a sound that could have been agreement or annoyance as he shoved his arms into the sleeves of his coat. "We have to go after him," he said. "He could lead us to Ian, and this whole thing could be over."

"What about the medallion?" Wharton asked as Martin gestured for the two of them to hurry.

"I suppose keep looking for it," Edward said over his shoulder, chasing Martin out to the hallway.

"I'll let you know what I find," Wharton called as they dashed away.

Edward had to have faith in the man, even if he didn't want to. They were running out of options, and he had the bad feeling Gleason had just gotten the better of them somehow.

CHAPTER 11

"Where did you last see Gleason?" Martin asked Edward as they shot out of the theater and skidded to a stop on the sidewalk. Several startled passersby jumped out of their way, exclaiming or shaking their heads before walking on.

Strangely, Edward didn't flinch at all the attention drawn to him or even seem to care. "He accosted me near the bank, about two blocks that way," he said, falling into a jog by Martin's side.

They hurried up the street, looking this way and that, searching for Gleason. Martin's mind raced as fast as his heart and his legs. Their chances of catching up with Gleason and putting a stop to whatever he was up to were minimal, but they had to try. A child's life depended on it.

"Did Gleason want anything else from you besides

the medallion?" he asked Edward breathlessly as they darted through traffic to cross the street.

Edward clapped a hand to his head to keep his hat from flying off, his eyes wide, as he followed Martin. "No, but he was adamant about what he did want. I told him I didn't have it."

"All this trouble for a medallion?" Martin dodged around a woman pushing a pram, spotting the bank in the distance. He patted the pocket of his coat to make sure the medallion was still there, then focused on reaching the bank. "I thought your brother was after money too."

"There has to be more to the thing than meets the eye," Edward echoed his thoughts. "That's the alley he dragged me into." He pointed to a shady passage between two dreary, rain-soaked buildings.

Martin's intention was to search the alley, though for what he didn't know. That idea died as soon as he spotted a short, suspicious figure with his collar pulled up and his hat pulled down, watching them from the corner diagonally across the intersection from the alley. He skidded to a halt and grabbed Edward's arm.

"Is that him?" he asked, turning Edward and pointing to the man he was certain was Gleason.

Edward blinked and scanned the modest crowd, then gasped, "By God, it is."

"Come on." Martin put a hand to Edward's back, encouraging him to run on and dodge traffic to cross the intersection.

Gleason saw them and broke into a run. He had the jump on them and seemed to know where he was going. Martin and Edward had to make it across the intersection and around several bystanders, who gawked and muttered at the impromptu chase that was interrupting their morning. More and more people paused what they were doing to see what was going on, which inadvertently put more obstacles in Martin and Edward's way as they raced after Gleason.

Slowly but surely, they closed the gap, aided by Liverpudlians getting in Gleason's way. Gleason was foiled altogether when a young woman selling flowers pushed her cart into his way, stopping his progress.

"Gleason, stop," Martin called out to him.

Edward jumped ahead of him, grabbing the sleeve of Gleason's coat before the man could dart away.

"Good job," Martin told him with a burst of pride before taking Gleason's other arm and wheeling him around until the man's back was against the wall of the building beside them. The flower seller and a few others gaped at the scene, but thankfully, no one attempted to intervene. "Why are you following us?" Martin demanded.

"And give me my wallet back," Edward added.

Gleason glanced between the two of them with an oddly calm look. He hardly seemed out of breath at all. "You know why I'm following you," he said, first to Edward, then deciding to address Martin. "I want the medallion, that's all."

"Well, you're not going to get it," Martin said.

"I told you, we don't have it," Edward added.

Martin tried not to twitch or show so much as a hint that the medallion was in his pocket. He did his best to forget about it himself, drawing on every acting trick he'd ever learned. "What's so important about the damn medallion that you would chase us halfway across England to get your hands on it? It's just a piece of ancient rubbish, from what I understand."

"It's not about the value of the piece itself, it's about how badly someone wants it," Gleason said.

"Ian can't have it," Edward growled. "Tell him this has gone on long enough. He needs to let this old rivalry go. It's become childish, petty, and criminal."

"And I personally am not inclined to negotiate with a man who holds a five-year-old boy hostage to get back at his father," Martin added, nodding to Edward as if to show they were in agreement.

"Anyone who would aid and abet a petty criminal like my brother isn't worthy of negotiating with either," Edward said, narrowing his eyes at Gleason. He took a half step toward the man and lowered his voice to continue, "I should petition The Brotherhood to have your membership revoked over this kind of behavior."

Gleason met the threat with a chuckle. "My business as a private detective and the confidentiality of my clients has nothing to do with my membership in The Brotherhood, and The Brotherhood is well aware of that."

"Are they aware of the lengths you've gone to in order to protect a kidnapper?" Martin asked.

"Are you going to run back to London and tell them all about it?" Gleason asked in return.

Martin had half a mind to do just that. He also reluctantly admired Gleason for his ability to remain completely unintimidated when accused of wrongdoing. The man looked as though the three of them were doing nothing more than discussing rival sporting teams.

"Look, all we care about is getting a message to my brother and begging him to release Lord Stanley to his father," Edward said, exhaling with frustration. "Selby is more than willing to grant Lady Selby a divorce. He's even willing to give Ian the medallion, once it's found. But he needs, we all need, a sign of good faith, that he actually intends to hand Lord Stanley over. Ian's trick with handing over just the girls in the autumn damaged his credibility and—"

Gleason pushed away from the wall and sprinted down the street as Edward spoke. Martin cursed himself for letting his guard down during the speech. They were left right where they started, chasing Gleason down crowded streets as the drizzle turned to a harder, icy rain.

"If I never run again, it will be too soon," Martin panted as they skittered around a corner, nearly plowing into a boy selling sodden newspapers.

"He's heading to the train station," Edward said, his eyes going wide. He slowed his steps and glanced around.

Martin did the same. They had chased Gleason all the way to the train station and were just in time to see the bastard dash through a crowd of people pouring out of the station. "He's going to leave Liverpool."

"Without the medallion?" Edward asked.

Martin stopped, rubbing a hand over his face. "He must think he can get it some other way. Or else he assumes we're too close and that we might catch him and turn him into the authorities for theft."

"He still has my wallet," Edward sighed. "What do we do?"

Martin thought fast. "We don't have much of a choice, do we? We have to go after him, catch him, and get him to tell us where your brother and Lady Selby are. He might be the only one who knows at this point."

"All right, then."

Edward started forward, but Martin grabbed him to stop him. "We should go back to the hotel, pack our things, and prepare to chase him over a long distance."

"Won't he get away if we don't go after him right this moment?" Edward argued.

Martin blew out a breath and frowned. "He might. But chances are he doesn't have a ticket for a train leaving immediately. He would have had to plan this whole encounter down to the minute if he did." He turned and hurried down the street toward their hotel. "My guess is that we have ten, perhaps fifteen minutes before he's able to purchase a ticket and secure himself on a train."

"We'd better hurry, then."

Martin had never packed his belongings and checked out of a hotel so quickly in his life. They were lucky that their hotel was so close to the train station and that they'd paid for their room in advance. Both he and Edward threw their things into their suitcases willy-nilly, then charged down through the hotel, returning the room key to the desk, then dashing out into the street, nearly upsetting a man selling fruit who had parked his cart just outside of the hotel.

Martin figured they had very little chance of spotting Gleason again once they reached the train station, but he figured there was a fair chance the man must be headed for London.

He was shocked when Edward grabbed his arm with his free hand and hissed, "There he is!" He let go of Martin's arm and pointed to one of the platforms where a train had just arrived and was disgorging passengers.

It was definitely him. Martin wasn't sure if Gleason saw them or not. "Platform four," he said, striding toward the ticket counter. "Can you tell where it's going?"

"The placard says Leeds," Edward said behind him. "It's heading east."

The line at the ticket counter was blessedly short and moved quickly. Martin had his wallet out and ready by the time they reached the window and purchased two tickets for the train leaving from platform four. The train was already boarding by the time he and Edward ducked and dodged their way to the platform. They were able to leap inside just as the porters began calling for all to be aboard.

"Now, where is the little bastard?" Martin growled as

they bumped and shoved their way down the crowded central aisle of third-class.

"It looks to be a long train," Edward sighed, craning his neck to see around a portly man who was trying to fit his overstuffed suitcase into a rack above the seats. "He can't hide indefinitely, though."

Martin could only push ahead a few more feet before being forced to admit they were stuck where they were for the moment. He growled under his breath and searched around for two empty seats together. Once he spotted two behind them, he pointed at them and gestured for Edward to take them. Edward nodded and hurried to secure the seats before anyone else could nab them, and Martin caught up to him, sitting by his side.

"Sitting still is a bad idea," Edward warned him.

"We're not going to get very far until everyone else is seated and the train is on its way, though," Martin agreed.

Edward hummed and nodded.

They sat still for a few seconds as the passengers around them bustled away, storing luggage and taking their seats. A conductor stepped into their car to help, and within a few minutes the chaos began to settle as the train lurched into motion.

"You have to admit," Martin said with a growing grin, "there's never a dull moment when you're with me."

"No, there's certainly not," Edward agreed. He then did something completely unexpected. He smiled. Then he laughed. Edward Archibald actually laughed. "This entire situation is completely mad," he said, shaking his head.

Martin's heart swelled in his chest to the point where he thought it might burst. He laughed along with Edward, reaching for his hand and squeezing it. "Most things in my life are completely mad," he confessed. "This is just Tuesday."

Edward laughed again, ending with a sigh. He turned and glanced over his shoulder. "The aisle is empty. We should continue our search."

"Or we could sit here for a few more minutes," Martin suggested, threading his fingers through Edward's.

Edward's smile vanished, replaced by a wary look. He was slow to pull his hand away from Martin's, which was all the victory Martin could hope for at the moment. Edward cleared his throat, then said, "We really should search."

Martin had to admit he was right. The train was now speeding along. The buildings of Liverpool were quickly giving way to outlying towns, and as Martin and Edward stood and walked slowly through the train car, bracing themselves now and then to keep their balance as the car jostled and jerked on the rails, it gave way to countryside.

"He has to be here somewhere," Edward muttered once they reached the far end of the train. They'd walked the entire length, passing through every car, but they hadn't caught so much as a whiff of Gleason.

"Are we certain we saw him board the train?" Martin

asked, a sinking feeling in his gut. Nothing seemed quite right. Nothing had seemed right since Edward had burst into the theater to tell him Gleason had accosted him. If he were honest with himself, nothing had felt right since that morning, and perhaps beyond.

"He had to have boarded the train," Edward argued. "He was on the platform, and I'm certain he didn't see us following him."

Martin wasn't certain that meant Gleason had boarded, but he gave Edward the benefit of the doubt. "Let's walk the length of the train again."

They did just that, though they received nasty looks from the conductor, who demanded to see their tickets, then ordered them to take their seats and stay there. As soon as the peevish man moved on to a different car, Martin and Edward stood and continued their search of the train.

"Perhaps he's hiding in the luggage car?" Edward asked once they'd traveled to the front of the train, then back to the end.

"Does this train have a luggage car?" Martin asked.

His question was cut short as the train slowed and pulled into a small, rural station. The rain had picked up, but he could still make out fields and a few farm buildings near the tiny station. They'd been speeding along for what felt like about half an hour, and already they were deep in the countryside. Only two people in the train car they'd just walked through got up to disembark.

"Martin, look." Edward grabbed his arm with his free

hand and tugged Martin to the nearest window, facing the station. "That's him!"

Sure enough, Gleason hurried down from the train two cars ahead of them and made a beeline for the tiny station house.

"Come on." Martin jumped forward, grateful they'd thought to take their suitcases with them through the entire search, unlatching the door near where they stood and leaping down to the platform, Edward right behind him.

Martin mistimed his jump and stumbled as soon as he hit the wet platform, but Edward kept him from falling. Once Martin had righted himself, as the train chugged into motion again behind them, the two of them raced into the rural station.

"Where are we?" Edward asked as Martin practically leapt over the turnstile on their way out of the station.

"I don't have the slightest idea," Martin called over his shoulder to him. "But there's Gleason, and he's getting away!"

Gleason was climbing into an unmarked carriage that had been waiting in front of the station.

"Stop!" Martin called out.

As expected, Gleason ignored him. As soon as he was inside, the carriage moved forward. A second carriage—one that looked like a cab—was parked behind it. Martin raced for it.

"Follow that carriage," he told the driver before throwing open the door and leaping inside.

"Yes, sir," the driver said.

Edward jumped into the carriage with Martin. As soon as they were seated, clutching their suitcases and panting, the carriage jostled into motion. Martin took a few seconds to catch his breath before shifting to the side, figuring out how to get the carriage's window unstuck and lowering it, then popping his head out to see how far ahead of them Gleason was.

"We're right behind him," he called back into the carriage to Edward.

Edward scooted as close to Martin as he could, though there wasn't room for him to stick his head out as well. "Are we at least gaining on him?"

"I don't know." Martin winced as cold rain pelted him. "Can you go any faster?" he called to the driver. "We need to catch that carriage."

The driver shouted back something indistinct and the carriage sped on.

Martin wasn't sure how long the chase lasted—easily over fifteen minutes—before they slowed at last. Once he felt the carriage slowing, he surged to the window and stuck his head out again.

"We've reached a cottage of some sort," he called back to Edward.

"Have we caught Gleason?" Edward asked.

"I think so," Martin said, spirits lifting. "His carriage just pulled to a stop in front of the place."

Moments later, their carriage stopped as well. The moment it was still, Martin grabbed his suitcase and stumbled out. His feet landed in a muddy puddle with a squish. Edward navigated the muck far more successfully when he climbed out, clutching his suitcase and wincing at the rain. They both raced for Gleason's carriage.

"Give up, Gleason," Martin shouted, reaching for the door handle of Gleason's carriage, feeling rather as though he'd reached the dramatic climax of a particularly adventurous play. "We've got you now," he added dramatically.

The carriage that had brought them to the cottage in the middle of nowhere launched back into motion, galloping away. Martin only barely registered how odd it was that the driver hadn't asked for payment before throwing open the door to Gleason's carriage.

Gleason's carriage was empty.

"What the bloody hell?" Martin muttered.

Edward raced up to his side, peering into the carriage with him. "My wallet."

Sure enough, Edward's wallet sat on the upholstered seat, a piece of paper sticking out one end. Edward lunged in to retrieve his wallet. As soon as he pulled back, stepping away from the carriage, the driver of that carriage snapped the reins over his horses' backs. The carriage launched into motion, knocking Martin right off his feet as it did.

Martin landed in a muddy puddle. Icy cold water soaked him before he could scramble to his feet, with Edward's help.

"What in God's name is going on here?" Edward

asked, hugging Martin's arm as if to keep them both from falling over.

The rain was horrible, and combined with the spill Martin had just taken, it chilled him to the bone. He pointed to the convenient cottage, and the two of them raced for the front door. Martin only intended to take shelter under the eaves, but Edward knocked, then tried the door handle. It was unlocked, so he let the two of them in.

It was obvious in an instant that the cottage was abandoned. It was cold and dark, with no fire in the grate in the front room and a musty smell. Martin didn't have time to take in the details, though. Edward muttered a sharp curse, and when Martin turned to see what had caused it, he found Edward reading a small note that had been tucked into his wallet.

"What is it?" Martin marched to his side and peered at the note over his shoulder.

The note read, *"Thanks for clearing out of Liverpool so I can search for the medallion in peace. Enjoy your accommodations for the night. Arthur Gleason."*

Martin snatched the note from Edward's hand and read it again, his eyes going wide. "Bloody fucking hell," he growled. "That bastard set us up."

CHAPTER 12

*E*dward felt as though he'd been punched in the gut.

"Gleason fucking set us up," Martin repeated, crumpling the man's cheeky note and throwing it at the wall. He'd never seen Martin so angry, though, to be fair, he couldn't in all honesty say he'd known the man long enough to see the full swing of his emotions. "The bastard led us on a merry chase, and we fell for it like green idiots."

Martin followed his pronouncement by letting out a frustrated shout and kicking a dusty basket of what looked like kindling that stood beside the door.

A moment later, that frustration turned into a yelp of pain, and Martin hopped back, favoring his right foot. Edward looked closer and saw the basket wasn't just filled with kindling, it was packed with solid logs as well.

"Sit down," Edward told him, dropping his suitcase

and prying Martin's from his hand as well. He slid an arm around Martin's back and steered him toward a wooden chair near the empty fireplace. "There's nothing we can do about it now."

He tried to sound soothing, but he was just as angry as Martin about the whole thing. Gleason had taken them, hook, line, and sinker. The bastard had probably planned the whole thing from the beginning. In fact, chances were that the entire encounter in the alley had simply been bait to lure them away from the theater, and then out of Liverpool entirely.

"I knew it was too easy," Martin growled, wincing as he sat, looking thoroughly miserable and rather like a drowned rat. "It was all too convenient. Gleason *wanted* us to see him in the street. He *wanted* us to follow him to the train station and to get on that train."

"I think you're right." Edward studied the fireplace. It had everything they needed to light a fire, including a box of matches on the mantle. He walked back to the basket by the door and fished out an armful of logs.

"And now we're stuck God knows were, in a driving, freezing rain, no way to get back to the train station but to walk."

"And who knows when another train will come by, heading back to Liverpool," Edward sighed as he piled the logs in the fireplace.

"Precisely." Martin flopped back in his chair with a frustrated grunt, rubbing his hands over his face so hard that he knocked his hat off.

Edward eyed him askance and set to work trying to light a fire. The trouble was, he wasn't very good at it. He'd rarely had to light his own fires in his life. Even at his flat in Westminster, a maid came in to take care of those things.

"Here, let me do that." Martin stood and hobbled his way over to Edward's side. "Have a look around this place and see what we're stuck with until this rain stops."

Edward backed away from the fireplace as Martin knelt to take over. He watched for a moment as Martin expertly rearranged the logs, added a bit of kindling, and reached for the box of matches on the mantle. He knocked the box off and sent matches scattering, but that somehow brought a smile to Edward's face. Of course Martin would spill matches everywhere while trying to light a fire.

He let out a breath and turned to study the cottage while Martin worked on getting the fire started. It was a small, one-room affair and likely very old. The ceiling was low, and the paint peeled away from the wall in places. It was clearly abandoned, but at the same time, it was well-stocked. The single bed in the corner was piled with blankets, and when Edward moved toward it for a closer look, he noted that it wasn't covered in dust, as though it had been sitting that way for months or years. In the candleholders there were fresh candles that had never been lit, both on the bedside table, on the small dining table that sat under one window, and on the counter in what might pass for a kitchen in the corner opposite the bed. Perhaps strangest of all, the shelves beside the cook stove were stocked with fresh bread, a side of bacon, eggs, various root vegetables, and a small, smoked ham.

"He furnished this place for us deliberately," Edward said as he opened the bottom of the cook stove to find it neatly set with coals, just waiting to be lit. "He drew us here on purpose."

Martin let out a wry laugh as he pushed to his feet. The fire was lit, though it would be a while before any warmth infiltrated the room. Martin brought the box of matches into the kitchen. When he saw that the stove was primed and ready, he set to work lighting that too.

"We played right into his hands," he said with a sigh. "But at least he had our comfort in mind."

"How could we have been so gullible?" Edward complained, turning back to the pantry shelves to see what else Gleason had left for them. A ridiculous twist of happiness hit him when he found tea, a small jug of milk, and sugar.

"Either we were too distracted by other things to think it all through or Gleason is just very good," Martin said, fiddling with the stove and making sure the fire started. "Oh look," he added, picking up the kettle that sat on the stove's top. "There's already water in the kettle and everything."

"And there's tea." Edward took the tin off the shelf to show Martin.

Martin laughed bitterly. "If it weren't for the obvious

fact that we're a pair of blind fools who now look like abject idiots, I would say this is quite a cozy, country retreat."

He sighed and shook his head as Edward set the tin of tea on the counter to be ready when the water boiled. Though considering how long it took for a stove to heat from cold to the point of being able to make tea, they were in for a good few hours' wait.

"We'd better get out of these wet things," Martin went on, slogging his way back to where they'd dropped their suitcases by the door.

A flurry of something warm and expectant, but also anxious, hit Edward's gut, even though there wasn't a single hint in Martin's words that he'd meant his comment to be more than a suggestion that they should change into something dry. The gnawing guilt he'd forgotten about from everything that had happened between them that morning flared anew. He should apologize. He should tell Martin he understood if he wanted to have some sort of a renewed dalliance with his friend, Wharton. He should let Martin know there would be no hard feelings if Martin was done with him already because he was more of a problem than a pleasure.

All of those thoughts and more weighed on Edward as he unbuttoned his coat and took it to the pegs by the door. He hung it and his sodden hat, then fetched his suitcase and carried it over to the bed, setting it there and opening it to see whether its contents had escaped the rain. All the while, he watched Martin out of the corner of his eye, waiting to see what Martin would say or do.

Martin was unusually quiet as he shrugged out of his coat and jacket, and tossed them carelessly over the back of the chair nearest to the fire he'd started. He slumped into that chair to remove his wet shoes and socks. The entire bottom half of his trousers were muddy and wet as well from when he'd fallen into the puddle. In fact, Martin was far more of a mess than he was.

When Martin stood to remove his wet trousers, Edward turned away. As much as he wanted to enjoy the sight of Martin undressing, to remember how Martin's body felt under his hands and against his own as they made love, Edward's emotions were too raw and in too much of a jumble to indulge.

"I can only hope that Gleason takes my message to Ian and that Ian comes to his senses and ends this whole thing," he said as he sorted through his clothes—which were, fortunately, dry. He selected the warmest items he'd brought to change into, setting them on the bed beside his suitcase. "This whole bloody thing could be over in a matter of days if Ian would just let go of this asinine grudge he's holding against Selby."

"Has your brother held grudges like this before?" Martin asked. The sound of his wet clothes coming off and dropping to the floor in front of the fire was as loud as a trumpet blast to Edward's ears.

"Yes," Edward said, sounding far too breathless for his own good. He raced through unbuttoning his jacket and waistcoat, and pulled his shirt over his head as quickly as he could. He thanked God the cottage was so cold that his important bits shriveled instead of expanding, although it felt like they were trying to do both simultaneously. The effect was wildly uncomfortable. "Ian has always held grudges," he went on. "He's the most stubborn man I know."

"It must run in the family," Martin said, a hint of amusement in his tone.

Edward made the mistake of glancing over his shoulder at the comment. He found Martin stark naked and bending to pick up his suitcase. The view of Martin's backside as he bent over wasn't just eye-opening, it was vivid. Edward's cock stiffened in spite of the cold, and his thoughts instantly scattered, overtaken by imagining what it might feel like to make full, carnal use of Martin's arse.

Unfortunately for him, Martin straightened and turned toward him, carrying his suitcase to the table, at just that moment. There was no point in denying that Martin could read him like a book, especially when the heated, impish look of desire that drove Edward wild flashed into Martin's eyes.

"You know, we could just skip the whole putting on dry clothes thing and go straight to bed," Martin suggested as he set his suitcase on the table and opened it.

Edward gulped, severely tempted. More than severely. He was ready to strip down and dive under the covers immediately. But old, tired anxiety wormed its way through him, freezing the newfound desire that he so desperately wanted to be able to embrace. The cottage wasn't completely abandoned. Someone must have been there a very short time before. Whoever they were, they could come back. He and Edward could be caught *in flagrante* again. This time, the police could get involved. His reputation, his entire life could be ruined. He could—

"It's all right, Shoe," Martin chuckled, shaking his head wistfully as he sorted through his suitcase. "I'm not going to force you to do anything you don't want to do. Even though I should."

Edward's mouth dropped open and he blinked. He couldn't think of a thing to say, though. Did Martin think he didn't want to go to bed with him? Did he think he'd forced himself on Edward that morning, or before, in Blackpool? He snapped his mouth shut and rushed through removing his wet clothes and putting on dry ones. Was Martin somehow under the impression that he'd coerced him into intimacy, that Edward hadn't wanted him or enjoyed every second of what they'd done together?

"You didn't force me, you know," he blurted when he couldn't stand the awkward silence between them any longer. "I was very willing."

"I know you were, Shoe," Martin answered his tense question with a grin and a wink. "Believe me, I know when the man in my arms is enjoying what we're doing."

Edward snapped his mouth shut and looked away,

shutting the lid of his suitcase. He was certain the comment was supposed to put his mind at ease, but it left him feeling sick, his mind filling with images of Martin entwined with Wharton and dozens of other faceless men. If Martin could have anyone he wanted, why would he bother with a damaged soul like Edward's?

"I'll see if the kettle is warm enough for tea," he muttered, marching to the opposite end of the cottage without looking at Martin. Though he caught enough out of the corner of his eyes to see that Martin had put on trousers.

"It's barely been ten minutes. There is no possible way the water is anything but ice cold still," Martin said, a wistful sort of humor in his voice.

Edward checked anyhow. Sure enough, the stovetop was still cool enough to touch. That filled Edward with impatience. He wanted his tea now. He wanted the whole, miserable affair with Ian and Lady Selby to be over and done with now. He wanted his feelings to be sorted and the confidence with Martin that he so desperately needed to be in place now. Waiting and wondering was going to drive him mad.

"Even though Ian has always been a prat who holds grudges against everyone, this whole thing with Lady Selby is too much," he blurted in what he was certain was a clumsy attempt to shift the mood in the room away from his inadequacies. "And it still surprises me that he's latched onto that medallion so much instead of just demanding money or a divorce for Lady Selby." He frowned. "I don't understand why that wasn't the first thing he asked for."

Martin had only just found a dry shirt in his suitcase but hadn't put it on yet. He was facing away from Edward, so when he shrugged, Edward was treated to the full sight of his shoulder and back muscles rippling. The sight made his mouth go dry and his trousers feel tight. Why was it so bloody impossible for him to just walk a few steps across the room and embrace the man the way he wanted to? What wicked force was denying him the power to ask for what he wanted from Martin and to indulge in it to the fullest once he had it?

Edward blinked and sucked in a breath, his gaze losing focus for a moment as he turned in on his thoughts. That might very well have been the first time he considered the force holding him *back* from acting on his urges to be wicked instead of the urges themselves. It might also have been the first time he felt as though desire and need were the champions in his internal drama and not the villains. It was almost as though his heart had turned a corner and wanted to rush toward passion instead of away from it.

He needed to test his theory.

"You don't suppose there's something else at play, do you?" Martin asked once he'd put his shirt on. Instead of tucking it in or throwing on a dry waistcoat and jacket, he moved to the chair where he'd thrown his wet things and picked up his damp jacket. "Has Ian ever mentioned—"

That was as far as he got. Edward stepped into him,

sliding his arms around Martin's waist and slanting his mouth over his, turning whatever else Martin had been about to say into a surprised sound of acceptance. The rush of power that surged through Edward was almost as delicious as Martin's mouth. He'd done it. He'd taken action, been bold, and embraced the way he felt about Martin instead of shrinking from it.

Nothing at all was shrinking between the two of them, which Edward could feel in an instant. He angled his hips against Martin's, pressing their constrained erections against each other. Of course Martin was already growing hard. The man was so free with himself and his body that Edward wouldn't have been surprised if he had the ability to make love in full sight of a crowd.

That thought did wildly sensual things to him, and he kissed Martin more fervently.

"I do want you," he spoke breathlessly against Martin's mouth between kisses. "I don't know what I'm doing. I feel like I've fallen off a cliff and am plummeting to the rocky ground. I'm terrified you don't want me back, that you want your friend or every other man who you so much as smile at, but I do, desperately want you."

"What other men?" Martin hummed, reaching for Edward's backside and gripping it tightly with one hand. He still held his jacket in the other hand and fumbled that clumsily as he kissed Edward, taking the lead and driving Edward to distraction with his lips and teeth and tongue. "There's only you, Shoe. There will only ever be you now."

Edward answered with a needy sound, digging his fingertips into Martin's back. He returned Martin's kisses with everything he had and reached for the fastening of Martin's trousers.

As he did, a sharp thunk sounded as something fell out of the pocket of Martin's jacket. Martin dropped the jacket and pulled Edward toward the bed, but as he tugged Edward's shirt from his trousers, Edward spotted a black and gold object on the floor.

He gasped and went rigid in Martin's arms, knowing in an instant what had fallen out of Martin's pocket.

"The medallion," he said, suddenly as stiff as a statue, and not in the good way. "Is that the medallion?"

"Yes, it is, love." Martin continued to kiss and caress him and attempt to undress him as though having the object they'd just spent so much time and effort looking for and being chased into the country over meant nothing. "Let's go to bed."

Edward jerked away from him. "You had the medallion all this time, through that entire, ridiculous chase, and you didn't bother to tell me?" His heart hammered against his ribs for all the wrong reasons. "Just like you didn't bother to tell me you knew Gleason had found us, that he was the one who picked my pocket?"

Martin met his eyes, face flushed with desire and guilt. "I can explain."

CHAPTER 13

Once, Martin had fallen off of a particularly high and precarious set piece in the middle of a performance. He'd crashed to the stage, interrupting the hero and heroine's love scene, injuring his shoulder, and bringing the entire production to a halt.

The situation he found himself in with Edward was a thousand times worse.

"There wasn't time to mention the medallion, Shoe," he said, reaching for Edward in an attempt to pull him close. If he could just feel their bodies together, if he could continue kissing and caressing Edward until they both forgot all about the silly misunderstanding, everything would be all right. "You were already in a state and ready to chase after Gleason when you reached the theater."

He brushed the side of Edward's face, his heart

pounding desperately against his ribs, and leaned in for a kiss.

Edward jerked away from him so fast that it left Martin reeling. "How difficult would it have been to say 'I have the medallion'? You could have told me at any point during the chase."

"I didn't think to say anything," Martin replied, hands outstretched, half in appeal, half in the hope Edward might change his mind and fall back into his embrace.

Instead, Edward narrowed his eyes and said, "No, you *don't* think, do you? You're too busy smiling and charming everyone within ten paces to actually *think*."

Martin recoiled as though Edward had slapped him. "I have been doing nothing *but* think since we set out on this journey," he said without a hint of softness in his voice. "Who was it who navigated the rail system, getting us where we needed to go? Who was it who figured out that the medallion might be worth more than anyone suspects?" He glanced to the useless thing on the floor, wanting to kick it for good measure. "Who sorted things after your pocket was picked and secured a hotel room without suspicion and realized Gleason was on to us and found the bloody medallion?" He shouted the last question, too furious that he'd been underestimated once again, and by the one person he wanted to impress more than anyone, to keep his anger in check. It was like every set-down from a schoolmaster or theater manager he'd ever had, but a thousand times worse.

Edward took a step toward him, his eyes flaring with equal amounts of anger—which was strange and unnerving, coming from him. "You hid all of it from me. You could have told me about Gleason last night."

"We were distracted last night," Martin growled.

"Yes, and by what? By your silliness and your games."

"By exhaustion and stress," Martin corrected him.

Edward didn't seem to hear the comment. "Am I nothing more to you than a toy to warm your bed? Do you think that little of me?"

Martin's jaw dropped at Edward's accusatory questions. To his heart, it felt as though the allegations came out of nowhere. They were good together. They wanted each other. Even now, boiling with anger and hurt, he would have tossed Edward across the bed and buggered him senseless, then begged to have the same done to him, in a heartbeat. His head, on the other hand, knew exactly what the motivation behind Edward's words was.

"This is all just an excuse, a distraction," he said, taking a step toward Edward. He pulled himself to his full height and stood with his shoulders squared, as if he were about to deliver one of Shakespeare's great, tragic monologues. "You're not really upset about me failing to tell you I suspected—*suspected*, not confirmed—that Gleason was the one who picked your pocket at the train station."

"Yes, I am," Edward shouted back, eyes going wide as he shifted away from Martin.

Martin continued to go after him. "No, Shoe. This is

about sex. This is about the fact that you're absolutely terrified of yourself, who you are, and what you want."

"It is not," Edward insisted with almost enough vehemence for Martin to believe him. Almost, but not quite. "This is about *trust*."

Martin shook his head and stepped toward him again. Edward continued to back away, but Martin wasn't having it. "What happened just now? You let yourself go. You began to grab what you wanted. And then, the second a convenient excuse showed itself in the form of that damnable medallion dropping, you backed away. You are a sexual coward, Edward Archibald."

Edward glared at him, and for a moment, Martin thought the man might strike him. "I am no coward. Up until your deceit was revealed, I fully intended to go to bed with you and let you do whatever you wanted to me, even things I never would have dared to dream about before."

Judging by the way Edward's face went bright pink, he was not only telling the truth, he would have enjoyed every second of Martin introducing him to the very deepest sort of intimacy. A part of Martin wept with frustration and loss, now that the opportunity was gone. Another part of him thought Edward was full of shit and needed taking in hand.

"I think you're lying," he said, advancing on Edward again. "Or at least fooling yourself." He backed Edward all the way over to the kitchen corner, where the stove was beginning to feel hot. "I think you want to believe that you're braver and more liberated than you are, but inside, you faint at the sight of your own reflection." He backed Edward up against the pantry shelves. A crock of butter caught his eye, and he reached for it. "I think you and I and this tub of butter need to have a deep, *probing* conversation about overcoming fears."

"Tub of—what in God's name—" Edward's eyes went wide. A moment later, his face contorted with fury. "You just proved my point," he snapped, skirting away from Martin and marching across the room to get away from him. "All you think about is sex. You have no respect for me as a person whatsoever."

"I have no—I only think—sex isn't just—how dare you say that?" Martin threw the crock of butter against the stove. It cracked and shattered as it fell to the floor.

"I dare because it's true," Edward shouted, looking more miserable by the second. "I was a fool to think that you, or anyone else, could love me."

Martin missed a step as he marched across the room, intending to try one last time to get Edward into his arms so that they could resolve the whole thing intimately. His heart lurched along with his steps. Every instinct he had screamed that Edward had just played a trump card and revealed crucial information that could resolve everything. But his anger was still towering, and the insult of Edward implying he was stupid pricked at him like hundreds of beestings.

"I care about you, Edward," he said in a grim voice.

"That is precisely why I have been bending over backwards to help release you from your fears."

"I don't need you to release me from my fears," Edward seethed, holding his ground for a change as Martin reached him. "Especially not when you think so little of me."

Again, Martin's mind reeled at the implication. Didn't Edward know that he'd fallen hard and fast in love with him? Hadn't he just said as much?

He rubbed a hand over his face, gaping at Edward. "You need someone to help you, Shoe. We all do. Personally, I think George was right when he said I should seduce the hell out of you and spend every spare second—"

"*George?*" Edward shouted, blanching. "You discussed intimate details about me with Wharton?"

Martin knew in an instant he'd lost the argument. He stepped away from Edward, his arms dropping to his sides. "I was at a loss," he said, the fight gone from his voice. "I love you, Edward, and I didn't know what to do. I had to talk to someone, get some advice about—"

"You accuse me of being afraid of my own shadow, and then you turn around and discuss that shadow with a former lover and a man I don't know?" Edward's voice dropped to a low hiss. "Knowing how much I dread being found out. Knowing my job, my livelihood, and my reputation depend on absolute secrecy."

"George won't say a word to anyone." Martin's gut

churned. He could see Edward's point with painful clarity.

"You know how sensitive I am about...about myself, and you used that as parlor conversation to reconnect with a former lover," Edward went on.

"I never said George was a former lover." It was an utterly lame and pointless defense. The fact that Edward had picked up on the connection without him having to spell it out suggested to Martin that perhaps Edward was savvier about sex than he'd given him credit for.

Edward shook his head and turned away, pressing his fingertips to his temples, as if he had a headache. "First Gleason, then the medallion, and now Wharton. Is there anything else you aren't telling me or any other details about my intimate life that you'd like to gossip about with the next stranger to come along? Did you take tea with Abigail and laugh over the size of my cock?"

"Absolutely not," Martin said. Against his better judgement, but because humor was his last resort in every situation, he added "Your cock is a perfectly lovely size."

Edward sent him the most withering look that had ever been directed at him.

"Look, Shoe, I'm sorry for everything." He took a pleading step toward Edward. His foot hit the medallion—which they'd completely forgotten about—and he bent over to scoop it up. "I was wrong. But this has been a mad-capped day, full of the most bizarre circumstances. I might not have made the best decisions in every situation we've faced, but I haven't done anything out of spite.

And look, we have the medallion." He held up the artifact.

Edward stared at him with narrowed eyes. Martin would have given anything to know what was going on inside the man's head. The room was too still, bristled with too much unresolved energy. And, God help him, he still wanted to forget the whole argument and fall into bed with Edward. With enough kisses and touches and several orgasms, they could make their peace with each other and continue on to grow their relationship the way it should progress.

Edward stepped forward and snatched the medallion from his hands. "We'll take this back to London in the morning and hand it over to John Dandie and Lord Selby." Falling back on full names and formal titles was not a good sign. "Then we can both be done with the whole, sorry business. We can go our separate ways."

Edward turned away from him entirely, marching to his suitcase and throwing the medallion inside. Without looking at Martin, he marched past him into the kitchen area and began banging around with the tea things.

Martin stood where he was, feeling as though he were drowning. The very last thing he wanted was to part ways with Edward. There was too much between them already that remained unresolved, and there was so much more that he wanted for there to be between them. Arguments were nothing. They were just another way to expose the truth and start important conversations. But if Edward didn't deem him worthy of battling through the jagged edges between them to come to some sort of an understanding, if the man thought he was as stupid and incapable of deeper thought, like far too many other people in his life, then there was nothing he could do about it.

He finally forced himself into motion, dragging himself over to his suitcase to finish dressing. The cottage was still cold, but the argument had heated him to the point where putting on layers of clothes was uncomfortable. He dressed anyhow, feeling as though he needed to put on as many layers of armor as he could to hide the bitter disappointment seeping through him.

The stove still wasn't ready, but Edward bustled around the kitchen area nonetheless. It was clear to Martin the man was trying to avoid him. He helped Edward along by finding a small shelf of books, selecting one, and plopping into the chair by the fire to read. When he realized that the volume in his hands was none other than *Sins of the Cities of the Plains*, an explicitly homoerotic work of pornography that was banned in much of England, he laughed out loud.

"What?" Edward snapped from the kitchen counter, where he was cleaning up the shattered butter crock, as though Martin had laughed at him.

"Gleason has a sick sense of humor," he said, standing and taking a few steps closer to Edward. When Edward flinched away from him, Martin's gut seized with bitter sadness. He scowled and threw the book at Edward, saying, "I think you need to read this."

Edward fumbled, failing to catch the book before it dropped to the floor, its spine cracking. "Did you just throw a book at me?" he demanded as Martin stomped back to the bookshelf.

"Yes, I did, Shoe," Martin said without looking at him.

He started to select another book from the shelf, but noticed they were all pornographic works of an inverted nature. He shook his head and huffed a breath. Either Gleason was mocking them or he had a sentimental streak and was trying to throw them into each other's arms. The man was as clever as the devil, Martin would give him that much. He'd planned to lead them away from Liverpool from the start. He'd likely spent the time Martin and Edward were in Blackpool furnishing the cottage and setting up the whole, miserable goose chase.

The rest of the evening passed in despondent silence. To Martin's surprise, Edward actually did sit down to read *Sins of the Cities of the Plains* as they waited for the stove to heat enough to boil water for tea. It took hours, but Edward seemed absorbed in the naughty book throughout the whole wait. That, or he was merely pretending to read it while stewing over what he likely saw as Martin's horrific betrayal. Martin thumbed through his own book, refusing to get out of his chair or say a word. But reading explicit descriptions of every manner of adventurous sex act only made him restless and desperate to find some way to make amends with Edward. At the same time, it wasn't lost on him that if he made any attempt to reconcile with

Edward, then followed it up by making advances and trying to get the man in bed, Edward would not only see right through him, it would start up the entire argument all over and appear to prove Edward's assertions that he was only interested in sex. He was damned if he did and damned if he didn't.

The silence was finally broken well after dark when Edward asked, "Do you want tea?"

Martin blinked up from his book, surprised to find Edward had not only made tea, he'd laid out a simple supper for them.

"Do you think I'm intelligent enough to figure out how to drink it?" he snapped, throwing his book aside and marching over to sit sullenly at the table.

"Stop being an arse," Edward grumbled in return, stabbing a piece of ham on his plate.

Martin speared a small potato. He deserved that. And when had Edward boiled potatoes?

"I should think you'll be glad to be rid of me when we reach London tomorrow," Edward said as their meal continued.

Martin glanced at him with a flat stare. "Now who's being the arse?"

Edward seemed genuinely surprised by the question, but neither of them had anything to add. That was the end of the conversation. It was the end of Martin's energy as well. He finished eating—knowing that he should eat, that he'd hardly eaten all day, but he hardly had any appetite—then checked to see how his wet things were drying. There was a fair chance the clothes he'd worn that day were ruined, just like his chances of creating something meaningful with the man he'd fallen so completely in love with at almost first sight. He glumly took his pajamas from his suitcase, washed up for bed, then climbed into the cottage's single bed and shifted to the far side. He knew full well he was acting like a child, but he was too exhausted to care.

"So there isn't even going to be a discussion about sleeping arrangements?" Edward asked, taking his suitcase from the foot of the bed.

Martin stretched his feet into the space that had been freed up. "No," he said over his shoulder. "It's either pack in with me or sleep on the floor. And I have a fair guess which you'll choose."

Edward made an irritated sound, but didn't say anything. Martin lay on his side, facing away, listening as Edward cleaned up and got ready for bed himself. He waited for Edward to come over and yank the blankets off of the bed so that he could make a palate on the floor, but was shocked to the point of flinching when Edward slipped between the sheets with him instead.

When he glanced over his shoulder with one eyebrow raised, Edward frowned at him and said, "I'm not sleeping on the floor."

"Fine, then. Don't sleep on the floor." Martin snapped away, facing the wall. His mouth split into a grin, but he tamped it down as quickly as he could, forcing himself to scowl at the wall.

Edward squirmed and wriggled, clearly having a hard time getting comfortable enough to sleep. At first, Martin could tell he was trying not to let their bodies touch, but given the size of the bed, that was impossible. Edward eventually gave up with a sigh and pressed his back against Martin's. It wasn't spooning, but at least it was physical contact. Martin closed his eyes and relaxed against him. In no time at all, he was warm and well on his way to being aroused, in spite of the lingering frustration and anger between them.

Although, on second thought, that frustration might not have been the bitter sort, and the anger might have been longing in disguise. Either way, there was nothing Martin could do about it. If he twisted around and attempted to start something, Edward would likely shout at him and start the argument all over again. If he sought relief by handling himself, Edward would know it and go right back to accusing him of being a thoughtless, oversexed imbecile. There was nothing he could do but lay there in agony, listening to the sound of Edward's breath. In the morning, they would pack everything up and head back to London. They had the medallion, true, but Martin's heart felt heavy, as though they'd lost far more than they'd gained.

CHAPTER 14

*E*dward barely slept a wink. He wanted to give in to oblivion and forget about everything pressing down on him, but sleep had other plans. All he could think about through the night, all he could focus on, was the sensation of Martin's body against his. It felt right. It felt good. Even if they were furious with each other. Even if it was only their backs that pressed together. More times than he could count throughout the night, he contemplated flipping to his other side and throwing his arm over Martin. He'd been brave enough to climb into bed with Martin the morning before, and he'd been rewarded for it with pleasure that had transported him to realms of happiness that he'd hardly known in his life.

And then he'd ruined it by shying away.

And then Martin had ruined it further by spilling the

most raw and intimate details of his life to a complete stranger. Martin might have had faith in Wharton not to say anything to anyone, but Edward had no such faith. He'd spent too much of his life being put down and denigrated for who he was—and that was without bringing sexuality into the equation. He couldn't bear the thought of having that repeated and magnified.

But he didn't feel as though he was in the right.

That niggling thought stayed with him through the long, tense night. He wasn't in the right, but he didn't believe he was completely in the wrong either. There was no wrong or right in the situation, there was just confusion, resentment, and disappointment. And to make matters worse, he was glaringly aware that Martin wasn't any more asleep than he was. All he had to do was flip over and embrace the man, or he could keep their physical positions exactly where they were and just open his mouth to apologize and talk things out to make peace.

If that was what Martin wanted. Experience had taught Edward that he was too difficult and complicated for anyone to put effort into. His parents, the very people who should have cared the most about him, had drilled into him the fact that he wasn't worthy of love, or even good opinion.

"You're being ridiculous, Shoe," Martin's voice sounded in his mind deep into the night. "You're a grown man. You shouldn't let the opinions of your parents rule your life."

Martin's voice was right. Martin was right. But

knowing something to be true and feeling it deep within one's heart to the point of changing decades' worth of ingrained thought were two different things.

When the first rays of dawn spilled through the cottage's windows, both Edward and Martin gave up pretending to sleep. Edward dragged himself out of bed, his head pounding and his body aching from clenching his muscles all night. He used the chamber pot, then shuffled into the kitchen to fix more tea. Martin rose silently after him and went through a similar routine. Neither of them spoke as they ate, packed their things, and set the cottage to rights so that it would be ready for whoever might end up there next.

"I feel as though we should leave Gleason a thank you note," Martin mumbled as they prepared to leave. The rain had stopped at some point in the night and the sun was making a valiant attempt to break through the clouds, but the air was brisk and cold.

"He doesn't deserve our thanks," Edward grumbled, opening the front door and stepping outside.

Martin didn't reply, though Edward could feel that he wanted to say something, as they walked out into the frosty morning. The muddy ground had frozen during the night. The icy chill was bitter, but at least they didn't have to slog through muddy puddles to reach the main road. The main road started to thaw as they walked, turning back to muck, but they reached the train station before soiling their already rumpled and dirty clothes.

The rest of the return journey to London felt like a

war of attrition. Edward and Martin had to wait for a train at the remote station to take them back to Liverpool. Once there, they had to wait again for a train to London. Though neither said anything to the other, they both kept their eyes peeled at the Liverpool station, looking for Gleason among the crowd. Edward was fairly sure that he would pummel the man into a pulp if they found him. Fortunately for Gleason, they didn't.

Sleep finally caught up with Edward on the long journey back to London. The result was that it felt as though the miles passed in the blink of an eye. He'd insisted on purchasing them a first-class compartment for the return journey—something Martin argued against, which made up the longest conversation they had between the cottage and Euston Station—which meant he could cross his arms, pull his coat tight and his hat down, and nestle into a corner to sleep for hours.

"Well, I suppose this is the end of the line," Martin said once they'd disembarked at Euston and walked through the station and out to the street.

Those simple words filled Edward with a dread that he hadn't expected. No. It couldn't be the end of the line. He still wanted Martin. He wanted the last few days to be erased. He wanted to go back to the point where things went wrong so that he could make them right.

Instead, he said, "I suppose it is," and glanced away.

"Edward, I hope you know that I—"

"If you hurry to the theater, I bet you'll be able to go on tonight," Edward cut him off.

Martin's mouth stayed open as he let out an exasperated breath. He closed his mouth, then opened it again, but nothing came out. He pressed his lips together, glanced off to one side in frustration, then snapped his head back toward Edward, meeting his eyes. "It doesn't have to be like this, Shoe."

Edward was at a complete loss for words. All he wanted was for Martin to drop his suitcase and throw his arms around him. He didn't even care that they were standing on a crowded street in the late afternoon, as city workers were rushing home to join their families for supper and a cozy night at home. That mental image made Edward's heart ache as it never had before. What would it look like, what would it feel like, if he could come home after a long day in Westminster to Martin, cheerful and cheeky, in his home? How lovely would it be if he knew Martin would lay beside him every night, that they could enjoy each other in every way possible with impunity or without question? What would he give to have that sort of a life?

But it was no use. He had a reputation to maintain, constituents to represent, and more fear rooted in his soul than he was proud of. It would never work, no matter how badly he wanted it.

"Goodbye, Martin," he muttered, then turned away, starting down the street toward a line of cabs, before he could do something he might regret.

"Edward!"

Edward thought he heard Martin call plaintively

after him, but he wasn't sure. He winced, clenched his jaw tightly, then finally gave up and glanced over his shoulder. Martin was walking fast in the other direction. The sight made Edward's heart sink. Martin hadn't called after him. It was all his imagination. He didn't want him after all.

Those glum thoughts carried Edward home and propelled him through the motions of unpacking his suitcase, changing into clean pajamas, and fixing bread and butter to fill his gnawing stomach. Eating only made him feel ill, though, and crawling into bed filled him with a sense of gloom instead of rest. His bed had never felt so cold and lonely. He was exhausted, but sleep continued to elude him.

He considered getting up, dressing, and cruising through St. James's Park in search of a companion for the night, but the thought felt repulsive as soon as it came to him. He might have looked for some kind of clandestine, anonymous relief a week before—just a week, it hardly seemed real—but there was no possible way his heart would let him now. It was Martin or it was nothing. How long that would last was a mystery to him, but for the present, he couldn't even think of another man.

So he didn't. He took himself in hand, stroking away as he thought of Martin—thought of his teasing smile, his joyful laughter, the impish light in his eyes when he attempted to seduce him. He thought of the way Martin kissed, the taste of his mouth and the power of command

Martin had over him. He thought of how perfect and right it felt to throw his arms around Martin, to dig his fingertips into Martin's arse, to feel their skin sliding together as they moved in search of relief. He thought about how close he'd come to that ultimate intimacy he'd always been so devilishly curious about, how it might have felt to have Martin inside of him. He would never be able to look at butter the same way again, especially since he'd missed out on the opportunity Martin had offered him. He even laughed aloud as he imagined Martin making a joke about hot buttered buns.

It was the suggestion of Martin's warm, rich laughter, coupled with the memory of how his mouth had felt while swallowing his cock, that sent Edward over the edge. But as much of a relief as the orgasm was, it didn't hold a candle to coming with Martin and feeling him come as well. It did the trick, though, and within minutes, Edward fell into a heavy sleep.

The problem hadn't gone away by morning. Edward got up, bathed, and fixed breakfast. He sorted his dirty clothes into a pile to be sent to the laundry and brushed dirt from his winter coat. It was life as usual, and yet, it felt like a pale imitation of being alive. He handled the medallion for a while, contemplating its mystery and wondering how valuable it truly was. He only hoped that Ian would come to his senses once he had it and return Lord Stanley. Otherwise, the whole, sorry episode would have been for nothing.

No, it couldn't have been for nothing. He'd had an adventure with Martin. In spite of everything, they'd enjoyed each other's company. They'd kissed and teased and made love. He'd never done any of those things before, and if he were honest with himself, he'd enjoyed every moment. He'd loved the way Martin had made him feel, and he loved the sounds of pleasure Martin had made that indicated his lack of skill and experience didn't matter, Martin had enjoyed making love with him as well. He would fly into Martin's arms again in a heartbeat if he could. He should have made an advance on Martin in the middle of the night, when they both couldn't sleep. Even if it was only for relief. He shouldn't have pulled away from him at the hotel in Liverpool, but he'd been so—

His thoughts stopped with a gasp. He sat at the small dining table in his flat, his tea gone cold, dangling the medallion in front of him.

"My God, Martin was right," he whispered.

He *was* afraid of his own shadow. He was terrified of his deepest desires. But Martin was safe. The same thoughts he'd had in the night came back to him, but with a new understanding. Martin hadn't once laughed at him or sneered in derision as he'd fumbled his way through sex. He'd enjoyed it all, even though Edward had been as green as a youth. And he'd attempted to seduce him over and over. He wouldn't have kept trying if Edward were nothing more than a toy to him. He would have leapt into Wharton's arms, like Gleason had suggested, the second Edward left the theater. But he hadn't. Instead, Martin had asked his old flame for advice. Advice about the two of them.

"I am a bloody fool," he sighed to the medallion, getting up from the table. He tucked the medallion into his jacket pocket, then crossed the room to fetch his coat and hat from the stand by the door.

He was a bloody fool, and he didn't know what to do about it. But someone else might. If Martin could go to a friend for advice, then so could he. He needed to deliver the medallion to John Dandie anyhow. Perhaps John would have some words of wisdom. He was one of the few people that Edward truly admired, truly trusted, after all, and he knew Martin.

He hurried through Westminster and up to The City in the middle of the morning crowd headed to work. Truth be told, he should head down to the Palace of Westminster to resume his seat on the back bench. Parliament didn't hold any interest for him at the moment, though. He wasn't sure it ever would again. But he would deal with that problem once he resolved all of the other messes on his plate.

When he reached John's office, he knocked on the door, then let himself in. The office was small and simple, with a pair of desks and several shelves of books and a stove in the corner. It had an air of not being entirely sorted since John had returned to London. It was also mostly empty when Edward arrived.

"Is John in?" he asked the attractive young man scribbling away at one of the desks.

The man, John's clerk, Cameron something or another, glanced up. "Er, no. Mr. Dandie isn't here," he said.

Disappointment crashed through Edward. He'd been so closed to resolution. "Do you know where he is?"

"At the club," Cameron answered. He stood. "Do you want me to take you there?"

"I know where The Chameleon Club is, thank you," Edward said with a kind smile.

Cameron looked relieved. "Good, because I don't like walking alone in London." He paused, then glanced sheepishly at Edward. "Would you mind taking me there? I have all these messages to take to Mr. Dandie." He grabbed a pile of folded slips of paper from the desk.

The man was endearing. He clearly didn't know what he was doing, which made Edward wonder why John had hired him. Then again, when it came to love, he didn't know what he was doing, but Martin had taken him on all the same. Sudden feelings of camaraderie filled Edward. "Certainly," he said with a kind smile. "Come along."

Hailing a cab and riding through London toward Hyde Park with John's green assistant felt somehow strange. It was too normal, too pedestrian for everything that Edward had gone through and was going through. Walking into The Chameleon Club and inquiring after John felt even stranger, mostly because, perhaps for the first time in his life, Edward hadn't thought about who might be watching him as he entered the building or who among the members of The Brotherhood might be some sort of a spy intent on exposing him to the public. He simply walked in, looking for John, his mind and heart filled with every other problem under the sun.

John was seated at a table in the club's huge dining room, having tea and talking to composer Samuel Percy. Edward tried not to be star-struck by the amazing composer. Not only was Samuel's music quickly becoming the talk of London, the fact that he was half black made that talk even louder. London society was so busy marveling over a black composer making such a splash that no one had stopped to consider he might be an invert as well.

"Edward," John greeted him, standing and offering him a hand. "You're back from the north."

John paused to accept his messages from Cameron and to tell the lad to help himself to tea and join them at the table. Edward noted the way Samuel smiled in amusement at Cameron and followed him with his eyes to the buffet as he piled a plate high with pastries. Edward wouldn't have bothered to find anything like that notable before, but after his own awakening, he now found it obvious that Samuel fancied Cameron. It had probably been equally obvious to sophisticated men like John all along that he fancied Martin. And here he thought he had been so careful at hiding the truth. The truth couldn't be hidden.

He shook his head as he slipped into a seat at the table. Martin had somehow poisoned his mind so that all he saw now was desire and innuendo. Or perhaps Martin had freed him to see the world as a place of love and pleasure.

"I have something for you," he told John, pushing aside his tumultuous thoughts, as John resumed his seat. He took the medallion from his pocket and set it on the table.

John's face lit into a wide smile. "So the mission was a success?" he said, taking the medallion and turning it over to study it.

"It was an utter disaster," Edward blurted, alarmed that it sounded like a sob.

John snapped his eyes away from the medallion to study him. "Since I'm holding this and since you're here by yourself, I take it the disaster was of a personal nature?"

Edward suddenly felt as though every eye in the room was on him, not just John's and Samuel's. But for a change, that didn't stop him from saying what he couldn't keep inside anymore. "Everything and nothing happened between Martin and I," he groaned. "And it could have been so much more, but I ruined it."

To Edward's surprise, and dismay, Samuel laughed. "Now there's a tasty tidbit to go with my morning tea. This is why I love dining at the club instead of at home."

Edward felt his face and neck heat. Samuel was the deciding factor. He'd gone completely mad. A week ago, he wouldn't have dared show his face at the club with his emotions in such a raw state. Now he was so desperate for some kind of advice, any kind of advice, that he was blurting out highly personal problems to a relative stranger.

"I trust that nothing I say here will go beyond this table?" he asked Samuel, one eyebrow arched.

Samuel held up one hand. "I do solemnly swear that my lips will be sealed."

Edward wasn't entirely convinced, but his doubt felt like the man he used to be, not the man whom he was trying to become. He sighed, rubbed the bridge of his nose, and turned back to John. "I stuffed it up," he said. "We were getting along so well at my parents' house in Blackpool, in spite of the fact that my parents were their usual horrible selves."

"Did you find out where Ian is?" John asked with a serious look.

Edward shook his head. "My parents are as disgusted with Ian as they are with me. All we were able to discover in Blackpool was that Ian ended up on the wrong side of several merchants in town and offended our parents to the point where they don't want anything to do with him." He paused and rubbed his hands over his face. "Granted, they don't want anything to do with me either, or so I assume, all things considered."

Edward expected John to ask for details, but before John could speak, Samuel hummed, nodding sagely, and said, "Family. They're supposed to be a source of joy, but they're rubbish more often than not."

"And you would know?" John asked him with a sly grin.

Samuel laughed warily. "I have a sister, mate. A twin sister. She's as beautiful as Venus and as wicked as a witch. It was just the two of us after our father died. We got on well enough, and then she got ambitious. Our father was a viscount, you know, and he acknowledged us in spite of his wife's objections. Samantha—yes, we're Samuel and Samantha, Mama thought she was being quaint when she named us—used that title and Father's connections to marry a wealthy industrialist with a penchant for collecting exotica. When he died, she set herself up as queen of the castle and—" He stopped and laughed, shaking his head. "Sorry, this is about your family problems not mine."

"Yours sound more interesting than mine," Edward sighed. "All I have are miserable parents and a missing brother who ran off with another man's wife and kidnapped his son. At least we have the medallion to lure him back. And with any luck, Gleason is still searching The Crown Theater for it."

"Gleason?" John snapped straight, his expression shifting from casual amusement at the stories Edward and Samuel were telling to something dark and bristling. "Did he follow you?"

Edward nodded. "He not only followed us, he led us on a wild goose chase to get us away from Liverpool so he could search for the medallion without interference." Edward's face flushed even hotter at the fresh, painful memories.

"So Gleason doesn't know you have the medallion, then?" John asked, his eyes lighting with hope.

"No, he doesn't." Edward frowned. "He demanded we hand it over, but I told him we didn't have it. I believed we didn't have it. Martin failed to mention that he'd found the blasted thing while searching with his ex-lover, Wharton." His tone turned bitter and he crossed is arms tightly. "He failed to mention he suspected Gleason was the one who picked my pocket at the Liverpool train station. He failed to mention a great many things until the eleventh hour, when I—" He stopped himself from spinning in circles and pressed his mouth shut.

John studied him with an understanding look and nodded. "So the two of you had a falling out because Martin held things back? Is that what you want advice about?"

Edward let out a breath and dropped his arms to his sides, nodding. He paused to consider, then shook his head. "No, we had a falling out because *I* held things back," he answered in a quiet, sullen voice. "Myself."

Samuel's brow shot up. "Why in God's name would you do that, mate? Martin Piper is a treat."

Twin feelings of jealousy and depression sucked all of the energy out of Edward. "So you've had him too, eh?"

"No, love." Samuel's look turned sympathetic. "I just

mean he's a jolly sort and not bad to look at. If it's advice you want, here's mine. If you fancy him and he fancies you, I can't think of a single good reason to hold back."

"I can think of a dozen," Edward replied. But when he opened his mouth again to begin listing them, he couldn't think of a single one. He shook his head and focused on John again. "Either way, my personal life is irrelevant. You have the medallion. I have no idea where Ian is. But you can hand that thing over to Selby, and he can pursue Ian and his wife without me."

He pushed his chair back and stood. "And now, gentlemen, I'm sure I have some sort of parliamentary session I'm supposed to be attending. I have a job I was elected to do and constituents who are relying on me to be as boring and unnoticeable as possible. And that includes not drawing attention to myself for my romantic entanglements or landing in the papers as the object of the latest police investigation into gross indecency. Good day."

As he walked away, John called after him with, "Edward, you don't have to leave. Samuel didn't mean anything by it. I still have advice to give you."

Edward knew Samuel didn't mean any harm, but he didn't slow his steps or turn around. Not even for the possibility of romantic advice from John. He didn't know what to do with himself now any more than he'd known what to do with himself in bed with Martin two mornings before. He wasn't just in over his head, everything he thought he knew about himself, his world, and the things that were expected of him had been shattered. All he could do was go through the motions of the life he'd been living before his bittersweet interlude with Martin had happened, but he knew his life would never be the same again.

CHAPTER 15

It was very possibly the worst performance of Martin's life, and that was saying something, after the way he'd stunk up the stage the night before. He walked off into the wings even before the crowd was finished giving Everett another standing ovation, swiping his costume cap off his head and smacking it against a set piece stored against the wall, then contemplated kicking a fake flowering bush sitting beside the set piece.

"What is that horrendous stench?" Jacob asked as Martin stomped past him on his way to the dressing rooms. Jacob answered his own question a moment later with, "Oh, that's you, Piper. Or at least your performance tonight." He sniffed. "They should sack you and let me take the part full-time."

"Go right ahead and ask Niall and see what he thinks about that," Martin snapped back without any of his usual joviality. Part of him hoped that Niall *would* sack him. That would certainly free up his time to stomp around London, kicking squirrels and ducks in St. James's Park to vent the towering frustration that he hadn't been able to shake since Edward walked away from him at Euston Station.

Edward walked away from him. Even now, as he turned the corner and stormed into the dressing room he shared with a few other actors and slumped into his chair in front of the long counter and row of mirrors, the gnawing, hollow ache Edward's dismissal of him caused was so painful that he couldn't think of anything else. Worse still, it felt as though there wasn't a damn thing he could do to win the infuriating man back. Their mission together was done, their paths had no reason whatsoever to cross, and even if they did, Edward was just as likely to pretend he didn't know Martin at all, and certainly not to admit they knew each other in the biblical sense.

He threw his cap at his reflection in the mirror, glaring at the silly spectacle he was in his comedic make-up. He couldn't have felt less comedic if he'd tried, which was exactly the reason his performances for the last two nights had been dismal. He wasn't even sure he could pull off a good dramatic monologue at the moment. What he needed was a role like Coriolanus, where he could march out onto the stage drenched in blood and chew up the scenery. He hadn't realized he was even capable of rage and bitterness like what he now felt. He'd always been cheerful, playful, affable Martin. Martin the idiot.

"Well if that wasn't a steaming pile of shite, I don't

know what was," Everett said, striding into the room with all the energy and bravado of his triumphant performance.

"I know," Martin said glumly, looking at Everett in the mirror.

"Patrick is funnier than that when he has a stomach ache," Everett went on, striding over to the counter and sitting against it. He crossed his arms and stared pointedly at Martin.

"I know," Martin repeated with more energy.

"And as much as I love him and worship at his feet, Patrick is not a funny man," Everett continued.

"I know," Martin snapped, scowling. "Where is your better half this evening anyhow?"

"Helping Stephen and Max investigate an orphanage in Limehouse that was reportedly mistreating their children, and possibly relocating some of them to Darlington Gardens," Everett said.

Martin felt guilty for biting at Everett and completely inadequate compared to some of his friends. He sank deeper into his chair, reaching for a cloth to begin removing his make-up with.

"A sigh like that can only mean romantic problems," Everett said, studying Martin closely. "I thought you and Edward Archibald were happily buggering away these days."

Martin's brow shot up, and he stared at Everett. "Where did you hear that?"

Everett answered with a wry laugh. "It's Brotherhood

gossip, darling. It travels faster than a locomotive these days."

Martin shook his head and sat straighter, focusing on his reflection as he removed his make-up. "It sounds as though Brotherhood gossip knows more than I know."

"So you and Archibald aren't taking it up the duff from each other?" Everett asked, too amused for his own good.

"Technically, no," Martin said in a flat voice.

Every one of his instincts begged him to confide in a friend, to talk about his problems and seek some sort of a solution, especially from a man he knew had gone through an emotional and romantic wringer that summer to get where he was. But he couldn't forget the betrayal in Edward's eyes when he'd learned about the way Martin had asked Wharton for advice. He'd made that mistake once, and as much relief as it would bring him to lay things out for Everett, Edward wouldn't like it.

"Technically," Everett said thoughtfully, then hummed. He was fishing, but Martin wasn't going to give in. Even when he said, "So do the two of you have an understanding, then?"

Martin concentrated on wiping make-up from his face. Understanding. Now there was a word. He didn't understand Edward at all. He understood how men like them could live in fear. He understood how a man who had waited as long in his life to give his heart and body away could have more reservations than someone like him, who couldn't remember a time when he hadn't felt like pleasure was something to give and take freely. He understood how Edward could have been badly damaged by his family, now that he'd met his parents. But he didn't understand Edward one bit.

"You know what I think?" Everett said, continuing on before Martin could so much as look at him. "I think you need to invite that fetching young stage hand, Robby, back to your flat tonight and let him suck you dry."

Martin scowled at Everett in the mirror as he dipped the cloth he'd been wiping his face with in the basin on the counter, wrung it, then continued cleaning up. A week ago, he probably would have done exactly that. Robby was a good kisser, but they'd never taken things further than that. Now the idea made him writhe with discomfort. "No, thank you," he said at last.

Everett laughed out loud. "Well, no wonder you bombed so egregiously these last two nights."

Martin glanced warily at him.

"Denied lust is one thing. Unrequited love is something entirely different," Everett went on in a teasing tone.

Everett was dead right, but it only made Martin's heart feel heavier. He tried to argue with himself that one week was hardly enough time to fall completely in love with Edward, but what a week it had been. Not to mention that it felt as though he'd known Edward his whole life.

He was spared having to take the conversation further as a knock sounded on the doorway.

"I'm not interrupting anything, am I?" John asked with a smile.

Martin's brow shot up, and he twisted in his chair to stare at John. His heart instantly leapt to a wild rhythm. John was the one who had sent him and Edward on their mission. He was the one who had thrown him together with Edward. He might have word of Edward or, he could only hope, a message from him.

"You're not interrupting anything," Everett said. "I was simply trying to get this pitiful excuse for a comedian to fess up about his erstwhile paramour, one Edward Archibald, Member of Parliament."

"Did you get anything out of him?" John asked with an amused grin. "I wheedled a bit out of Edward himself this morning."

Martin's heart did a belly flop into his stomach. Edward had talked to John? He needed to know what Edward had said, needed to know how Edward had said it, how he'd looked when he said it. He needed to know if there was a way he could fix things, if Edward had given the slightest hint there was a way to patch things up between the two of them.

He needed to stop acting like a ridiculous schoolboy with his first crush.

"I take it Edward told you we found the medallion?" he said instead, acting his heart out as he pretended nonchalance.

John reached into his pocket and drew the medallion out, letting it dangle from his fingers. Everett leapt to grab it and ogle over it. "I sent word around to Blake and Niall for them to meet us here so I can hand it over."

"Why here?" Martin asked, grateful that the conversation was steering away from him and Edward.

"Blake doesn't like to go anywhere outside of Darlington Gardens except for the theater," John said. "He's afraid someone from his former life will drag him aside and ask about Lady Selby or ask if all the rumors making the rounds about him are true."

A pinch of unexpected guilt hit Martin's stomach. Edward had the same fears. Unlike Blake, a duke, though, he had to live his life in public. He couldn't hide in the relative safety of Darlington Gardens.

"Hopefully the whole thing will be resolved soon," he said, facing the mirror again and wiping off the last of his make-up. He didn't like how pale and wan he looked without a layer of paint to hide the dark circles under his eyes.

"Speaking of things that need to be resolved." John snatched the medallion back from Everett and tucked it into his pocket. He strode forward, sitting on the counter on Martin's one side while Everett moved to sit on the other. Martin instantly felt surrounded. "What the devil happened between you and Edward up north?"

"I was just trying to pry the same thing out of him," Everett said, lighting up, as though he would finally get his gossip.

Martin sighed and glanced resentfully from Everett to John. "I've already been taken to task once for discussing private things with a former lover," he said, praying the two would leave him alone.

"We aren't former lovers," John argued.

"Speak for yourself," Everett muttered.

Martin felt himself blush and wanted to sink into the floor.

"Really?" John asked Everett, looking highly amused. "The two of you?"

"Darling, I've slept with everyone," Everett told him with a proud grin.

"It was years ago, and it was just because we were bored," Martin muttered, unable to look either man in the eye. He didn't know why he suddenly felt so bad about dallying with Everett. It had only been a few times. They'd both wanted it. They'd both known it was just for fun. They'd had a good time, and it hadn't impacted their friendship in any way.

But, of course, he *did* know why it bothered him now. It bothered him because of Edward.

"Look, the whole thing is a mess," he told both of his friends. "There are feelings involved."

"Yes, that makes everything complicated," Everett said with a wry grin. The glint in his eyes said he was serious, though.

"You do realize that the two of you are perfect for each other," John added. "I wouldn't have played matchmaker and thrown you together if I didn't believe that."

Martin jerked straight, staring at him with wide eyes. "You threw us together *on purpose*?"

"Of course, I did," John laughed. "Just like I've been amusing myself by throwing young Cameron at Samuel Percy."

"That adorable rube of an assistant you hired?" Everett asked John over Martin's head. "And Samuel Percy?"

"I know," John laughed, a gleam in his eyes. "Poor Cameron won't know which way is up, but there's far more to him than meets the eye. Samuel won't know what hit him."

"Clever," Everett said, nodding to John as though John had won a point in a tennis match.

"Well, if you're the one I have to thank for the current state of my heart and my balls, then you get no thanks at all," Martin snapped at John, refusing to feel any shame for pouting and feeling sorry for himself. "Edward wants nothing to do with me now, and I'm not sure I'll ever recover."

"Nothing to do with you?" John sputtered, gaping at Martin. "The man could barely keep himself together at the club today. He's pining for you harder than I've ever seen anyone pine."

"Pining like a Norwegian forest?" Everett suggested. "Or perhaps he's harder than a Norwegian pine?" Now the man was just being silly at Martin's expense.

Martin huffed out a breath and stood. "I'll thank you to stop meddling in my personal business," he said. In actuality, his heart thundered with hope. Could Edward truly be pining for him? Perhaps their argument was only a bump in their road and not a trough that they couldn't cross. Of course, Edward would never be the one to admit as much and fly back to him. Fear gave men feet of lead.

"What exactly did Edward say?" he asked John.

John didn't get a chance to answer. A commotion in the hall was followed moments later by Blake and Niall rushing into the room. Blake held a letter of some sort in one hand, and both of them were red-faced and out of breath, as though they'd run to the theater from Earl's Court.

"Glad you could join us," John said in a conversational tone, reaching into his pocket. "Look what I have."

Before he could draw the medallion from his pocket, Blake interrupted by blurting, "They're here. They're here in London."

"Where?" John asked, pushing away from the table and meeting Blake and Niall in the center of the room.

Blake handed the letter to him and said, "It's unclear. It was delivered by messenger to Selby House. My housekeeper there said the footman received it, but he was slow to bring it to her."

"You keep a staff at Selby House?" Everett asked, still sitting against the counter, arms crossed. "When you don't even live there?"

"It's for appearances," Blake said distractedly. "London houses always keep a minimal staff when the family is in the country. Mrs. Englewood knows which way the wind is blowing, and she's been helping me maintain the appearance that I'm living at Selby House with the girls, but that I'm not home to company. Ian Archibald must believe that's where I'm staying."

Martin listened to Blake's explanation with only part of his attention. He shifted to John's side to read the letter over his shoulder with the rest of his attention, taking the letter from John once he'd finished it. Within the first few sentences, Martin's instincts said something wasn't right.

"*Dear Blake. I know that things between us are difficult right now, but you must believe me when I say that I am truly sorry everything has come to this point. I will not pretend I condone the choices you have made with your life at all, but I will admit that I have made mistakes myself. I never should have married you, for one. Ian upbraids me for it every day. All I want to do now is rectify the situation and return home to Papa in New York. But to do that, Ian says you need to hand over the medallion and give him the money he demanded. And really, that small a sum cannot be too much to ask. You used to give me that much as pin money every year. So please, give Ian what he wants and I will make certain Alan is returned to you, a divorce between us is finalized, and then I will leave England forever*." The short letter was signed simply, "*Lady Selby.*"

"...cannot possibly just hand over that much money to Archibald," John was in the middle of saying when Martin forced his attention back to the conversation. "It's a ludicrous sum."

"How ludicrous?" Everett asked, his eyes alight, as

though he were watching a particularly melodramatic play.

"He wants five hundred thousand pounds," Niall answered on Blake's behalf with a disapproving frown.

"You gave your wife five hundred thousand pounds a year in pin money?" Martin asked with a frown.

"No." Blake blinked at him in surprise. "Nowhere near that."

"But she said—"

"Perhaps this will help the situation." John reached into his pocket and produced the medallion before Martin could finish puzzling out the contradiction in Lady Selby's letter.

"The medallion!" Blake snatched it from John, turning the piece over in his hands with a light of triumph in his eyes. "This is it. This is definitely it." He handed it to Niall.

"That's it, all right." Niall's expression was as full of the promise of victory as Blake's. "All we have to do now is figure out where in London they are."

"What sort of connections does Ian Archibald have in the city?" John asked aloud.

Blake and Niall frowned, pondering. Even Everett looked as though he were thinking things through, though Martin didn't think he knew Ian at all.

"I don't know who Ian knows in the city, and I have no idea what the man's current financial status is," Martin chimed in, "but it cannot possibly be good. Not if he needs that sort of money. But regardless, it's clear this letter is from Lady Selby, not Ian Archibald."

"They're together," Blake said with a dark scowl. "And Annamarie may be many things, but she is not capable of orchestrating this entire thing on her own."

"From what I know of Archibald," Niall added, "he is not only capable of this sort of treachery, he thrives on it."

"Are we certain Lady Selby didn't send this letter of her own volition?" Martin asked on. "It doesn't sound as though Ian dictated it to her. Are she and Ian still together?"

"Of course, they are," Blake said. "She mentions him explicitly in the letter."

That much was true. Martin glanced through the letter again. "She does say he upbraids her every day," he muttered, then shook his head. "I'm still not convinced Ian was a part of sending this letter."

"We need to question your footman to ask if he remembers details of who delivered the letter," John said, ignoring Martin's thoughts. "Perhaps someone in the neighborhood, another servant, saw the messenger. If we could trace them, we could follow them."

"Did anyone else think it odd that Lady Selby doesn't seem to be fully aware of the amount of money Ian is asking you for?" Martin asked. "If she's unaware of that, what else is Ian keeping from her? And what is she keeping from him?"

"Annamarie has always kept herself blissfully ignorant of anything she doesn't want to know," Blake said with a frown.

Martin fought the twist of indignation in his gut at being brushed off. Yet again, his insights were being ignored. Perhaps it only struck him negatively because he was already irritated with everything after having his life turned upside down and his heart inside out in the last few days, but it still stung.

"Edward Archibald might know where Ian could be hiding in the city," John said, glancing to Martin with a mischievous grin. "Someone should probably approach him about it and tell him Ian is in London."

"Perfect." Everett leapt toward Martin with an equally giddy and meddling smile. "And I think that person should be Martin."

"It should absolutely be Martin," John said, his grin widening.

Blake and Niall exchanged looks that said they didn't know what was going on, but that they supported the idea of throwing Martin at Edward again.

Martin opened his mouth and raised his hands to protest, but something stopped him before he could beg off and separate himself from the whole mess for good. Why shouldn't he go knocking on Edward's door again? What rule said he had to slink away, licking his wounds, simply because he and Edward had a fight? That fight had laid far more cards on the table than would have been laid if they'd kept their hurt and resentment a secret when they parted ways. And was he really inclined to let the best thing that had happened to him in recent memory just walk out of his life?

No. No he wasn't.

"All right," he said, lowering his arms and breaking into a determined smile. "I'll call on Edward and get him involved in this whole mess again. I'd like to give the man a piece of my mind while we're at it."

"And a piece of something else, I'd wager," Everett added in an undertone.

"Did we miss something?" Blake asked, glancing from Martin to Everett to John, who was having a hard time keeping a straight face.

"Not yet," Martin said, marching across the room to where his street clothes hung. "Not if I have anything to do about it."

CHAPTER 16

"If you ask me, we should all be focusing much more on the murmurings I've been hearing about Germany, Austria, and Italy renewing their commitment to that blasted Triple Alliance of theirs," Mr. Golding said to Mr. Lambert with an imperious sniff, "instead of bothering with that sad business in the Transvaal."

"Surely you're joking," Mr. Lambert replied. "South Africa is important to the empire. We should be expanding our influence there instead of worrying what a few backwater states on the continent are up to."

"Backwater states? Where is your brain, man? Bismarck has made Germany into a force to be reckoned with, and I'd wager that it'll be a real problem within our lifetime, especially with all these alliances."

"Alliances mean nothing and are easily broken," Mr. Lambert snorted.

"Poppycock."

Edward hung back, listening to the conversation that was taking place in St. Stephen's Hall in the Palace of Westminster during an extended recess from proceedings in the House of Commons. He wasn't truly a part of the debate, and if he were honest, he didn't care—which was a terrible sign when it came to deciding whether a political life was his true calling. All the same, he did his best to pay attention. It was better than letting his thoughts drift to the one and only topic they'd wanted to dwell on for the last two days—a certain someone's laugh, the clever way he spoke, and the feel of his mouth devouring Edward's own.

Edward shook his head and stared hard at Mr. Golding, as if that would discipline his thoughts. There was nothing at all even remotely attractive or interesting about the dusty old gentleman, from his outdated sideburns to his dry, papery skin.

"As soon as it comes up for a vote, I plan to put my full weight behind diverting as much funding as possible to investigating ways to counter the Triple Alliance," Golding said with a sniff.

"Wouldn't it be better to put the crown's resources toward domestic matters?" Edward asked. "Infrastructure and improving conditions in factories, for example."

He had once felt strongly about the need to help the people of England, but when both Golding and Lambert laughed at him as though he were a child, it barely offended him, because it wasn't the sole focus of his new world.

"My dear boy, perhaps you don't understand because you are only from York—" Golding exchanged a look with Lambert as though they both knew what sort of an inferior position that put Edward in. "—but our duty is toward the Empire and fighting for its interests first and foremost."

"I would think that our duty is toward our people before it is to an abstract concept," Edward said.

"Abstract concept?" Lambert flinched as though Edward had threatened him, but Edward barely noticed it.

In an instant, Edward's full attention was drawn to the far end of the hall, near the door, as Martin strode in, as easy as you please. He wore what looked like a new, woolen coat—the other one had probably been ruined by all the mud up north, after all—and a smile that felt as though he'd let the sun into that side of the hall. Of course, the brilliant effect of the entrance was marred slightly as he knocked into a stand of umbrellas, sending several of them flying. One hit a parliamentary clerk in the shin, and when Martin reached out to see if the man was all right, he nearly clocked a passing Lord in the process.

Edward grinned, his chest swelling with adoration, before he could stop himself. But as soon as he had the reaction, he snapped his features to neutrality and tried to focus on what Golding and Lambert were saying.

"The Empire is the only thing that matters." Lambert pounded his fist into his hand with vehemence. "It is our pride and our joy. It is what sustains us and tames the wild savages of the world. It is our duty to bring civilization to the darkest parts of the dark continents. Without the proper funding for those endeavors—"

Edward's attention floundered again. Martin spotted him. His face lit into a determined smile that sent a shiver through Edward for dozens of good and frightening reasons. Warm desire pulsed through Edward along with a sharp sense of dread. Martin strode boldly across the hall toward him. The madman had come to Westminster specifically for him, though God only knew what that would mean.

"...and if you cannot grasp that, perhaps you should return to York and take up blacksmithing," Lambert finished with a laugh that sounded more like a bark.

"You're right, of course," Edward said. He nodded curtly to his two fellow MPs, then walked away without any further words of parting. They stared after him as though he were a curiosity, but Edward didn't care.

"What are you doing here?" he hissed at Martin as their paths met in the middle of the crowded, echoing hall.

"I've come to find you, of course." Martin's usual grin had a decidedly prickly aspect to it that told Edward in an instant he was in deep trouble for everything he'd said and done and the way the two of them had parted.

"You could have waited until I was at home or sent a

note around." Edward grabbed Martin's arm and goose-stepped him to the quietest corner of the hall that he could spot.

"Ah, but time is of the essence, Shoe," Martin said, shaking out of Edward's grip but staying dangerously close to his side. He leaned far too close to Edward and whispered, "We have to find your brother."

"I don't know where he is," Edward said, glancing around to see whether anyone was observing them, and if so, what they thought of things. Fortunately, most of the men lingering in the halls seemed absorbed in their own concerns, and the few who did glance in their direction didn't seem to care what they were seeing. It brought to mind everything Martin had said in the train station at Liverpool, how no one really cared at all.

He was startled out of his thoughts when Martin said, "He's in London," in a definitive voice.

Edward cut short his scan of the hall and met Martin's eyes, his brow lifting. "How do you know that?"

"Lady Selby sent Blake a letter yesterday, and it was clearly delivered from within London," Martin said.

Edward's concerns for being found out slipped away as the thrill of the mystery he felt invested in unraveling zipped through him. "How do they know they're in London?"

"The letter was delivered by a messenger, not the post." Martin crossed his arms. Something about his smile shifted slightly, but Edward had too many thoughts flying through his head to grasp what it was.

"And how do they know Ian is with her? She could be here on her own," he said.

"That's what I thought too." Martin suddenly lit up like the night sky. His smile was genuine and joyful for a moment before dropping. "Of course, no one listened to me when I suggested Lady Selby might have sent the letter without your brother's knowledge."

"What made you think she might?" Edward asked.

"She seemed unaware of the full amount of money Ian is asking Blake to pay."

Edward shrugged. "That could mean she and Ian aren't as much in league as we're assuming, but it could also just mean she's flighty."

"True." Martin sighed, letting his arms drop. His energy renewed a moment later as he grabbed Edward's sleeve and tugged him toward the door. "Come on. Get your coat and hat. We've a job to do."

Edward let him pull him a few steps before digging his heels in. "What job? And I cannot simply leave Westminster in the middle of a session to go gallivanting all over London."

"And why not?" Martin smiled. "Haven't you told me before you're just a back-bencher and that your presence isn't required in there?" He nodded past Edward to the doors to the Commons Chamber.

"What if there's a vote?" Edward protested, but his heart already knew which activity it wanted to be involved in that afternoon. Given a choice between suffering through dry speeches about topics he didn't care about and running around London with Martin, there wasn't really a choice at all. Which was a bad sign.

"You're the only one who might know where your brother is hiding, Shoe," Martin said, a tempting twinkle in his eyes. "Come on, now. Where are his haunts? Where does he like to stay when he's in town? Does he have any friends here? Where are we going to catch the little bugger?"

Edward nearly choked on the last question. "Ian isn't the bugger of the family," he muttered as he started toward the coat room.

Martin laughed loud enough to draw attention. "Heavens, Shoe. Did you just make that sort of a joke in the halls of Westminster? I call that progress."

Edward shot him a scathing, sideways look.

The problem was, Martin was right. In spite of the fact that there hadn't technically been any buggery at all between the two of them...yet. The fact that Edward could joke about it, that he could think about such things without turning beet red and wanting to hide behind the nearest tapestry was some sort of progress.

As soon as he'd collected his winter things and they were out on the street, looking for a cab, Martin asked, "Where are we going? Where might your erstwhile brother be hiding?"

Edward lowered his hand as a cab noticed him and the driver brought it around to fetch them. "He could be anywhere," Edward sighed. "Ian isn't a gentleman, and if he's asking Selby for money, he doesn't have the funds to stay anywhere grand."

"So we can rule out Mayfair and Kensington," Martin said with a nod.

"He wouldn't stoop to stay anywhere in the east end, though," Edward figured on. "But that still leaves masses of the city to search and millions of people to sort through."

"Who are his friends in London?" Martin asked as the cab pulled up in front of them.

Edward rubbed the back of his neck. "I don't know if he has any left. There might be a few old chums who haven't deserted him. Rogers, for one. We can start with him." When the cab stopped and the driver hopped down to open the door for them, Edward told him, "Can you take us to Baker Street, Marylebone?"

"Yes, sir." The man nodded.

As soon as they were safely inside the cold carriage, Edward had second thoughts about everything.

"This is cozy, isn't it?" Martin said, settling on the forward-facing seat beside him, looping his arm through Edward's, and nestling close as the carriage jolted into motion.

"For God's sake, man, what are you doing?" Edward attempted to shake him off, but Martin refused to detach himself. In fact, he inched closer.

"I'm cold," Martin said with a teasing laugh.

Edward stared flatly at him. The temperature had been the instigating excuse in every one of the times they'd ended up naked, sweaty, and panting in each other's arms. "You are incorrigible," Edward muttered.

"And you're a right pain in my arse," Martin snapped back with enough anger to surprise Edward. When Edward stared incredulously at him, Martin went on with, "Well, you are. Trying to walk away from our relationship without so much as a by your leave." He *humphed*.

Edward gaped at him. "We do not have, as you call it, a relationship of any sort."

"Tell that to my prick," Martin bit back, though there was just as much humor as frustration in his tone and his expression. It dawned on Edward that Martin couldn't settle on an emotion because he was as confused as he was about everything. It was such a small thing, but it felt huge to know he wasn't alone in confusion either.

The realization made Edward go hot and cold, wanting to both leap out of the speeding carriage and throw himself against Martin, pin him to the seat, and kiss him until they were both silly. "Who's the pain in the arse now?" he demanded, feeding his irritation instead of his desire, if only out of habit and the need to defend himself—possibly from himself. "You don't ever give me time to think, you just push and push and push until I don't even know who I am anymore. And do *not* go making a sexual euphemism out of those words," he added as Martin opened his mouth, a mischievous gleam in his eyes.

"You don't know what you want, Shoe. I'm merely helping you along," Martin insisted.

"I *do* know what I want," Edward shouted, startling Martin to the point where he flinched. "I know exactly what I want, you fool. I just don't think I can have it."

"Whyever the fuck not," Martin said in a paradoxically calm voice. Edward could tell he'd hit a nerve, though. Martin was not the sort to casually use obscenities.

"We've already been through this," Edward grumbled, yanking his arm out of Martin's grasp and crossing his arms. "And you just saw my place of work, the men who were, even as you arrived, judging me and finding me wanting without knowing the full, damning story."

Martin scowled. "How were they judging you?"

"For being from Yorkshire and thinking the resources of the precious Empire should be used to better the lives of its citizens instead of engaging in foreign wars and entanglements."

Martin leaned against the wall of the carriage, his eyebrows going up. "That's very noble of you, Shoe."

"It's why I entered politics in the first place. To help people."

"No, you entered politics because you thought it would make your parents love you."

The simple statement, delivered so casually, shook Edward to his core. He turned his head to stare at Martin, as if gold coins had suddenly started pouring out of the man's ears.

Martin blinked at him. "You didn't already know that?"

"I chose a political life because—" Edward stopped. Because it was the only thing his parents had talked about for his future as he grew up. Because it would bring honor and respectability to a family that was already diminished by his father's poor investments. Because if Edward pleased him, they might care for him after all. "I wanted to help people," he finished, certain of that much.

"Then get out of politics and help people in a way that actually helps them," Martin said.

"You don't know what you're talking about," Edward sighed, sinking in on himself.

"Oh, of course I don't," Martin said with toweringly disproportionate bitterness, throwing up his hands. "Silly Martin never knows what he's talking about. He's a buffoon who can sing well and fuck well, but he's not worth anything else. He's certainly not any sort of mental giant." Martin pushed himself out of his seat and plopped onto the rear-facing seat, hugging himself tightly and glaring out the window.

Edward's jaw dropped open. "I didn't mean it like that. Stop being so sensitive."

"Then you stop being such a coward," Martin snapped at him.

Anger welled within Edward, but he stopped himself just short of lashing out. It was as if his heart had reached up from his chest and grabbed the harsh words he'd been about to say, warning him to truly pay attention to what had just happened.

He clenched his jaw and stared thoughtfully at Martin as the carriage rattled on. After what could have been an hour or thirty seconds, he couldn't tell in the charged environment of the carriage, he said, "Do you really think you're not that bright?"

"I don't think it, everyone else does," Martin muttered, hunkering down in his seat. "I know that I'm quite clever. You used to think so too, or so you told me the night we met."

Edward shrugged and shook his head. "I still think you're clever. I've seen first-hand how clever you are. You're brilliant."

The look that passed over Martin's face, settling in his eyes, was like nothing Edward had ever seen from him. It warmed so quickly that for a moment, Edward was certain Martin would launch himself across the carriage and ravish him. But just as quickly, it vanished. "You're only saying that because—"

Edward waited for him to finish, and when he didn't, he prompted, "Because?"

Martin was slow to answer. So slow that the carriage lurched to a halt before he could say anything. As soon as it did, Martin took one, guilty look at Edward then threw open the carriage door and hopped down to the street. Edward sighed and followed after him. A tiny part of his heart was astoundingly relieved, though. He wasn't the only one with a mountain of irritating problems within himself to overcome.

"Right," Martin said once they were both standing in the chilly street. "Let's find your brother."

Rogers, the man who lived on Baker Street, was a friend of Ian's from university that Edward remembered. Unfortunately for them, the man claimed to barely remember Ian. He didn't have the first clue where Ian could be. Another friend Edward remembered from growing up lived relatively close by, but he hadn't seen hide nor hair of Ian in years either. They managed to keep the services of the same cabbie through the entire afternoon, paying the man a handsome sum to sit and bask in the cold, January sunshine, more often than not.

After the third failed attempt to ask after Ian, Edward began to grow restless.

"This is futile, you know," he told Martin.

"Yes, but at least it's allowed us to spend the day together," Martin grumbled, his tone and the way he hunched in his coat and hugged himself seemingly at odds with each other. Edward could tell that Martin genuinely was glad for them to be spending the day together, and as mad as it was, he was glad too.

"Yes, we're spending the day together wasting time." Edward scrubbed a hand over his face, glancing around. For a change, he wasn't looking to see who might be watching them. He was desperate for clues of any sort.

His perusal of the area hit a spark of inspiration when he realized they were across from Regent's Park. A corner of the park had been set up with what looked like a fair of some sort.

"Do you think a five-year-old boy would enjoy a fair like that?" he asked, nodding to the park.

Martin turned his scowl to the park. Mere seconds after seeing what Edward was looking at, he straightened, his expression lightening again. Aside from feeling encouraged that Martin must have grasped what he was thinking, Edward was amused and mystified by how fast and how frequently Martin's moods could change and how expressive he was with every last emotion he had. It was rather endearing, actually, especially since he himself was such a dull stick in the mud.

"Lady Selby has Lord Stanley with her," Martin spoke Edward's thoughts aloud. "As I understand it, she isn't a particularly fond or attentive mother."

"And Ian hates children," Edward said.

Martin turned to him. "What sort of blackguard hates children?"

"You like them?" Edward's brow inched up.

"Children are perfection." Martin burst into a smile. "Haven't you ever spent time at Stephen and Max's orphanage? I saw you at the Christmas party last month."

"I—" Edward's mouth hung open for a moment. Of all the times for Martin to point out that he'd noticed him at a party a month ago, ostensibly before they were introduced. That meant he'd been noticeable enough to catch Martin's eye. And that moment was the absolute worst for information like that to come into play. "Focus, man," he said with a frown. "What do you think the odds of Ian and Lady Selby taking Lord Stanley to the park or a fair like that to keep the lad occupied might be?"

"Better odds than us wandering around London searching for the next week and a half," Martin said with a shrug.

They exchanged another look, then marched on toward Regent's Park. Edward didn't expect anything, and if he were honest with himself, after over an hour of wandering the park and searching through the fair—which they had to purchase tickets for—his assumptions were proven right. It was too cold for the park or the fair to be crowded, so it wasn't as though Lady Selby and Lord Stanley or Ian would have much of a crowd to hide in. It had been a solid idea, but they weren't there.

"Where else might a bored duchess who cannot show her face in public because of the infamy of what she's done take a restless little boy to entertain him while her nefarious and skint lover skulks about?" Edward asked after what felt like an eternity of searching.

"Isn't there a zoo nearby?" Martin asked, looking equally as put out by the whole thing.

"Or a theater specializing in productions for children?" Martin would know about that.

Martin growled in frustration and rubbed his hands over his face. "This whole thing is so achingly pointless," he said, then dropped his hands to his sides. "If you ask me, we would get much further and have loads more fun if we went back to my flat and—"

Edward clapped a hand on his arm, stopping him in the middle of what he was certain would be a ribald suggestion designed to force the issue of whatever it was between them. He'd spotted Ian standing at the corner of one of the fair's tents, staring right at them.

"Ian!" he shouted, grabbing Martin's sleeve and rushing toward his brother. "Ian, you prick, what in God's name—"

He didn't get any further than that. Ian slipped behind the tent, getting away from them.

"So they're here after all?" Martin said, laughing. "What a perfectly convenient turn of events."

It was convenient. Too convenient. So much so that Edward was instantly suspicious. He dashed around the corner of the tent with Martin on his heels, just barely able to keep Ian in sight. Ian kept looking over his shoulder, as if he wanted them to follow.

As last, he darted inside one of the tents. Edward was certain they'd cornered him at last, but when he and Martin raced inside the tent after him, they found themselves in a particularly devilish hall of mirrors.

"Ian, you rat, where are you?" Edward called out.

"Do you have the medallion?" Ian's voice echoed through the tent.

"Not on us," Martin answered. "But we do have it. How in the hell did we get lucky enough to find you?" he asked in a much quieter voice.

Ian's derisive laughter sounded as Edward and Martin moved through the maze of distorting mirrors.

"You think you found me? I've been following the two of you for the last two hours. Jensen was kind enough to alert me that you were searching for me."

Edward swore under his breath. Jensen was the second of Ian's friends they'd visited in search of him. Jensen told them he didn't know where Ian was, hadn't heard from him in years, but that had clearly been a lie.

"Ian, this has gone on long enough. Return Lord Stanley to his father at once. Selby wants to divorce Lady Selby, so you can have her," Edward called out, beginning to feel dizzy from the mirrors. He caught glimpses of Ian here and there, so he knew his brother was listening, but whoever had designed the mirrored maze was devilishly talented.

"The medallion," Ian repeated. "And the money. I want both. Blake gets nothing until I get the medallion and the money he's promised me. You go find him and tell him that."

"This is ridiculous," Martin called out to the mirrors. He took a few quick steps in one direction only to come within inches of smashing into his own reflection. "Give us an address of where you're staying. Let Selby see his son. We don't even know how to get the medallion and the money to you if we don't know where you're staying."

A pause followed that remark, then Ian called out, "Tell Blake to bring the medallion and the money to Lady Norwich's ball tomorrow evening."

"Lady Norwich's ball?" Martin turned to Edward

with a scrunched up, confused face. "Of all the daft things...."

"It will be crowded," Edward said, understanding dawning. "They'll be able to stage a hand-off in public, which is often more anonymous than private." The statement again made Edward think of how few people either noticed or cared about the way he and Martin interacted with each other. But that was not the time to travel down that particular rabbit hole. "All right," he called out. "We'll take the message to Selby. We'll tell him to be at Lady Norwich's party tomorrow night with the medallion and the money."

"Good," Ian said. "Tell him I'll have his son there and that I'll hand the brat over to him. But only if he stays true to his word without any tricks."

"We'll tell him," Martin called out.

"Ian, this has to end. You cannot keep—"

Edward was cut off by the sound of something falling over and shattering near the edge of the tent behind them. They whipped around and skirted their way through the mirror maze in search of whatever had made the sound, but Edward knew instantly what it was. Ian had slipped away and was gone.

CHAPTER 17

There was no reason whatsoever for Martin to miss yet another performance of *Love's Last Lesson* to attend a society ball where almost no one would lower themselves to speak to him and where the only conversations he found himself in were about Everett Jewel. But Martin would have rather fallen into a dozen muddy, icy puddles in the middle of nowhere outside of Liverpool than miss what he was certain would be the endgame of the drama between Blake and Ian Archibald.

And it didn't hurt that he got to see Edward dressed to the nines as part of the deal.

"You're looking rather fetching, Mr. Archibald," he said, sidling up to Edward's side as one of Lady Norwich's footmen presented Edward with a tray of wine glasses. Martin pretended his motivations for being there were to take a glass of wine for himself, then schooled his expression so that any outside observer would think any conversation with Edward was strictly a matter of chance as the footman moved on. "I could just eat you up the way you're looking tonight," he said with the conversational tone one used while talking about the weather.

"Don't start with me, Mr. Piper," Edward said in an equally polite tone, adding a pained smile that the blessed man probably thought passed for nonchalance. "We aren't supposed to speak with each other tonight. We aren't technically even needed here."

"But John secured us invitations in case the hand-off ran into trouble." Martin reminded him, sipping his wine and pretending to observe the crowd of nobs. "Personally, after what I've seen so far, I think this party could use a little trouble."

"Haven't you caused enough trouble already?" Edward asked, sipping his own wine and turning his body away from Martin just enough to make it look as though they weren't directly involved in conversation, and as if they were hardly aware of each other.

Which was a gigantic lie. Martin couldn't have been more aware of Edward if he'd tried. Especially after the delightful afternoon they'd spent together the day before. The two of them were born to form some sort of investigative duo, like the heroes in those new stories by Mr. Arthur Conan Doyle that were all the rage at the moment. As far as Martin was concerned, Edward should throw off Parliament and become some sort of social crusader who solved mysteries on the side. Martin would gladly take up the position of his Watson any day. He would be particularly good at the task of keeping Edward in peak physical condition through a rigorous routine of gymnastic activity that would—

"Will you stop staring at me with that wolfish look?" Edward hissed, snapping Martin out of his thoughts.

"No," Martin answered, but did anyhow, taking a sip from his wineglass. "Not after you told me you thought I was clever yesterday."

Edward sighed. "You are clever. I don't know why you ever doubted it."

Rather like Martin wondered why Edward ever doubted he was desirable. But those were mountains to climb on another occasion. At the moment, they needed to keep their eyes peeled for Ian.

"Does John have the medallion still or did he hand it over to Blake?" he asked, lowering his voice and inching closer to Edward.

"Last I heard, he gave it to Selby," Edward said, shifting to face Martin. "Selby is the one Ian is here to negotiate with, after all."

"And have you seen Lady Selby?" Martin raised one eyebrow. It seemed increasingly unlikely that his theory about Lady Selby not being a part of Ian's plans, or at least not knowing fully what they were, was correct. She would have to at least release Lord Stanley into Ian's custody if they wanted to complete some sort of trade at the ball that evening.

"I haven't seen her," Edward sighed.

They took another look around the ballroom. The event was every bit as grand and complicated as Martin had ever imagined a high society ball to be. He recognized half of the faces smiling, simpering, and preening around the room from etchings that had appeared in the papers or from the most expensive boxes in the Concord Theater. Everyone who was anyone seemed to be there that evening. Which was probably the point of Ian orchestrating the hand-off at that sort of event. Lady Norwich's ballroom was massive, but the lords and ladies, industrialists and heiresses, were packed in like sardines all the same. The room was bright with electric lights and decorated with flowers, bunting, and glittering strands of faux gems that caught the light. An orchestra that was nearly the size of the one at the Concord Theater played at one side of the room as valiant guests battled the milling crowd to make space for dancing.

"You wouldn't fancy a turn about the dance floor, would you, Shoe?" Martin asked to deliberately tease Edward.

Edward merely frowned at him.

"Next time The Chameleon Club hosts a ball, then," Martin said with a nod.

"Is there any point in telling you not to discuss those things so loudly in public?" Edward grumbled.

"No point at all, Shoe, because as I am always telling you—"

"—nobody cares," Edward finished for him.

Martin turned to him with a delighted smile. So Edward did listen to him after all. Perhaps one of these days, he would actually start to believe him when he said that everyone in the world could get away with any number of things society at large disapproved of as long as they didn't draw too much attention.

No sooner had the thoughts crossed his mind than the volume of conversations throughout the room diminished and all eyes turned to the wide doors that marked the entrance to the ballroom. The source of the crowd's sudden hush was painfully apparent at a glance. Blake had just entered the room.

An unexpected tightness took over Martin's gut. Blake was dressed perfectly and didn't have a hair out of place. He wore his usual affable grin and smiled and nodded to several of the guests. Guests who turned away from him in deliberate snubs as he did. But still, Blake's smile remained in place as he put one foot in front of the other, parting the crowd of party-goers as he did. Parting them as though he were a leper. He was alone. Niall was nowhere in sight. Martin couldn't decide if he felt sorry for the man for not having his heart's companion with him or if having Niall there would have made matters worse. Because it was obvious to a blind man that the rumors about Blake and his choice of lover had spread through London society like the plague. Only, Blake was the one who looked as though he was about to die of it.

"What do we do?" Martin murmured as Edward repositioned his body again to make it appear as though there were distance between the two of them. "Should we go to Blake's rescue somehow? This is like watching the man commit social suicide."

"Wait until someone of unimpeachable reputation approaches him first," Edward muttered back.

"What the devil is that supposed to mean?" Martin threw caution to the wind, turning to frown at Edward.

Looking irritated at his boldness, Edward turned back to Martin. "The cat is out of the bag for Selby. Not only did his wife leave him, but half of Yorkshire society saw him with Niall in the fall and drew their own conclusions. Particularly since Selby then disappeared. But if what I've been hearing lately is true, he and Niall have been spotted together several times in spite of taking care and keeping mostly to Darlington Gardens." He nodded across the ballroom to where Blake was still parting guests like the Red Sea as he made his way deeper into the room. "That is what happens when one of our sort who is too high to be arrested and put on trial is exposed for being what we are."

For once, Martin had no desire whatsoever to make a joke. His heart went out to Blake. The man looked so thoroughly alone moving through the ballroom, everyone avoiding him. No, not avoiding him, spiting him with looks and turned backs. If Martin's guess was right, Blake was searching for Ian's face in the crowd, probably thinking of nothing but his son, but Ian hadn't arrived or made himself known yet. Watching a man like Blake ostracized by his peers had Martin feeling sick. Suddenly,

Edward's fears didn't seem so frivolous or unfounded after all.

"Can you believe the cheek of the man?" a blustery gentleman whom Martin didn't know strode up to Edward's side. "Showing his face in a respectable place like this? It's disgusting. Even if he is a duke."

Martin pivoted so that his back was to Edward in an effort to make their association seem as random as possible.

"I hardly think having one's wife leave you is cause for such treatment," Edward said with a decidedly innocent tone.

Martin's lips twitched into a proud grin. Feigning ignorance was the highest road Edward could have taken in the situation and still retained his innocence without blatantly speaking against Blake.

The man Martin didn't know snorted. "It's more than just that. The Duke of Selby has been exposed as a reprehensible sodomite."

"Has he?" Edward shrugged slightly. "I tend not to listen to society gossip. It doesn't pertain to me."

Again, Martin grinned in spite of himself. A lifetime of being terrified of being discovered had made Edward highly adept at deflecting uncomfortable conversations.

"Word amongst people in the know is that Selby has audaciously taken up residence with his male lover, in spite of every law of nature and decency," Edward's friend went on. "No wonder his wife left him."

"She ran off with my brother," Edward said in a flat

voice. Martin was shocked that Edward would suddenly associate himself so closely with the gossip. His friend seemed shocked too, but Edward went on with, "I know for a fact that Lady Selby and my brother had been carrying on an adulterous affair for years before they stole Lord Selby's children and ran off together."

Edward's friend made a choking sound and flapped his jaw uselessly for a few seconds before saying, "Well, it's no wonder, if Selby is the way he is." Martin smirked at the "if" that had made its way suddenly into the conversation, but his temptation to gloat was stopped when the man glanced to him and said, "What do you think?"

Martin winced internally. He'd been caught listening in, which meant there was a chance the lout might put two and two together to figure out he and Edward knew each other. And suddenly, against everything Martin thought he believed, he didn't want to put Edward's reputation at risk by giving even the slightest impression that they knew each other, let alone *knew* each other.

"What is this?" he asked, feigning total ignorance, just as Edward had, as he pivoted to join the conversation.

"Good lord," the lout said, his expression brightening. "Aren't you Martin Piper, the comedian? I saw you in *Love's Last Lesson* right before Christmas. You were brilliant, astounding." He thrust out his hand, as if meeting Martin was the highlight of the entire evening. "Charles Hepplewhite, MP for Swindon, at your service."

Martin put on his best, most flattered smile and shook the man's hand. So he was one of Edward's so-called work colleagues, was he? "The pleasure is all mine, sir."

"And what do you think of a reprobate like Lord Selby," Hepplewhite said without letting go of Martin's hand. He put on a sly smirk that implied he already knew and that they were all about to have a jolly time tearing Blake to shreds together.

Martin shrugged and pulled his hand away from Hepplewhite's. "Live and let live, eh?"

Hepplewhite was clearly disappointed by Martin's reaction. Disappointed and then dismissive. "Of course, you would say that," he sniffed. "Theatrical sorts are weak in the head and full of every vice known to man."

"Are we?" Martin asked, an edge in his voice. He turned to Edward with a questioning look, then stared hard at Hepplewhite. "And how many theatrical sorts are you acquainted with, sir?"

"Plenty," Hepplewhite laughed. "I'm a particular favorite of the chorus girls at the Savoy, don't you know." He elbowed Edward and winked.

"Oh," Martin said, pretending to have understanding dawn in his expression, though what he was certain shone from his eyes was fury. "You must be the walrus stuffed into a suit that they were telling me about."

Hepplewhite's jovial expression dropped. "Now see here, man. I don't know who you think you are—"

"Yes, you do. I'm that brilliant, astounding comedian

you paid money to see in a show before Christmas," Martin snapped.

"Mr. Piper is not only a talented actor, he's one of the most intelligent men I know," Edward added. "Not weak in the head at all."

A rush of joy shot through Martin's heart like an arrow. Not only had Edward just endorsed him as being intelligent—and after the things that were said during their carriage ride the day before, Edward had to know that was a sore point with him—he'd acknowledged knowing him. Him. An actor. And everyone knew all about actors.

"I—I'm sorry to have given offense," Hepplewhite said, looking more baffled than sorry. "It's just that you must admit, a man like Selby shouldn't be mixing with polite society."

"Why?" Edward asked, his face a mask of banal innocence.

"Because he's—you know what they're saying—and his wife left him for it," Hepplewhite stammered.

"I just told you that his wife left him because she ran off with her lover of many years, my brother," Edward said, his eyes going cold as he stared at the man. "A man who certainly wouldn't stop at spreading rumors as a way to prime the courts to grant Lady Selby a divorce."

Martin nearly choked on his wine, which he still had in hand and had taken a gulp of to calm his nerves. *Well done, Shoe*, he thought to himself. *That definitely deserves a reward. Now, if we can just find a quiet corner for me to give it to you.*

He glanced around the room with a heated grin, looking for a way to rescue Edward from the boorish conversation and to give them a chance to be alone. They had so many things to sort out, and Martin would be damned if he let Edward wiggle away from what they both knew was inevitable between them now.

His gaze landed on a short, nondescript man standing near one of the French doors that led out to the terrace. If he'd been sipping his wine then, he would have spit it out.

Gleason.

"Bloody hell. You must be joking," he clipped before he could stop himself.

Edward and Hepplewhite both turned to him with entirely different looks of alarm.

"Is there a problem?" Hepplewhite asked.

"I've just seen an acquaintance of Mr. Archibald's and mine," he said, then stared fixedly at Edward. "Gleason."

Color splashed Edward's face, and he set his wine glass on the tray of a passing footman. "You cannot be serious," Edward said, completely ignoring Hepplewhite.

"Who is Gleason?" Hepplewhite asked, looking put out to not be in the know.

Martin deposited his wine glass on the tray as well, searching the room to see where Blake had ended up. He spotted John talking with a trio of middle-aged ladies much closer by, while Blake was all the way across the room. Martin nodded for Edward to head toward John.

"Who is Gleason?" Hepplewhite asked again, but with more feeling.

Both Martin and Edward ignored him as they cut their way through party guests to reach John. Martin was able to catch John's attention, and he broke away from his companions, weaving through the crowd to meet them.

"I knew it was another double-cross," Edward sighed before the three of them met up. "Ian is too much of a snake to stay true to his word."

"At least it isn't entirely unexpected," Martin sighed. He glanced back at Edward with a smile. "You're a gem for standing up for me back there," he said.

Edward flushed, but this time it was adorable. "I cannot abide that man," he grumbled. "And I'm sick of men like him disparaging men like Selby, men who are a thousand times better than them."

They didn't have time to say more. They met up with John in a slight clearing in the crowd.

"Gleason," Martin said, glancing toward the French doors.

"Where?" John frowned in that direction, but Gleason dipped around the corner before John could spot him.

"Go tell Blake Ian is trying to trick him again," Martin said, resting a hand on John's arm and pushing him toward the far end of the ballroom. "We'll catch Gleason. I have a score to settle with that man."

"We both do," Edward growled.

"I believe a queue of people who want a piece of Gleason is forming," John said, then headed off across the ballroom.

"Hurry," Martin said, tugging Edward's sleeve as they started toward the French doors. "This time, I am not letting that bastard get away."

CHAPTER 18

*E*dward had done more running in the past week than he'd done since his mediocre attempts at cricket and football at university, but as he shot through the French doors, a step behind Martin, he understood why so many men went in for sports. Moving, feeling his muscles work and his blood pump was exhilarating. Rather like another activity that involved the same rush of blood and stretch of sinew.

He laughed at the thought in spite of the fact that dozens of startled party guests stopped their conversations and lowered their wine glasses to see why on earth two men were dashing through the frosty courtyard outside of the ballroom and into the street. It wasn't his thoughts they were seeing and judging. Any two men could have caught their attention without doom raining down on them for who they were behind closed doors.

"There he is," Martin gasped, pointing ahead to the corner of the house at the end of the street.

"We are not letting the bastard get away this time," Edward growled, feeling a rush of power through his body that he'd never felt before.

He pushed ahead of Martin, sprinting to the corner and skidding on the icy pavement as he turned it. Gleason was still ahead of them. He slowed his steps at an alley between two stately homes, paused to glance over his shoulder at Edward and Martin, then dashed on.

"Where is he headed?" Martin asked, catching up to Edward's side as they ducked into the alley. "And why?"

"Into the mews, I imagine," Edward called back to him. "He probably has a carriage ready to whisk him away, now he knows he's caught."

The alley spilled out into the mews at the back of two rows of Mayfair townhouses. It was late, so they were mostly abandoned, though a few servants cleaning up from their masters' suppers glanced up from scrubbing pans or shaking out tablecloths to watch the chase fly past. Again, Edward's instinct to cringe at being seen doing something highly unusual flared within him, but he tamped it down even faster this time. Worry was a useless emotion when there were far bigger things at risk.

Gleason dashed out the far end of the mews and onto another street at the edge of Mayfair.

"Is he trying to reach Soho?" Martin asked, though Edward didn't think he was after an answer.

Edward kept his eyes glued to Gleason as he dodged in and out of alleys, backtracking now and then, but always moving east. The man had remarkable stamina and an uncanny ability to leap over stray crates or barrels in the alleyways. He had no trouble at all gaining on Edward and Martin, but always paused just before slipping out of sight to make certain they were following. Edward's lungs burned from exertion, but he couldn't shake the feeling that they were minutes away from catching Gleason. If they could just keep up for another block, race him around another corner—

It hit him like a cannonball in the gut when Gleason hesitated at yet another corner before dashing on.

"Stop!" Edward flung out his arm to stop Martin and ended up grabbing the sleeve of his formal jacket. "Stop," he panted, bending over and resting his hands on his knees. His body ached and his lungs burned, but it was the twist of shock in his gut that made his blood boil and had him growling out loud in indignation.

"Stop?" Martin gasped for air as he stared from the corner Gleason had disappeared around to Edward. "But we're so close. The bastard will get away."

"Don't you see?" Edward continued to pant, leaning on his knees for a moment before wincing as he straightened. "We are the biggest fools that ever lived."

A wry grin tugged at the corner of Martin's mouth in spite of the difficulty he was having catching his breath and the sweat that dripped down his face. "I won't dispute that one, Shoe, but we'll be even bigger fools if we came this close to nabbing the prick and let him slip away."

Edward shook his head and laughed. "It's Liverpool all over again." He wiped his own overheated, sweating face with the back of his sleeve. Sweat was pouring down his back in spite of the chill in the air, and already he was beginning to feel the full extent of the cold. "He lured us away from Lady Norwich's party on purpose. He must have known we were there to back Selby up. Just like it was easier for him to search for the medallion without us in Liverpool, he probably believes the handoff between Ian and Selby will be smoother if Selby has no one watching out for him."

"Divide and conquer," Martin sighed.

"God only knows where Gleason was trying to lead us," Edward finished.

Martin started to protest, but got no further than opening his mouth. His eyes bulged as the truth hit him. "That damnable pillock," he said at last, shoving a hand through his hair. "We fell right into that one, didn't we? Again."

Edward nodded, slapping a hand on Martin's arm. They looked like complete idiots standing in a dark alley in formal suits, panting and sweaty, but Edward burst into laughter. The whole thing was utterly mad. It was so far from what he could have seen himself doing a fortnight ago. The old version of himself would have been shocked, but the man he was now couldn't stop laughing. He hadn't had so much fun in years, possibly ever. He rested his arm on Martin's shoulder and buried his head against it, laughing until he was dizzy.

"Oh, dear," Martin said, humor seeping into his own voice. "He broke you, didn't he?"

Edward lifted his head and shook it. "I've never felt more alive in my life," he said.

Martin made an incredulous face and eyed him askance. "Who are you, and what have you done with my Shoe?"

The question was tender and light. Martin's eyes shone with a curious sort of happiness in the cold, dim moonlight. It was all so perfectly absurd that there was only one thing Edward could do. He shifted to stand in front of Martin, clasped his hands on either side of Martin's face, and pulled him close for a deep and searing kiss. He'd never wanted to kiss anyone so desperately in his life. They were standing in the middle of a public street with a huge, bright moon above them, and the only action he felt capable of was kissing Martin until they were both sighing with longing, their tongues mingling and their lips hungry for each other.

"We should chase wily detectives through the streets of Soho more often," Martin gasped between kisses, drawing Edward into his arms and taking command of the kiss.

They only had a few, glorious seconds of communion

before a voice hissed from one of the windows above them and a woman leaned out to say, "Psst! There's a copper right up the street. Take that elsewhere."

"I don't even know where we are," Edward laughed, leaning into Martin's warmth in spite of the danger, and meaning it both literally and figuratively.

"Lucky for you," Martin said with a wink, "I do. Thanks, Moll!" he called up to the woman in the window.

"Just lookin' out for you, Marty," she replied before pulling inside and shutting the window.

Martin took Edward's hand and hurried off down the street in the opposite direction Gleason had gone in. He moved with purpose, turning left at the corner, then continuing on along a row of terraced houses.

"Shouldn't we return to the ball?" Edward asked. "If Gleason truly did trick us into leaving so Ian could tackle Selby alone, wouldn't it be better if we went back?"

"Blake isn't alone," Martin reminded him. "John is still at the ball. And do you really want to walk back into a society party attended by people who know you in the state you're in?"

Edward glanced down at his mussed suit in the light of a streetlamp as they marched past. He was certain his face was red and sweaty as well, and he didn't trust how he smelled after dashing through the streets of London. "You have a point," he said. "I trust John to help Selby without us."

"As do I," Martin agreed with a nod.

They walked on, the cold lamplight and the distant moon all they had to light the city around them. "All right, where are we, then?" Edward asked, threading his fingers through Martin's. He could lie to himself and say it was for warmth, but the truth was he wouldn't have had it any other way.

"We just so happen to be in my own neighborhood," Martin said, heading for the door to one of the buildings. They stepped inside, but rather than going up the staircase in the front hall, Martin knocked on the first door on the right. It was answered by a middle-aged woman with a thick shawl around her shoulders. "Sorry to disturb you, Mrs. Evans, but I don't have my key on me. Could you let me into my flat?"

"Right-o, Martin." She nodded, ducked back into her flat, then came out with a ring of keys and pushed in front of Martin and Edward to head up the stairs. She barely even looked at Edward, even though Martin was still holding his hand.

"Shouldn't we...." Edward didn't know what question he wanted to ask, let alone what to do about it.

He and Martin followed Mrs. Evans up two flights of stairs to the door of what Edward assumed was Martin's flat. She unlocked the door for them without so much as blinking. "Do you need a new key made, love?" she asked as Martin opened the door and tugged Edward inside.

"No, I'll just go fetch my coat and keys from where I left them tomorrow. Thank you, darling."

That was it. Mrs. Evans said goodnight and headed back downstairs and Martin shut the door of his flat and turned the lock. As soon as that was done, he grabbed Edward by his lapels and pulled him into a passionate embrace.

The whole thing was such a giddy whirlwind that Edward didn't have the presence of mind to do anything but kiss Martin back. He barely took in his new surroundings except to note Martin's flat was smaller than his. He fumbled with the buttons of Martin's jacket so that he could slide his arms around the solid warmth of his torso and made a sound of approval deep in his throat as Martin devoured his mouth.

"Wait," Martin said a staggering heartbeat later, throwing Edward completely off balance. Martin leaned back, eyeing Edward suspiciously. "This isn't the Shoe I know. Where's the flinching and the anxious looks? Where is the hesitation?"

"Stuff hesitation," Edward said, grabbing Martin and pulling their bodies flush against each other. "I've been a right fool, and I'm thoroughly ashamed of myself."

He slanted his mouth over Martin's, drinking him in and reveling in the lust that pulsed through him, warming him after the dash through the cold, dark night. Martin kissed him back, looping his arms over Edward's shoulders, but only for a moment.

"This really isn't like you at all," he said breathlessly, pulling away slightly but keeping them in an embrace.

"Did something happen that I should know about? I feel like I'm waiting for the other shoe to drop."

"You happened," he said. He leaned in to kiss Martin again, but changed his mind. "No," he corrected himself. "I happened. Because of you. And because of the way Blake was treated at the ball. And because of my parents, because of Ian's audacity, because of my jealousy over every other lover you've had, because of the damnable laws of this country, and because I cannot go another second living my life at the bottom of a hole I dug for myself."

The vehemence of his words had Martin's eyes alight with excitement. Martin shifted his hips to press against Edward's and drew his hands down to undo the buttons of Edward's jacket and waistcoat. "I like this new Shoe," he said, passion thick in his voice. "This is the Shoe I saw underneath the old Edward Archibald all along. Who do I have to thank for shaking that old, useless armor off and setting this man free?"

"You," Edward said, kissing Martin with everything he had and burying his fingers in his hair. "Always you. Forever you. You're the Other Shoe that makes us a pair."

Martin laughed even as Edward tried to kiss him. He pushed Edward's jacket off his shoulders and followed that with his waistcoat. "I'm never going to live that metaphor down now, am I?"

"No," Edward said, wriggling out of his clothes and letting them drop to the floor, then reaching for Martin's trousers. "I'm so tired of being afraid all the time. I'm exhausted from seeking other people's approval. I want to be myself now, not the shell of a person society wants me to be, as if that would gain my parents', or anyone else's, approval. It doesn't matter how perfectly I fit into the mold they make for me, my parents will never be happy with me. I'm done with that. I want to be happy for myself, as myself."

"You make me happy," Martin said, the timbre of his voice dropping sensually as he undid Edward's trousers and pushed his suspenders from his shoulders. "You make me so happy, and all I want to do is give that back to you and then some."

"Give away," Edward said, a flash in his eyes. "I'm ready to receive it."

Martin made a wicked, delightful sound, meeting Edward's eyes with a spark of lust. "Are you sure about that, Shoe? You'll be walking around tomorrow with a sore bum. Aren't you going to worry that everyone you meet will see right through you and know what you did to earn it?"

"Nobody cares, Martin," Edward scolded him. "Why, I'd wager half the men in the halls of Westminster are walking around with sore arses from being buggered silly on any given day."

Martin laughed out loud at that and leaned into Edward, kissing him soundly and tugging his shirt from his trousers so that he could smooth his hands along Edward's naked sides. It felt so glorious to finally give in to the desire that inflamed him that Edward could only sigh and let himself be touched and kissed and more. He drew in a sharp breath when Martin slipped a hand into his trousers to cup his balls and then stroke his swiftly growing erection. He batted away every residual worry and fear that what they were doing was wrong. It wasn't wrong, it was the rightest thing he'd ever done in his life.

"You really are lovely, you know," Martin whispered against his ear as they tugged each other's clothes off and moved clumsily through the tiny apartment to the bedroom at the back. "I'm going to need hours just to kiss you and touch you and learn every nook and cranny of your magnificent body."

"Would years do?" Edward asked. It might have been too much for the moment they found themselves in, but it felt so right to say.

Martin smiled and kissed him with a whole new level of passion, making Edward's head spin. "Years would be perfect."

They tore off the rest of their clothes somehow. Edward barely paid attention. He knew what he wanted, and the sooner he got it, the better. Martin's bed was small, but that somehow made everything better as they tumbled into it, bodies entwining. He touched Martin everywhere he could, not satisfied to keep his hands in one place for long. He wanted to memorize the muscles of Martin's back, learn the lines of his sides and the swell of his arse. He slipped a hand between them to stroke Martin's cock, drawing impassioned moans from Martin as he did, feeling its impressive length and girth. The fact that he wanted that cock inside of him was pure madness and sent a shiver through him, but he'd never been more certain of what he wanted in his life.

"I want you," he whispered against Martin's ear, nibbling his earlobe. "I want all of you. I want to be yours."

"You have no idea how wildly good that sounds," Martin said in a rich and resonant voice. He shifted so that he covered Edward's body with his and brushed his hands up Edward's arms until he had his arms pinned above his head. The hint of surrender in the position had Edward panting in expectation. "You are going to be astounded at how good it actually feels to be fucked," he went on with a wicked glint in his eyes. "And once you've been had a few times and are used to it and can't imagine what life was like before that, we're going to turn the tables and you're going to fuck me, because I *do* know how good it feels and I've been imagining you doing it ever since we met."

"Really?" The single word came out shaky and full of expectation.

Martin laughed. "Of course, Shoe. Taking turns and taking care of each other is what two men do when they're in love."

The words sank into Edward's heart and spread through him like the summer sun. "You love me?"

"Yes, yes, I know." Martin rolled his eyes teasingly. "It's barely been more than a week and love at first sight is an invention of storybooks and all that. But no, I reject that. I knew you were the one for me the moment I laid eyes on you skulking through Covent Garden, about to land in trouble."

Edward's heart raced, and tears stung at his eyes—not because he thought Martin was lying or making fun of him, but because he knew he wasn't. He knew and was certain of the fact that Martin loved him. He was loved. Finally.

"I loved you from the moment I first saw you on stage," he confessed with a laugh. "Does that count? Or should we count from the moment you rescued me from a fate worse than death."

Martin's eyebrows raised. "A right hero I am, then. And what did I save you from?"

"You rescued me from myself."

A sentimental gleam joined the mischief and lust in Martin's eyes. "Well, if that doesn't beat all," he said, then bent down to kiss Edward with searing passion.

Edward gave in to that kiss. He surrendered all of his fear and all of his trepidation into Martin's hands, into his body, to be more precise. Nothing had ever felt better than to put fear aside in exchange for trust. He trusted Martin with everything he had, even when he pulled up and cheekily said, "Now, roll over. I'm going to play with that sweet arse of yours and get you limbered up and ready to take me to the hilt."

Edward laughed even as his prick jumped in anticipation. He did as he was told and rolled over, stuffing Martin's pillows under him to lift his hips the way Martin wanted them. He had no real idea what to expect and trembled slightly in anticipation as Martin took out a small jar from his bedside table.

"It's not butter, but this will make it much easier, believe me," he said with a mock serious look, taking some of the clear ointment from the jar and spreading it against Edward's arsehole. Edward gasped and tightened at how cold it felt at first, but as soon as Martin began toying with him in earnest, penetrating him with one finger, then two, he heated in a hurry. "There we are, love," he cooed as he stretched Edward further. "Relax as much as you can."

"It feels good," Edward insisted, wriggling to spread his hips and lift them into Martin's touch. What it felt was wildly intimate and personal. He didn't think he could possibly have shared anything so intense with anyone else and never would for the rest of his life. He'd never been so vulnerable or liked it so much, and he vocalized those emotions with abandon.

Martin laughed at the sounds he made, but there was an edge of impatience to his laughter. "You're testing my patience, Shoe," he said breathlessly. "Believe me, this view is the most amazing one I've ever seen." Before Edward could come up with a cheeky reply, Martin withdrew his hand, reached for the jar, and slicked his cock. "I can't hold off anymore."

A last gasp of anxiety shot through Edward as Martin grabbed his hips and lifted them, gripping tightly. Martin didn't give him time to worry for long or come anywhere close to losing his nerve and changing his mind. Edward sucked in a breath and tensed slightly as he felt the head of Martin's cock press against his hole, then let out a long, ragged sigh as Martin thrust in. It was odd, almost terrifying, and surprisingly uncomfortable at first. For the space of a heartbeat, Edward wondered why anyone in their right mind would do such a thing. The stretch and the burn was—was actually astoundingly erotic after the first startling moments. A soon as Martin began to move, sliding in and out of him and pressing deeper with each thrust, Edward let go of his inhibitions and relaxed. A few more thrusts as Edward adapted to the sensation of being filled, and everything turned to absolute gold. He moaned aloud as Martin shifted and pressed up against an uncommonly pleasurable spot inside of him.

"That's right, love," Martin murmured, curling over Edward and kissing his shoulder as he thrust. "God, yes."

His kisses turned to gentle bites as the pleasure grew deep inside of Edward, seeming to spread from his groin to every part of his body. Martin matched the sounds he made, then reached around to grasp Edward's prick.

That was all it took to bring Edward to the edge. Martin's touch, the way he filled him, igniting that spot inside of him that drove Edward mad beyond his wildest dreams, and the pure joy of being one with the man he loved had Edward coming hard into Martin's hand. It was better than anything he'd ever experienced, and even that joy was tripled when Martin cried out sharply and thrust hard as he, too, came. The symbiosis of it all was shateringly good, and when Martin pulled out and sank to his side, gathering Edward into his arms as they lay entwined together, gasping for breath and trying to kiss each other senseless at the same time, Edward felt truly happy and unencumbered for the first time in his life.

CHAPTER 19

*T*he morning sunlight filtering through the curtains had never felt so warming and wonderful to Martin. He lay on his side in bed with Edward in his arms, Edward's back snuggled against Martin's chest. It was a reversal of the way he'd awakened with Edward spooning him at the hotel in Liverpool, but unlike that morning, Martin was absolutely certain Edward wouldn't bolt as soon as he woke up.

That certainty was proven as Edward slowly woke up and stretched. Martin reveled in every tiny detail of the way his lover's body moved against his—their thighs brushing, their arms sliding against each other, Edward's back flexing against his chest, and his delicious backside grinding against Martin's swiftly-growing erection. Edward made a sound of surprise and moved his hips to tease Martin more acutely.

"Don't you start, Shoe," Martin scolded him sleepily,

a smile on his face. "You're probably too sore for any of that until at least tonight at any rate."

"Don't tell me what I am and am not ready for, Other Shoe," Edward growled in return, rubbing mercilessly against Martin's cock.

Martin burst into laughter, sliding his arm farther around Edward's belly and hugging him close. He buried his face against Edward's shoulder, smelling the salt musk of his skin and resting his lips against Edward's neck. Edward moved his hand to rest over Martin's, their fingers entwining. He then decisively nudged Martin's hand down to his own morning erection and sighed in contentment.

"Well, that's a complete turn-about, isn't it?" Martin grinned against Edward's shoulder as he cupped his balls.

"I want you to make me come," Edward said, not nearly as asleep as he had been just moments before. "And then I want to do the same for you."

Martin lifted himself on one arm enough to glance down at Edward's heavy-lidded eyes while stroking his cock. "Don't tell me that, now you've overcome your fear of intimacy, you're going to become an insatiable demon."

"I think I might," Edward sighed, rolling lazily to his back. His face pinched with pleasure and he smiled as Martin played with him. "That feels amazingly good."

"Isn't this what I've told you all along, Shoe?" Martin smiled down at him, aroused at the look of pleasure that Edward wasn't even trying to hide.

Edward's breath grew tense and shallow as pre-cum

beaded on his head. Watching the process of his lover letting himself go and enjoy a little morning fumble had Martin's blood feeling like fire in his veins, especially when Edward jerked his hips subtly into Martin's touch, as though he wanted more.

"This is a far cry from the man who shied away from my kisses a few days ago," Martin said, letting go of Edward so that he could wedge himself between his legs and kiss his way down Edward's chest to his belly, then tease Edward's prick with licks and kisses.

"Oh, you are a devil, Martin," Edward groaned, burying his hands in Martin's hair as Martin took all of him in. "But you're my devil."

Martin laughed. He had Edward's cock deep in his mouth as he did, and he suspected that the vibrations did wild things to Edward, based on the way he sucked in a breath, then let it out on a moan. It was simply marvelous to suck and swallow Edward, using his tongue and lips to pleasure him and to listen to the increasingly desperate sounds he made until he came with a jerk. Martin swallowed, then hummed in victory as he kissed his way back up Edward's relaxed and loose body to nibble on his neck and shoulder, then to kiss him.

"Move your hand to—yes," he sighed when Edward grasped his cock and balls with both hands without further instruction. "Just like that."

He was so fired up that it took only minutes until he came apart in Edward's hands, then let out a long, satisfied sigh and rested on top of him. He lay there covering Edward, Edward's hands caressing his backside in the most insanely delightful way, until sense got the better of him.

"I'm not crushing you, am I?" he asked, balancing above Edward. As soon as he looked down at him, he couldn't help but smile.

"Not at all, Other Shoe," Edward smiled. "Your weight makes me feel safe, like I won't suddenly go flying off into the ether."

"In that case," Martin grinned, dipping down to steal a kiss, "I'll stay right where I am."

He nipped at Martin's lips, then kissed his cheek and jaw and neck. In the past, he'd known fairly quickly whether a lover would stick around for just the night or for a few weeks, but he'd never had the feeling he had that morning, as if it were part of his bones and his blood, that Edward would stay with him forever.

"So what do we do next, Shoe?" he asked between kisses, unable to keep his smile inside.

Edward kissed him back, digging his fingertips into Martin's back and even lifting one leg over Martin's hip to bring them closer together. "I suppose we should return to Lady Norwich's house to fetch our coats and hats," he said.

Martin laughed, stealing a particularly long kiss and feeling a stir in his groin that hinted they could have quite an entertaining morning if they wanted to. "Yes, that," he said, gazing down at Edward's sleepy face with a smile.

"But after that. Tomorrow. And the day after that. And next year. And ten years from now."

Edward's eyes snapped wide. "You're already thinking about ten years from now?"

Martin shrugged. "Ten years, ten seconds, it's all the same to me. I want you this way always. I want you about three dozen other ways too," he grinned, then flickered one eyebrow suggestively.

"But we've barely begun this affair," Edward argued, though there was no real fight in the hazy way he spoke. "Are you sure you want to put up with me for that long?"

"I'm sure I want to put up with you and for you to put up with me until the final curtain falls and we get our standing ovation for the brave way we've lived our lives."

Edward met his words with a smile that reached deeper into the man than any smile Martin had seen yet from him. It gave him hope and made him feel like a man caught up in the throes of first love. Perhaps this was his first time. It felt like his first time for true and abiding love.

"We'll have to be exceedingly clever if we want to carry on while I'm still in the House of Commons," Edward said, thought filling his eyes. "Though, if I'm honest, I want out of that job as quickly as possible."

Martin's brow rose, and he lifted higher above Edward. "You mean I won't get to strut around London bragging that I'm sleeping with a Member of Parliament?"

Edward laughed. "If you did that, we'd both land in

prison within a week." He reached up to brush a stray lock of hair out of Martin's face, love vivid in his expression. "God, you're lucky I'm such a coward when it comes to appearances. I have a feeling it will be my forbearance that keeps us out of more than a few jams."

"It absolutely will be," Martin agreed, his heart singing. He leaned in for another kiss, closing his eyes like a green lad as he took what he wanted and then some. His heart wasn't sure it could stand the perfection in his arms.

"You know," he said, wriggling his hips against Edward's to test where they both were in terms of bouncing back from their first, passionate explosions, "we don't have to get those coats right away. We could stay in bed all morning and challenge ourselves to see how many times—"

A short, sharp knock on his flat's front door stopped him in the middle of his thought. He let out a breath and lowered his head in casual defeat as Edward tensed under him.

"Don't make fun of me for saying this," Edward clipped, "but is there any chance that's the police?"

"No, none at all."

Martin dipped down to kiss him quickly, then muscled himself off of Edward and out of bed. He was badly in need of a wash after everything he and Edward had done in the last twelve hours, including their race through London, but he ignored that for the moment, threw his robe on, tucked his feet into his slippers, and shuffled out to the flat's main room.

An envelope lay on the floor just inside the door, as though someone had knocked, delivered the letter, then gone on their way. He bent to pick up the letter, then unlocked and cracked open the door, just to make certain no one was waiting in the hall. As he suspected, the hall was empty. He closed and locked the door again, then glanced at the envelope.

"Huh. Shoe, it's for you," he said, an uncomfortable shiver shooting down his back, as he read the name "Edward" on the envelope.

Edward was seated on the side of the bed, the blankets pulled over his waist, his eyes wide and wary, when Martin entered the room. "How does anyone know I'm here?" he asked the incredibly valid question.

"It has to be from Gleason," Martin said, handing him the envelope. "That man is a fiend when it comes to knowing people's business. And who knows? Considering what we found in that cottage, he might have been deliberately leading us home, knowing the inevitable would happen."

Martin thought it was a very good guess, but the contents of the letter told another story.

"It's from Ian," Edward said, glancing to Martin with wide eyes. "Gleason must have told him we were together." He looked down, then read the letter. "*Dear Edward. I shouldn't be at all surprised to discover what a perverted villain you are, or that you chose to commit horrible sins with your theatrical lover instead of ensuring Selby upheld his end of our bargain by attending Lady Norwich's ball last night."*

"What is he talking about?" Martin frowned. "We were at the ball—at least, the beginning of it—and Blake was there as well."

"Ian seems to be under the impression none of us were there," Edward said, looking thoroughly confused. "Which doesn't explain why he knows the two of us are together here, in your flat."

"Is it possible he was lurking at the ball, watching the two of us and waiting for Blake, and that he followed us when we left to chase after Gleason?" Martin asked.

Edward shook his head. "Selby arrived before we left."

He read on, finding the answer to the puzzle in the letter. *"I should have known you were as twisted and damaged as Selby. I saw you and that wretched actor rushing out of the Norwich's as I arrived. If I hadn't thought you had the medallion, I never would have chased you. And then to see you snogging, like common whores. No wonder Father and Mother never cared for you."*

"That's rich, coming from him," Martin said, hating the bastard even more. "And he's an idiot for assuming we had the medallion and not Blake."

"Strategy has never been Ian's strong suit," Edward said. "If it were, he wouldn't be in his current mess. But there's more to the letter." He read on. *"That is why it rankles me that I still must rely on you for help that might very well save my life."*

"Oh, now he's asking for your help?" Martin began pacing in front of the bed.

"Stop interrupting and let me read the entire letter," Edward scolded him. *"If you have any human feeling left and not just evil impulses, you will uphold your end of the bargain and convince Selby to hand over the money and the medallion at once. I should have known you couldn't be trusted to carry out such a simple mission. I will never forgive you for sending that wretched detective in Selby's place. That man is as wicked as they come, and if you think for one second that you can discover my whereabouts by—"*

"Hang on," Martin stopped him, feeling as though he'd been punched in the gut. He stared hard at Edward, wondering if he'd caught it too.

"Ian thinks Gleason is working for us," Edward gasped, eyes wide, proving that he had picked up on it after all.

"Which means he isn't working for your brother," Martin said, shoving a disbelieving hand through his hair. "But he's definitely trying to locate the medallion."

"If not for Ian, then for who?" Edward asked exactly what Martin was thinking.

"Something tells me we're not going to like the answer to that question."

Martin leapt toward his washstand, practically dumping the pitcher of cold water waiting there over his body in his haste to clean up enough to dress. "We have to take that letter to John Dandie right away," he said.

"And we have to find out what happened to him and Selby after we left the ball last night," Edward agreed, standing and rushing to the wash stand as well. "But there's more to the letter," he said, glancing at the document before setting it down on the wash stand and taking the spare rag Martin handed him. "Ian must still believe we are Selby's agents. He wants to try the exchange again, this afternoon, in Hyde Park."

"Did he say where in Hyde Park?" Martin asked as he scrubbed away the remnants of last night's activities hurriedly, then reached for a towel. "It's a big park."

"He gave a location near the Serpentine. He said he'll give Selby the address where Lady Selby and Alan are staying as long as he has absolute proof that the money and the medallion are his."

"I still say Lady Selby doesn't know what's going on," Martin said as he rushed through dressing. "Especially now that we know Gleason isn't working for him."

"Something is very wrong about this entire situation," Edward agreed.

Edward dressed in his formal suit from the evening before while Martin put on fresh, warm clothes. He would have loaned Edward something from his own wardrobe, but he didn't have time to offer before Edward was fully dressed. They made an odd pair as they rushed out of the building and into the cold morning without coats, one of them looking as though he were ready for the opera and the other for a brawl in Limehouse. Fortunately for them both, they were able to hail a cab to take them on to John's office in relative warmth, though it was still cold enough that Martin nestled unapologetically against Edward as they waited impatiently for the journey to be over.

"Aren't you going to scold me for hugging you in the back of a cab when anyone might look in through the window and see us together, Shoe?" he asked with a teasing grin when they were stopped at an intersection to let morning traffic by.

Edward let out a wry laugh and snuggled closer to Martin. "I'm so cold I was just about to suggest we snog a bit to warm this carriage up."

Martin was so proud of the corner his darling lover had turned that he went ahead and snogged him anyhow. Devilish, daring Edward was ever so much more delightful than timid, jumpy Edward, and as soon as they put the entire business of Ian and his damned medallion behind them and saw to it that Alan was back in his father's arms, he intended to begin Edward's carnal education in earnest.

Their kiss was brought to an end as the carriage lurched into motion. Martin considered it a fair loss, as it took them one step closer to John's office. As lovely as it would have been to keep a carriage warm in the naughtiest way possible, he was relieved once they made it to the office and the warmth that greeted them there, along with some truly awful coffee prepared by young Cameron.

"I shouldn't be surprised that Gleason fooled and double-crossed us all," John growled after reading Ian's letter and hearing Martin's take on it. "And I don't like the fact that there's someone else involved in this whole thing who we haven't even considered."

"I might have an idea who it could be," Martin said, reaching back into the mad jumble of events from the past week for answers. "That Mr. Jeffers fellow at your parents' boring supper party said the medallion is part of a set and that the set is owned by a private collector."

"Clearly it's the private collector," Edward agreed. "Jeffers didn't say who that was, did he?"

"No." Martin sighed.

"That doesn't explain the five hundred thousand pounds either," John added as he dashed into the back part of his office. He emerged with Martin's and Edward's coats and hats. "I took the liberty of getting these back from Lady Norwich's footman," he said. "I didn't think it wise for them to remain together after every other garment had been claimed. Not when so many people saw the two of you leave together."

Martin glanced to Edward, concerned and fearful on his behalf. "What happened after we left? I take it we were noticed together."

"You were," John said, fetching his own coat and tossing Cameron's to him. "But the remarkability of your exit was quickly replaced when Lord Grantchester threw a glass of red wine on Blake."

Both Martin and Edward gasped. "He didn't," Martin said, ready to go to battle for his friend.

"He did," John said grimly as they all put on their coats and headed out the door.

"I take it Selby left afterwards," Edward said. "Which would explain why Ian thought he was never there at all. He must have returned to the party after following us."

"He did," John said as they reached the street. He paused, then turned to them and said, "We have just enough time to go to Darlington Gardens to get Blake and Niall up to speed before your brother's appointed meeting time in Hyde Park. Unfortunately, Blake will have to think twice before showing his face in public for a while, but I don't think he'd want to miss out on this."

"No, he wouldn't," Martin agreed.

"Then we'd better hurry," John said. "The sooner we get this over with, the sooner we can all move on with our lives, and the sooner I can hunt Gleason down like the dog he is and wring his scrawny neck."

CHAPTER 20

In the last twenty-four hours, Edward's life had changed beyond recognition. That morning, he should have been warming his spot on the back bench in the House of Commons Chamber, but instead he was marching through Hyde Park with his lover at his side and four other men, all of whom would have been arrested and sentenced to three years of hard labor if anyone had an inkling of who they were or how they lived their lives. But he didn't care. He'd been transported in Martin's arms the night before, slept peacefully with him through the night, and greeted the new day in the very best possible way—not because of the sex, although he couldn't complain about that, but because he'd awoken feeling loved, desired, and wanted.

With feelings like those fueling his heart and his body, Edward felt unstoppable.

"We will need to take serious care with Ian," he said as the six of them—him and Martin, John and Cameron, and Blake and Niall—paused near the spot Ian said to meet. "The man is an arse and a blackguard, but he's also clever, and like any dark horse, he spooks easily."

"Will he stay away if he sees all six of us here?" John asked, glancing around with a frown.

"I believe he will." Edward nodded.

"From everything you've told me about the man, I wonder if he'll show up at all, considering how crowded the park is today," Martin said, hunkering into his coat.

Edward smiled at him in spite of the tense situation. Martin would certainly need warming up once the entire, mad business was done, once Ian had his medallion, and Blake had his son back. Edward could think of several ways he wanted to do the warming. There were so many things he hadn't done yet—things he had shied away from in the past—that he was desperate to try with Martin now. The world had absolutely been turned upside down.

"Blake and I will head over that way," Niall said, nodding to the less-crowded end of the Serpentine, his hands tucked under his arms for warmth. "Blake's got the medallion, and really, he's the one Ian wants to talk to anyhow. Perhaps we can draw him away and get him to tell us where Alan is if he spots us in an area with fewer people." He glanced to Blake with a look of concern.

Blake hunched in on himself, a hunted look in his

eyes, staying quiet. Edward felt bitterly sorry for him. Clearly, Blake was worse for wear after the humiliation he'd endured the night before. Watching the painful incident had changed something in Edward's heart, and he now felt comfortable referring to the man by his Christian name instead of by his title, which was more proper. They had a bond, even if they weren't friends, which was what the Brotherhood was all about. Blake had had everything Edward feared most happen to him, and it showed. But he also had Niall. It was as clear as the frosty sky above them that Niall was wounded on Blake's behalf, and that he was determined to bind his wounds with love and give Blake everything he had.

Edward peeked sideways at Martin as John went on to say, "Cameron and I will search the other side of The Serpentine, just in case. We'll loop back around and meet here in fifteen minutes."

The rest of them nodded, and the others went on their way. Edward was still studying Martin, his heart feeling as though it were too big for his chest, and turned to face him. Blake had been through the worst, but Edward still envied him. He had love. But for the first time in his life, Edward was certain he had love as well. It didn't matter what happened to him. Let the blackmailers and society prigs rain disaster down on him if they dared. He had Martin. Everything else was inconsequential.

"Shoe, if you keep looking at me like that, we're going

to be arrested," Martin said with a sparkle in his eyes, hitting close to Edward's thoughts.

"Who cares?" Edward shrugged. "Let them arrest me. Let my name be splashed all over the papers. You wouldn't forsake me, would you?" A momentary pinch of fear gripped him.

It vanished before taking hold as Martin laughed and said, "Good Lord, no, Shoe. You cannot get rid of me now."

"Nor you me." Edward grinned from ear to ear and set to work scanning the crowd of bundled up men and women cutting through the park on their way to one errand or another and nannies with whining children who didn't understand why fresh air was still good for them when it was so cold. It was all so normal and domestic, but so was he. So were he and Martin, together, as a single unit.

"What is this strange new emotion I feel emanating from you, Shoe?" Martin asked, hugging himself against the cold and inching closer to Edward as he, too, studied the people around them, searching for Ian. "Could it be peace, contentment?"

"Do you know, Other Shoe, I think it might be," Edward replied, his smile widening.

Martin dragged his eyes away from the milling people around them, smiling at Edward. "It suits you, you know. It makes you glow pink and your eyes shine with a light that is damn near irresistible."

Edward felt himself blush at the compliment and sent Martin a coy, sideways look. "I owe it all to you."

"Yes, of course you do," Martin said, feigning casualness with a shrug. "I have those sorts of powers, after all, as your sore bum likely attests to."

Edward laughed. He *was* a bit sore still, come to think of it. The sensation was oddly enjoyable and only made him want to be sorer. "We need to have a serious conversation once this whole business is done," he said, leaning toward Martin.

"Oh?" Martin's joviality faded for a moment.

Edward loved the man. He adored the way Martin's emotions shifted from moment to moment, but how he was always happy somehow, miraculously, underneath it all. "I'm thinking of quitting my job, you see," he went on.

Martin's brow shot straight up. "Can you just quit Parliament?"

Edward shrugged. "I'm certain there's a way, though it would be better if I hold off until I can make the exit in as unobtrusive a way as possible."

Martin turned more fully toward him. "But why? In spite of all the joking, I thought you liked being a stuffy MP."

"I don't," Edward snorted. "I never did. But I like helping people. And something you said a while back struck a chord in me that I haven't been able to ignore. There might be better ways for me to help people, ways that extend beyond me keeping a bench in a dark corner of the Commons

Chamber warm. Ways that might allow me to live my personal life in a more personal way. I would have to move house, of course. I hear there are still several flats and townhouses available in Darlington Gardens." He sent Martin a significant sideways look. In the last year, mentioning Darlington Gardens to one's lover had turned into a sort of code for lifelong commitment and domestic bliss.

Martin flushed and beamed as though it were suddenly summer. "Darlington Gardens, eh? I hear that's become quite the fashionable residence for—"

His blushing, affectionate smile dropped, and immediately, Edward saw why. Ian was striding swiftly toward them, dodging pedestrians, hunched into his coat.

"Where is it?" Ian asked before he reached them.

Edward's emotions shifted from cozy and domestic to wary and anxious so fast that it felt as though he'd been knocked by a speeding carriage. "Where is Lord Stanley?" Edward asked in return. His heart beat like a drum against his ribs, and he clenched his fists in his coat pockets, desperate to get the encounter right.

"We don't have time for this," Ian hissed. He stopped only a few feet in front of Edward, sending both him and Martin a seething look. "Just give me the medallion and the money I want and I'll tell you where the brat is."

Dread and suspicion squeezed in Edward's gut, but it was Martin who answered, "I say, that's a bit rich, don't you think? We should have at least some sort of proof that you're being honest this time."

"There isn't time for that." Ian's eyes were wide with

a sort of fear Edward had rarely seen in his brother. "Do you have the medallion and the money or not?"

"We don't have them with us," Edward said, "but Blake does. He and Niall went to search the other end of The Serpentine for you."

Ian swore under his breath and yanked his hands from his pockets. He grabbed Edward's arms and shook him. Martin moved as if he would step in, but Ian growled, "I don't have time for your nonsense. Don't you understand? My life is at stake here."

Edward's eyes snapped wide. "I hardly think running away with another man's wife is cause for your life to be at risk."

"Annamarie has nothing to do with this," Ian shouted, then pulled away, glancing around as if snipers had rifles pointed at him and he'd just alerted them to his location. "She doesn't know what's going on," he continued in a lower voice.

For a moment, Martin looked victorious. His theories might not have been so wild after all.

"What *is* going on?" Edward asked.

"I'm in trouble, Edward," Ian said, barely above a whisper, darting a glance around as though that trouble would descend on him at any moment. "Deep trouble."

"What sort of trouble?" Edward didn't know if he wanted to strangle the man or help him.

Ian gave up searching the area with a sigh and faced Edward fully. "A few years ago, I borrowed a great deal of money from...a questionable source."

"Let me guess." Martin crossed his arms. "Five hundred thousand pounds?"

Ian sent him a withering look. "Less than that. Interest has accrued over the years. The investment failed miserably. Needless to say, I haven't had the means to earn that money back so as to pay off the debt."

"So you thought you could kidnap Blake Williamson's son and hold him for ransom in order to pay that debt?" Edward hadn't thought his opinion of his brother could sink any lower, but there it went.

"The brat was a convenient stroke of luck," Ian said. "I was hoping to get the money from Annamarie's father in New York."

"Is that why you ran off with her so unceremoniously?" Martin asked.

"I love her," Ian snapped with surprising intensity. "I have always loved her. Far more than that mistake of nature she married. But I suppose the two of you would know all about that." He sneered between Edward and Martin, lip curling as though he might be sick. "I should have known all along you were twisted and defective that way," he told Edward. "No wonder Father and Mother never thought much of you."

"Never mind Father and Mother," Edward said, more annoyed than hurt, which was the biggest sign of the change in his life yet. "Why did you kidnap a child if you could simply get the money from Mr. Cannon?"

"I didn't kidnap the brat," Ian argued. He slumped his shoulders and looked guilty a moment later. "At first.

Annamarie found out what kind of a pervert Blake was and demanded I take her and the children away from the vile situation. I obliged, thinking the time had come to fly off to America, secure the money to pay off my debt, and start anew in a new land. But Annamarie doesn't care much for those whining brats, particularly when the girls began making demands and bothering her."

"So why didn't you return all three of them?" Edward asked. "And why not leave for America immediately? Why bother blackmailing Blake, ruining his reputation, and dividing his family?"

Ian seemed to shrink in on himself even more. He shot another look around and moved closer, as though he feared they would be overheard. "Annamarie knows the boy is Selby's heir and that he would do whatever we want to get him back, but apparently, her father also likes the brat. She thinks we'd get more money from him if the boy was with us. As for the timing, my debt was unexpectedly called in. The...the person to whom I owe the money demanded it immediately. With consequences if I didn't comply. Sh—they made it impossible for me to leave England. But they offered me a compromise. They want that stupid medallion from university, the one Professor Carroll had made from an artifact from Thebes."

A rush shot through Edward, as though he might finally get an answer to questions that had baffled them all.

"The private collector," Martin gasped, sensing it too.

Ian looked at them as though they were mad, then narrowed his eyes. "You know about The Black Widow?"

"The what?" Edward blinked.

Ian's face suddenly splotched with color. "Never mind. Forget I said anything. Just give me the medallion and the money or tell me where Blake is so I can get it from him."

"Why do you need both?" Martin asked with a suspicious look.

"Insurance," Ian snapped.

"This Black Widow wants both now," Edward guessed.

"She wasn't pleased when I failed to secure the medallion the first time," Ian growled.

It all made sudden, astounding sense to Edward. Ian was a damned fool who had gotten himself in over his head. He'd borrowed money from the underworld and his investment had failed. Now he was beholden to someone, someone who called herself The Black Widow, who was determined to hold him to his debt.

"I still don't understand why you're ruining Blake's life over this instead of begging for the money from Annamarie's father," Edward said. "Blake is more than willing to offer her a divorce. You could marry her and get the money as a dowry or something."

Ian shook his head. "Annamarie doesn't know. She thinks Blake is refusing to pay the small amount of money we need to book tickets for America."

"Which explains her letter," Martin said, smiling.

"What letter?" Ian frowned.

"I knew it!" Martin exclaimed. "I knew she sent that letter without you knowing."

"Annamarie sent a letter?" The color began to drain from Ian's face. "Is she going to go back to Blake?"

A twist of compassion hit Edward's gut. Ian truly did love Annamarie. He could see it, even if everything else about the bastard was reprehensible. "Blake wouldn't take her back, even if she did. You've already ruined his reputation, and he's moved on to a different life."

"And we all know what that means," Ian sneered. A moment later, he shook his head as though it didn't matter. "You say Blake has the medallion and is here, in Hyde Park?"

"He is," Edward answered. He stepped to the side to search for Blake and Niall. As luck would have it, they were watching the confrontation from the opposite side of The Serpentine, near the road. "There they are." Edward nodded to them.

"This had better not be another trick," Ian muttered, shooting off toward them.

Edward glanced to Martin, and the two of them launched into motion, chasing after Ian. They drew all sorts of attention as they rounded the end of The Serpentine and dashed up to the road on the north side. The passing pedestrians jumped out of their way, but continued to watch as Ian tore toward Blake and Niall. John and Cameron stood several yards behind them, looking ready for battle.

"Give it to me," Ian shouted, dodging a passing carriage as he approached Blake. "Give me the medallion and the money. Now."

"Tell me where my son is and it's yours." Blake strode forward to meet him, a look of fury in his eyes.

"I won't let you trick me that way again." Ian raised a fist as they all came together by the side of the road. A passing carriage had to veer sharply to avoid smashing into their group. "I want the money."

Blake pulled the medallion from his pocket and held it up, almost as if taunting Ian. Ian swiped at it, but Blake held it out of his way. "Where is my son?" he asked in crisp, dark tones.

"Where is my money?" Ian countered.

Niall reached into his pocket and pulled out a thin envelope. "We'll give you the medallion first," he said. "Then you give us an address where we can find Alan. Once that's been done, we'll hand over the bank draught."

Ian hesitated, eyes narrowed, shifting from one foot to the other. "How do I know you aren't trying to give me a false medallion again?"

"Blast it, man. Here." Blake stepped forward, nearly throwing the medallion at Ian. "Now where is my son?"

Ian fumbled the medallion in his gloved hands for a moment, his eyes going wide. He gripped the chain tightly, staring with wide eyes at the scarab that made up the heart of the medallion. "That's it," he said, blinking in amazement. "That's actually it."

"Are you satisfied?" Niall asked, glowering.

"Tell me where my son is," Blake said.

"You're a damned fool, because he's been under your nose this whole time," Ian laughed. "He and Annamarie are at—"

The roar of a speeding carriage approaching stopped Ian cold. The carriage was drawn by four huge, black horses and was far too big to be driving casually through Hyde Park. The driver was dressed all in black and had a muffler pulled up over his face. Edward was certain they'd all be crushed by the monstrous vehicle, but the driver pulled it to an unexpected stop. They'd all leapt to the side of the road to avoid being crushed, but the sudden burst of movement put them at a disadvantage, particularly when the door flew open and two burly men leapt out. They went straight for Ian, hoisting him up under his arms and dragging him into the carriage.

"No!" Ian shouted as he disappeared inside the carriage. "I have the medallion. He's about to give me your money. I have what you asked for! You must spare me."

Edward couldn't move, couldn't decide whether he should save his brother or leave him to his fate. He could only gape when a woman with mahogany skin and eyes that flashed like stars in the dark, night sky appeared in the carriage's doorway. She wore a rich, fashionable gown under a black coat that was trimmed with black fox fur. She was stunningly beautiful, and her wicked, cunning smile hinted that she was devilishly clever as well.

"Thank you, boys," she told the six of them in a rich alto. "You've helped me complete my late husband's collection at last. As for this one—" She glanced over her shoulder into the carriage, "—I'll deal with his duplicity my own way."

She winked at them, then pulled back into the carriage. A meaty hand reached for the door, shutting it, and a moment later, the carriage shot forward once more. It raced away before Edward's mind could fully catch up to what had just happened.

"The Black Widow," Martin said breathlessly. He blinked as they all watched the carriage speed out of Hyde Park. "Damn, the woman knows how to make an entrance *and* an exit."

"Ian didn't tell us where Alan and Annamarie are," Blake said, eyes wide with horror, visibly shaking. He was the only one of them who didn't look astounded or impressed. He instantly began pacing and breathing heavily as his face splotched with color. "He didn't tell us, and now he has the medallion. Alan could be anywhere. He could be in danger, and we might never be able to find him."

"Calm down, love." Niall leapt to his side, grabbing Blake's arms to steady him. "Ian gave us enough clues to find her. They're right under our nose, which means he and Annamarie are in London. We can find them."

"And if whoever that was holds Ian prisoner or worse," John added, sending an unexpected shiver down Edward's spine on behalf of his brother, "Annamarie is as likely as not to show up at Selby House if she feels she's been abandoned."

"Or she'll board the next ship heading for New York to return to her family," Blake said, his panic growing instead of lessening. "In which case, Alan will be gone."

"Ian said The Black Widow was keeping him from leaving England," Martin added, looking reluctant to say anything. "The woman wouldn't have any reason to keep Annamarie in the country."

"How difficult are international custody battles?" Edward asked, looking to John.

"We have to go after them." Blake started off in the direction the carriage had gone without waiting for John to answer.

Niall caught him and held him in place. "There's no way we'll be able to chase a carriage like that. We either have to figure out who that woman is and, dare I say it, rescue Ian so that he can tell us where your son is, or we have to wait for Annamarie to come to her senses and return to Selby House."

"As much as I want to believe my brother gets what he deserves," Edward said with a wince, "I'm not sure I could live with myself, after what I just saw, if I don't at least try to rescue him."

"We don't know who that woman was," Martin said with a frown.

"I have a suspicion," John said rubbing a hand over his face.

"Who?" Niall asked.

"I'd be willing to wager that was Samantha Percy," John said.

"Samuel Percy's sister?" Niall frowned at the idea.

"The only way to find out for sure is to ask Samuel," John said, starting down the path toward Hyde Park Corner. "He's usually at the club this time of day. He might just have the answer."

CHAPTER 21

Martin loved the feeling that he and Edward and the others had stepped right out of ordinary life and into the pages of some sort of thrilling and dangerous novel. He shouldn't have. Blake's son was at stake, and even though he didn't think much of the man, Edward's brother might be in danger. All of them could be in danger, and any number of things could have gone wrong. But, God, it was thrilling.

"Is Samuel Percy here?" John asked the man behind the front desk as the six of them burst into The Chameleon Club.

A few men were loitering in the front hall, and they, as well as the man at the front desk, flinched in surprise as their group stormed the place.

"He arrived at his usual time for breakfast," the man behind the desk said.

That was enough for John. He nodded and dashed down the hall.

"Is breakfast still being served?" Martin asked the man at the desk over his shoulder. "Do they have those blueberry scones today?"

"Focus, Other Shoe," Edward grumbled at him, grabbing the sleeve of his coat and tugging him on. Edward's face was stony with purpose, but the twinkle in his eye that had been there since before their adventure started that morning still shone.

"I'm starving," Martin complained to him quietly as their group made their way to the club's vast dining room. "We haven't eaten so much as a bite since running through the streets of London last night, fucking like rabbits in heat, and dashing through Hyde Park again just now. Any one of those activities leaves me hungry enough to eat a house, but all three?"

"You're incorrigible." Edward shook his head, laughing in spite of himself.

Martin promised himself that as soon as they had two seconds to sit and breathe, he was going to shower Edward with all the love and affection he could possibly muster. And feed him. Feed both of them. They would need all of their strength for what he had in mind for the afternoon.

"Samuel!" John's urgent shout snapped Martin back to the matter at hand. Samuel was seated at a table near the far end of the room, chatting with a strappingly handsome man that Martin recognized as a dancer from the ballet currently being staged down the street from the Concord Theater, Alexander something or another that sounded Russian. "Samuel, we need to talk to you."

Samuel dropped his conversation and turned to their charging group as though he were about to be assaulted. "Good God, man. What's the matter?"

John came to a stop beside the table, and the rest of them skittered to a halt around him. Martin couldn't have blocked the movement better himself if he'd been given full directorial control of the scene. But then John hesitated.

"This might sound awkward," he said with a wince, "but by any chance is your sister The Black Widow?"

Samuel went from looking startled to alarmed. Then his expression flattened into an irritated scowl. "What's the little tart up to now?"

"So she *is* The Black Widow?" Niall gaped at him.

"When she's feeling particularly cheeky, yes." Samuel's expression hardened by the second. He pressed his lips together and shook his head. "I take it you had a run-in with her?"

"She kidnapped my brother," Edward said, looking far more awkward than upset about it.

Samuel suddenly wasn't as cavalier about his sister. "Kidnapped?" He shook his head. "Could we perhaps go one month without someone being kidnapped? What exactly did she do?"

"Ian was on the verge of telling us where my son and Lady Selby are," Blake said, still looking as though he might implode with anxiety, in spite of the fact that Niall had his arm fully around him, now they were in the safety of the club. "I'd given him the medallion, but before he could tell us, a huge, black carriage pulled up, two thugs dragged Ian inside, and a black woman dressed in furs thanked us before speeding off. We still don't know where Alan and Lady Selby are."

Through the entire explanation, Samuel's expression flattened more and more. Instead of being alarmed and upset by the turn of events, like the rest of them were, Samuel reacted as though they were telling him the story of a child's game gone wrong. "That little minx. I always knew she'd go too far one day."

Martin wanted to laugh. Truly, the turn of events was so theatrical that it was hard to stop himself. And Samuel seemed to be taking things so cavalierly. But the rest of them, including Edward, gaped at Samuel as though he'd told them Death was at the door.

"Will she harm my brother?" Edward asked. "Granted, the louse probably deserves to be strung up by his balls, but he is family."

"I have issues with your family, Shoe," Martin muttered. "I think we need to change the definition of who deserves to call themselves your family entirely."

"Yes, but not now, darling," Edward whispered back.

The simple endearment had Martin's heart soaring. Which was utterly out of place with the seriousness of the matter before them. He never had been any good at seriousness, though, and if Edward was his to have and hold forever now, he didn't think he'd ever be able to be serious again.

"We have to find Ian," Blake said, agitated in spite of the way Niall rubbed his back. "He has to tell me where my son is."

"We could also search London for them or wait until they come out of hiding," Niall said softly.

"If they don't flee the country first," Blake said.

"I wish I could help you," Samuel said, "but Sammy and I haven't exactly been on the best of terms lately. I don't know where she's currently living."

"Derbyshire," Cameron said, seemingly out of nowhere. "She's living in Derbyshire."

A tight silence fell over their group as everyone turned to gape at the wide-eyed young man.

"And how do you know that, love?" Samuel asked, standing and moving to within touching distance of Cameron.

Martin had never seen a man blush as hard as Cameron did when Samuel addressed him. Cameron was fair and blond to begin with, and his blush turned him a vivid shade of pink. It was a charming enough reaction that Martin had to subtly cover his grinning mouth with one hand to keep from outright giggling at the adorable reaction.

"I...I know the carriage," Cameron stammered. "Seen it all the time back up home. Mr. Thorne used to tear about the countryside in that thing, terrorizing good farm folk with it. Everyone knew about his dark wife too, begging your pardon, Mr. Percy." He blushed even harder and shied away from Samuel. His eyes darted back to the man, though, as if he couldn't get enough of looking at him.

"That's definitely her," Samuel said. He winked at Cameron—Martin thought the young man would expire on the spot at the gesture, or come in his trousers—then glanced from John to Blake to Edward. "Thorne was her late husband. But they owned several houses, not just in Derbyshire. She's obviously in London now, but she could take your brother back to Derby or to her summer home on the Isle of Wight, or she could whisk him off to the continent, for all I know."

"Can you call on her?" Blake asked. "I don't care what happens to Ian as long as you can find him and get him to tell you where my son is."

Samuel winced, rolling his shoulders in discomfort. "If it were anyone else, I would tell you to go fuck yourself. But I know what you've been through, my friend." He sighed. "All right. I'll see if Sammy is still in London."

"And if not, are you willing to travel to Derbyshire to see if she's there?" John asked. Samuel continued to wince and writhe, as though it were the last thing he wanted to do. "I'll send Cameron along with you," he added, as if sweetening the deal. "The poor man hasn't been home to see his family in ages."

"What? I...Mum won't...." Cameron gulped hard, staring at Samuel as though he'd just been offered up as supper.

Martin was reasonably certain he had, especially when Samuel answered, "I'll do it," with a wolfish gleam in his eyes. "As long as it doesn't interfere with the concert next month. I'm debuting a new work at the Royal Albert Hall."

Martin's brow shot up. A black composer debuting a work at the Royal Albert Hall?

"In the meantime, we'll continue to search London for Annamarie and Alan," Niall said, hugging Blake from the side. "We'll find them. We will."

Blake nodded, sending Niall an adoring look.

"Do you need us for anything else?" Martin asked John, his gaze drifting past John to where the club's footmen were setting out lunch on the long buffet table against one wall. He had the distinct feeling his and Edward's work was done, and everything that came next in their lives was calling.

John glanced over his shoulder to see what Martin was looking at, then grinned. "I believe we can continue on without you. And many thanks for your help."

"Thank God," Martin breathed out in relief.

"If you need any more of that help," Edward began.

He didn't have a chance to finish. Martin grabbed his hand and jerked him off toward the buffet table. "Eat up, Shoe," he said, handing Edward a plate, then plopping a ready-made roast beef sandwich on it. He fixed the same for himself. "We're going to need all our strength for that *talk* you mentioned us needing to have, now that our part in this whole thing is over."

Edward laughed and shook his head, but went along with Martin's admittedly silly antics. They helped themselves to a table as Blake and Niall, John, Cameron, and Samuel continued to talk about their whole tangled mess at the other end of the room. Martin was concerned for them all, of course. He wasn't completely unfeeling. If he had it within his power to rescue Blake's son, he would have dropped everything to do so. But his part in the mission was over, and in spite of Edward's brother still being missing and part of the whole mess, he felt as though Edward's part in it had ended as well.

"That was delicious," he said as soon as they were finished with their lunches. He stood, gesturing for the young man near the table to come clear their plates and taking a bill from his pocket to compensate him, then grabbed Edward's hand. "Now we're going back to my flat for our *discussion*."

"You really are mad, Other Shoe," Edward sighed, letting himself be led on with an adoring grin.

As far as Martin was concerned, it had never taken so long to make his way home. They found a cab easily, traffic through the city wasn't particularly busy, and no one waylaid them after he paid the cab's driver and yanked Edward into his building and up to his flat. As soon as they were alone with the door closed and locked behind them, Martin practically threw himself at Edward with so much force that Edward stumbled backward until his back hit the door. Martin pinned him there, slanting his mouth over Edward's and sighing with relief as he kissed him to within an inch of his life.

"This, Shoe, this," he panted between increasingly amorous kisses, holding Edward's face one moment, then racing through the buttons of Edward's coat, jacket, and waistcoat the next. He was still wearing the formal suit from the previous night's ball, which had seen better days, but that hardly mattered. Neither of them would be dressed for long. "This is what life is all about." He finished his thought with one long, luxurious kiss that devoured Edward whole.

Martin could have gone on forever, but through the haze of impending passion, he sensed Edward was tense. When he opened his eyes and leaned back, he was treated to the sight of Edward looking utterly gobsmacked, gripping the doorframe for support, his eyes heavy-lidded and hazy.

"Yes," Martin said from the bottom of his heart. "This is how I want you. I want you like this always."

"Like what?" Edward managed to say, straightening slightly.

"Bowled over," Martin said, stealing another kiss. "Bamboozled." He pushed Edward's coat and jacket from his shoulders, then tugged him away from the wall by his tie. "Helpless and hopeless."

He only managed a few backward steps before losing patience and sliding his arm around Edward's waist. He pressed their bodies together, smiling through more kisses as he felt the evidence of Edward's desire grind against his own erection. A time would certainly come when Edward was as confident as he was about sex, but until then, Martin intended to enjoy every moment of surprise and exploration that the two of them would enjoy together.

Within minutes, they were naked and tangled up in Edward's already mussed bed.

"Good thing we didn't bother tidying up this morning before dashing off," he panted as he rolled Edward to his back and wedged himself between his legs. He wasn't going to last long if he didn't pace himself, but the idea of speeding to a quick and messy conclusion thrilled him.

Edward didn't answer with words, but the heady sound of surrender and pleasure that he made as Martin kissed him and reached between them to stroke him was all the answer he needed. Edward would never pull away from him again, that much was certain. In fact, he seemed as eager as Martin was to rush to the finish. And since there was no point in holding back, Martin encouraged him, encouraged them both, by closing his hand around both of their cocks and moving frantically until Edward cried out as he came.

Martin let himself go, beyond aroused by Edward's climax, and came as well less than a minute later. It was every bit as much of a whirlwind as he'd anticipated, and every bit as magnificent. He let every last emotion that filled him vent with sighs and a particularly colorful oath as he dropped to Edward's side, gathering his stunned and smiling lover into his arms.

"Now," he said at last, before fully catching his breath. "What did you want to talk to me about?"

Edward laughed. The sound was rich and resonant. It blended with his heartbeat and reached into the most intimate places of his soul as Edward shifted to his side and threw an arm and a leg over Martin. Edward nestled his forehead against Martin's neck and drew in a deep breath.

"Do you know, Other Shoe," he said, still slightly breathless, "I'm not sure that I actually want to talk."

"No?" The faintest hint of worry made Martin lift his head slightly and twist so that he could look into Edward's eyes.

"What needs to be said that we haven't already said with our hearts and with our bodies?" Edward grinned at him.

"Shoe, that's extraordinarily poetic for an MP." Martin grinned.

"Perhaps I'll become a poet when I leave Parliament," he said with a satisfied sigh, nestling closer to Martin. "Although I should probably take up some profession that provides me with enough of an income to rent one of those places in Darlington Gardens." He lifted his head enough to glance up at Martin, hope in his eyes, continuing where they'd been interrupted in Hyde Park.

Martin felt everything behind Edward's casual statement loud and clear. "Good Lord, man. We've barely known each other two weeks. Are you trying to tell me that you are suddenly willing to throw off your entire life and lease a flat in a notorious neighborhood with me?"

"It wasn't my life," Edward said. "I've spent far too long trying to live as someone else has told me I should live. The moment I met you, I knew that wasn't what I wanted. I want you."

Martin smiled with his whole heart. "Are you certain? I mean, it would be quite a change." Edward's sated smile dropped, so Martin rushed on with, "Don't misunderstand, Shoe. There's nothing I want more than to leap into the greatest role I will ever play in my lifetime, Edward's Other Shoe. I couldn't imagine my life any other way. But are *you* certain?"

Edward surprised him with a show of strength, pushing Martin to his back and straddling his hips. The rush of excitement that pulsed through Martin at having Edward on top had his blood running hot and his cock hardening all over again at record speed. It was simply glorious when Edward swooped down and captured his mouth in a searing kiss.

"I have never been more certain of anything in my life," he said, eyes filled with adoration, then leaned in for another kiss.

That kiss turned into another, and then another after that. It felt as good to be ravished by Edward as it did to take the lead, even if Edward wasn't entirely sure of himself yet. There would be time for that. Plenty of time. Martin envisioned an entire future of the two of them switching off driving each other wild. It made everything so much better between them in the moment.

Edward eventually broke away from his mouth and shifted down Martin's body, nudging his legs apart as he went. "I doubt I'll be very good at this to start," he said as he took Martin's prick in hand, stroking it until Martin was half-crazed with lust. "I might not know much, but I know it takes practice to get to the point where you can put the whole thing in your mouth."

Martin laughed, even as he broke out in a fine sweat from the way Edward was teasing him. "It's not about how much you can put in your mouth," he said, although he wouldn't throw Edward out of bed if he got to the point where he could take all of him, "it's about what you do with what you can handle."

"Oh?" Edward arched one eyebrow, then bore down on Martin before he could give further instructions.

He took only Martin's tip into his mouth, but that was plenty. He licked and kissed him, taking more of him, bit by bit. And even though Edward was a complete novice, to Martin, it was still wonderful.

"Darling," he sighed, raising one arm to grip the bedpost behind him. "That's lovely, it's—oh!"

Edward used his tongue to tease Martin in exactly the right way. Martin was deeply grateful that they'd spent themselves quickly once before getting to the real show. He would have come unceremoniously down Edward's throat then and there if they hadn't. Instead, he was treated to Edward's precocious efforts for far longer than he would have been able to hold out otherwise.

"I had no idea this would be so arousing for me as well," Edward panted, rocking back in what Martin interpreted as an effort to catch his breath. Sure enough, his cock stood up, proud and ready and practically begging Martin to touch him.

"You learn something every day." Martin muscled himself up, throwing his arms around Edward and pulling him down for a long and powerful kiss.

He would never be able to get enough of the feeling of Edward's body against his or the way his muscles moved as he embraced Martin in return and flexed against him, looking for more. Now that the shackles of fear had been removed, Edward was eager and desperate for it. There were so many things Martin wanted to do and so many ways he wanted to make his dear, darling lover scream that he hardly knew where to begin.

He settled for flipping Edward to his back and reaching for the jar they'd left on the bedside table the night before.

"Stuff that pillow under you to lift your hips up," he directed Edward with a gleam in his eyes as he coated his cock with lubricant.

Edward looked momentarily confused. "You don't want me to...." He shifted to his side and lifted his hips a bit to present his arse.

Martin nearly cried at the willing gesture. "No, love, I want to see your face when I come inside of you."

Edward's eyes lit with excitement at the prospect, and he followed Martin's instructions. The whole thing was so wildly erotic that Martin was inches away from coming apart before he even positioned Edward's legs, spread his arse, and slicked it. The complete trust in Edward's eyes as Martin grabbed his thighs and plunged into his arse was devastating in its beauty. The way Edward gasped and cried out in pleasure sent his heart soaring.

At least, until Edward started laughing as Martin moved in him with abandon.

Martin paused with his cock buried deep. "What the devil are you laughing for, man?" he demanded, panting.

"We must look ridiculous," Edward continued to laugh.

Arguably, they did. They were a jumble of bodies, legs sticking out at ridiculous angles, flushed with passion, sweaty, and so utterly happy that nothing could have wrenched them down from the heavens. Martin laughed along with him as he resumed thrusting. It felt so good, so pure to give and take as much pleasure as either of them could stand with a man whom he truly loved with his whole heart.

Edward's laughter turned into cries of pleasure that grew more intense by the moment. The sight of his lover so close to bliss reached straight into Martin's soul, turning every part of him into pure light.

"I love you, Edward," he said, feeling the tell-tale sign of impending orgasm tighten his body. "God, I love you."

Edward came with a cry that went straight to Martin's heart, cum spilling across his belly. The sight of it and of Edward's face contorted in pleasure sent Martin over the edge. He gasped as orgasm raged through him, spilling deep inside of Edward. It was so beautiful and so complete that he didn't have a lick of strength left when it was done.

With a contented sigh, he collapsed by Edward's side, pulling him into his arms. They lay there, panting and happier than either of them had ever been.

"I love you so much, Shoe," Martin gasped, twisting so that he could kiss Edward solidly.

"And I love you too," Edward sighed and kissed him back. "Always and forever."

EPILOGUE

John Dandie's list of problems to solve was quickly growing as long as his arm. He'd handed off responsibility for contacting Samantha Thorne to Samuel, and if things progressed the way he expected, Samuel and Cameron would be making a trip to Derbyshire soon. Which was as much an excuse as anything else to give his assistant the push that the young man needed to put aside his naïve, country ways and to grow into the man John knew he could become. Along with that, Niall and Blake were intent on finding Annamarie and Alan, though John agreed with Niall that it wouldn't be long before Annamarie sought Blake out.

That left John himself with the biggest and most difficult problem to solve on his own. Which was how he ended up concealed in the shadows outside of The Journeyman pub in Brompton well after midnight. It had taken him days of careful observation and discreet asking around to figure out where he would be able to catch Arthur Gleason unawares, and at last, the moment had come.

Gleason stepped out of the pub and into the icy, January night exactly when John expected him to. He turned up his collar, glanced this way and that without seeing John, thrust his hands into his pockets, then started along the street, heading north. John slipped out of his hiding place and fell into step behind him, careful to keep his distance until Gleason crossed in front of the entrance to the cemetery. As soon as he did, John picked up his pace, closing in on Gleason fast.

Not fast enough, as it turned out. Gleason spun to face him at the last minute, grabbing John's arm and twisting. John was ready for him, though. He countered the move by pivoting and striking Gleason's forearm. Gleason hadn't expected the move and cried out, losing his grip on John. That gave John the advantage. Gleason might know fancy techniques learned during his time in the orient, but John had pure, brute strength on his side. He grabbed Gleason by the collar and hauled him into an alcove just inside of the cemetery wall.

"Where are they?" he demanded, slamming Gleason's back against the stone of the alcove.

Gleason grunted, then laughed. The cemetery was dark, but John could still make out the spark of challenge in the bastard's eyes. "You'll have to narrow it down a little," Gleason growled. "From what I understand, you've let quite a few people slip out of your reach lately."

The man was right, but John wasn't in the mood to hear it. He wedged his forearm across Gleason's collarbone and leaned into him. Damn the man for smelling like good beer and even better food. And something else John couldn't put his finger on. Something that made his mouth water.

He breathed through the sudden wave of lust that unnerved him and said, "Lady Selby and Lord Stanley. Where are they?"

"I haven't the faintest idea," Gleason answered, sounding too calm for his own good.

"You're lying," John growled. "You were working for Ian Archibald, trying to find the medallion for him."

Gleason laughed. "Who told you that?"

"I—" John paused. If he was honest, he wasn't certain. They'd assumed as much from the beginning. Except Martin. Martin had expressed doubts about who Gleason was really working for days ago, but John hadn't truly listened to him. "Who else could you be working for?" he asked.

"Come now, John," Gleason said, as though they were in the middle of a friendly discussion. "I thought you were cleverer than that." The bastard's eyes shone with mischief in the dark.

Several things that Martin said flashed through John's mind. He inched back, still pinning Gleason, but wanting a better view of his face. "You're working for The Black Widow."

Unexpected tension pinched Gleason's face. "If I had known she'd given herself that moniker in advance, I might not have taken the case."

John frowned, leaning back even more. "What does she have you doing?"

"What do you think?" Gleason asked. "She hired me to locate the missing piece of her Egyptian collection, the medallion that you all seem to think is so precious."

"But she has that now."

"Very good, lad," Gleason said in a sing-song voice. "Top marks for that one."

John pushed him into the wall again. "Don't mock me. You're up to something."

"What could I possibly be up to?" Gleason laughed. "I'm a private detective. I specialize in locating things and people for those who have misplaced them."

"You're in league with a criminal," John growled, bringing his face close to Gleason's.

"She's not a criminal," Gleason argued, though there was a hint of doubt in his eyes. "She's merely…eccentric."

"She kidnapped Archibald."

Gleason shook his head. "Don't be so dramatic, love. She didn't kidnap him, she offered him a ride."

"She yanked Ian Archibald off the street and dragged him away to God only knows where," John argued.

"So you care about Ian Archibald now?" Gleason arched one eyebrow. He writhed against the wall, shifting his feet in a way that brought them closer to John's.

John blinked. In truth, he didn't care one whit about Archibald. "I care about the information he has," he said instead. "He knows the whereabouts of Lady Selby and Lord Stanley."

"Apparently," Gleason said.

"And now he's missing."

"So sad." Gleason dripped with sarcasm.

"And it's your fault," John finished in a low growl.

"Is it, though?" Gleason asked, tilting his head to one side. "Or is the whole thing no longer my business, now that my client has what she was after?"

He could have had a point, but the restless pulsing inside of John felt as though it told a different story. Gleason was dangerous. He'd gotten in John's way once, and there was no doubt he would do it again.

"I want you to find Archibald and get him to tell you where Lady Selby and Lord Stanley are," John demanded.

"Is that what you want, love?" Gleason said in a deceptively coy tone.

"Yes, that's—"

Before John could finish, Gleason grabbed his wrists and twisted out of John's grip. More than that, he kicked John's feet apart and spun him so that he was the one with his back against the wall, knees buckling so that he could barely stand. His and Gleason's faces were level with each other, and Gleason managed to slam John's hands against the wall above his head. He surged into John, slanting his mouth over his and kissing him with a force that scrambled John's brain and fired his senses.

In all his life, John had never been kissed like that. He didn't have the first clue how to respond to Gleason's tongue in his mouth or his lips molding to his own. He felt powerful and helpless at the same time, alive and yet captive. He fought with everything he had not to kiss the bastard back, but it was a losing battle. He wanted the devil too desperately.

Without John truly realizing it, Gleason shifted one of his hands to the buttons at the front of John's coat. He undid enough to slip his hand inside. John gasped when Gleason cupped his erection, stroking him for a moment to make him harder.

A groan had only just formed in John's throat before Gleason pulled away entirely with a throaty laugh. "I thought so," he said, hoarse and panting. "I'm going to enjoy spreading you, like jam on a bun, and fucking you until you cry."

"You won't—" John panted, hot and scattered. "I would never—"

Gleason winked and walked off before John could find words to deny that was exactly what he wanted.

No, it wasn't. Not even close. Gleason was a villain, and John wanted nothing to do with him.

Except that he couldn't get the scent of the man out of his nose or his taste out of his mouth.

And he was just standing there, cock throbbing, while Gleason disappeared into the darkness.

Damn the man. John cursed under his breath, straightened, and turned to slam his hand against the wall. His blood pumped wildly through him and he couldn't stop his head from spinning or his body from throbbing. Gleason was the very devil, and whatever happened with the cases they were both wrapped up in, he would make the man pay for his insolence.

🦢

I HOPE YOU ENJOYED EDWARD AND MARTIN'S STORY! They were so much fun to write, and I'm thrilled that they got their happy ending, that Martin will always have someone who knows how smart he is, and Edward will always feel loved. But the hunt for Annamarie and Alan continues! And what happened to Ian? Was he really kidnapped or did he actually go with The Black Widow willingly? And what sort of mischief is Samuel's sister, Samantha, up to anyhow? Find out soon in *Just a Little Gamble*. Will Samuel be able to convince his sister to give up her mischievous ways and help get Alan back? And how will things turn out between Cameron and Samuel? Is this a case of a naïve country boy falling for a sophisticated city composer, or is there more to Cameron than meets the eye?

BE SURE TO PREORDER JUST A LITTLE GAMBLE NOW!

If you enjoyed this book and would like to hear more from me, please sign up for my newsletter! When you sign up, you'll get a free, full-length novella, *A Passionate Deception*. Victorian identity theft has never been so exciting in this story of hope, tricks, and starting over. Part of my West Meets East series, *A Passionate Deception* can be read as a stand-alone. Pick up your free copy today by signing up to receive my newsletter (which I only send out when I have a new release)!

Sign up here: http://eepurl.com/cbaVMH

Are you on social media? I am! Come and join the fun on Facebook: http://www.facebook.com/merryfarmerreaders

I'm also a huge fan of Instagram and post lots of original content there: https://www.instagram.com/merryfarmer/

Click here for a complete list of other works by Merry Farmer.

ABOUT THE AUTHOR

I hope you have enjoyed *Just a Little Madness*. If you'd like to be the first to learn about when new books in the series come out and more, please sign up for my newsletter here: http://eepurl.com/cbaVMH And remember, Read it, Review it, Share it! For a complete list of works by Merry Farmer with links, please visit http://wp.me/P5ttjb-14F.

Merry Farmer is an award-winning novelist who lives in suburban Philadelphia with her cats, Torpedo, her grumpy old man, and Justine, her hyperactive new baby. She has been writing since she was ten years old and realized one day that she didn't have to wait for the teacher to assign a creative writing project to write something. It was the best day of her life. She then went on to earn not one but two degrees in History so that she would always have something to write about. Her books have reached the Top 100 at Amazon, iBooks, and Barnes & Noble, and have been named finalists in the prestigious RONE and Rom Com Reader's Crown awards.

ACKNOWLEDGMENTS

I owe a huge debt of gratitude to my awesome beta-readers, Caroline Lee and Jolene Stewart, for their suggestions and advice. And double thanks to Julie Tague, for being a truly excellent editor and to Cindy Jackson for being an awesome assistant!

Click here for a complete list of other works by Merry Farmer.

Printed in Great Britain
by Amazon